The dogs growled, reminding Tess that she was tough

A survivor. Plus she had two big dogs and a gun.

She could see her visitor through the slit in the curtains. He was of average height and weight—as her attacker had been.

Tess unlocked the dead bolt and opened the door a crack, reassured by the dogs behind her.

"Hi," the guy said. The corners of his mouth tilted up and the result was rather breathtaking. In another time or place Tess could have appreciated this man. Blue eyes, incredible angles to his face, dark hair under his cowboy hat.

But not now. She did not smile back. "Can I help you?"

"I'm Zach Nolan. I called yesterday about renting your pasture for my cows."

And she'd said no. So what was he doing here?

Renting the pasture meant the dogs getting used to the sounds of someone being around. Which seemed like a good way to compromise her safety.

"I'm sorry. I'm not interested."

Zach stared at her in seeming disbelief as she pushed the door shut and then snapped the dead bolt in place.

Believe it, cowboy.

Dear Reader,

I'm delighted to announce exciting news: beginning in January 2013, Harlequin Superromance books will be longer! That means more romance with more of the characters you love and expect from Harlequin Superromance.

We'll also be unveiling a brand-new look for our covers. These fresh, beautiful covers will showcase the six wonderful contemporary stories we publish each month. Turn to the back of this book for a sneak peek.

So don't miss out on your favorite series—Harlequin Superromance. Look for longer stories and exciting new covers starting December 18, 2012, wherever you buy books.

In the meantime, check out this month's reads:

#1818 THE SPIRIT OF CHRISTMAS
Liz Talley

#1819 THE TIME OF HER LIFE
Jeanie London

#1820 THE LONG WAY HOME
Cathryn Parry

#1821 CROSSING NEVADA
Jeannie Watt

#1822 WISH UPON A CHRISTMAS STAR
Darlene Gardner

#1823 ESPRESSO IN THE MORNING
Dorie Graham

Happy reading!

Wanda Ottewell,

Senior Editor, Harlequin Superromance

Crossing
Nevada

JEANNIE WATT

HARLEQUIN®

entertain, enrich, inspire™

Recycling programs
for this product may
not exist in your area.

ISBN-13: 978-0-373-71821-4

CROSSING NEVADA

Copyright © 2012 by Jeannie Steinman

ABOUT THE AUTHOR

Jeannie Watt lives off the grid in a historic Nevada ranching community. Before being published, Jeannie made Western belts and bridles out of hitched and braided horsehair, and her gear was featured in several Western art shows and museums. Jeannie no longer has time to make cowboy gear—instead she gets to write about cowboy life, which she likes even better. She still displays gear at the occasional rodeo, where she spends most of her time observing the participants and dreaming up story lines.

Books by Jeannie Watt

HARLEQUIN SUPERROMANCE

*Too Many Cooks?

Other titles by this author available in ebook format.

CHAPTER ONE

IT HAD been another in a long string of sleepless nights.

Tess O'Neil finally drifted off from sheer exhaustion just after sunrise, only to be awakened by a sharp bark and the bounce of the mattress as her dogs leaped to the floor.

For one terrifying second she thought Eddie had found her, and she automatically reached for the weapon she kept under the bed. Her hand had just touched metal when the phone rang again and she realized what had sent her dogs on alert.

The two Belgian Malinois shepherds, Blossom and Mac, stood shoulder to shoulder next to her bed, their amber eyes fixed on the bedroom door on the other side of the room, ears pricked forward at the unfamiliar sound of the phone. Tess pushed back the covers, heart pounding. It had to be a wrong number, but if it wasn't…

The ringing continued as she and the dogs crossed the hall to the old-fashioned ranch house kitchen where the plain white phone hung on the wall next to the refrigerator. She'd had the landline connected so she could send and receive faxes and have ridiculously slow internet. She never expected the damned thing to actually ring.

Tess hesitated for a few seconds, decided it was better to know than not, and snatched the receiver off the hook.

"Hello." She fully expected to hear her stepfather's drug-roughened voice either threatening or taunting her and unconsciously put a hand on Mac's head for reassurance.

"Ms. O'Neil?" The voice was deep, somewhat hesitant, definitely not Eddie. But how the hell did this guy know her name? Or rather, her assumed name?

"Who is this?" Tess demanded, then instantly regretted her tone. *Brittle. Edged with fear.* She didn't want to sound fearful, didn't want to give Eddie the satisfaction if the guy on the other end of the line was one of his minions. But it was hard to sound normal when her heart was beating a hundred times faster than usual.

There was a brief, quite possibly stunned, silence before the caller said, "I'm Zach Nolan. I live across the road."

"I see." Tess took hold of the phone cord. Anyone could say they lived across the road.

"I was wondering if you have plans for your fields and pastures?"

It took Tess a moment to wrap her mind around the unexpected question. "My fields and pastures?" she asked blankly.

"Yeah. The big green things surrounding your house."

There was a touch of gentle humor in his voice, as if he was trying to make a connection, reassure her. Tess instantly drew back. No connections.

"Why?"

"Until you took over the place, I grazed my cattle on those fields and paid a rental fee. I was wondering, if you aren't using the fields, if we could make a similar arrangement."

He'd barely finished his sentence when Tess blurted, "No." She let go of the phone cord and pressed her fingertips against the thickened skin on her left cheek where the stitches had been, felt the residual pain from the torn and stitched muscles below then dropped her hand. It was a habit she was trying to break.

"You're sure?" The touch of humor was gone, replaced

by irony bordering on sarcasm, triggered no doubt by her instant and adamant response.

"Yes."

"Well, thanks. Sorry to have wasted your time."

"No problem." Tess hung up the phone without saying goodbye and put a hand on her forehead, pushing the bangs back and wishing she'd asked how he'd gotten her name. It had to be from that overly friendly lady who ran the local post office.

Tess O'Neil was the authorized signature for the Angstrom Land Company, the limited liability corporation that had leased the small ranch where she was living. If you could call it living. More like hiding.

In reality, Tess *was* the Angstrom Land Company, but no one knew that—the beauty of an LLC in the state of Nevada. She could conduct her financial business without using personal, traceable credit cards or her real name— Terese Olan to her former employers, Terry to her handful of friends. But her grandmother had called her Tess and that was who she'd become. If she was skirting the law by informally becoming Tess O'Neil in addition to hiding behind the LLC, she'd take that chance. It beat the alternative.

She didn't know if Eddie would go so far as to hire a private detective, but he had a lot of nefarious contacts. Not knowing his reach was one of the things that kept her awake at night.

Tess walked over to the sink and started the tap running into the enamel basin before she opened the back door. The screen door wobbled on its loose hinges as she pushed it open and the dogs raced outside. They stopped in tandem a few feet from the bottom porch step, black ears pricked forward, muscles tensed and ready for action. It was a morning ritual they'd developed since moving into the house thirteen days ago. They were city dogs, still acclimating themselves to the sights, sounds and smells of the country. As was Tess.

She watched and waited until the dogs finally dropped their guard, first Mac and then Blossom. They began snuffling in the grass, checking out the action they'd missed the night before as they headed for the taller grass to do their business.

All clear.

Tess closed the door and filled a glass with water, turned off the faucet and leaned back against the counter. If the dogs were relaxed, she could relax. In theory anyway.

Her heart rate still wasn't quite normal. Had the caller really been the guy across the road?

She set the glass down and opened the drawer where she'd spotted the printed paper with local phone numbers while unpacking her meager kitchen supplies a few days ago. She traced a finger down the list. Nolan. Zach. Okay. He existed.

But was it him?

Her hand only shook a little as she dialed the number. Halfway through the second ring he answered.

Same voice.

Tess hung up.

ZACH SET DOWN the phone with a shake of his head. A prank call at eight in the morning was a first, as was the oddly defensive phone conversation he'd just had with the new neighbor. Defensive to the point of rudeness. What the hell?

Let it go. The woman was perfectly within her rights to say no to his offer. She could work on her delivery, but...

Zach grabbed his work gloves off the table, trying to focus on the day instead of how much hay he was going to have to buy to tide things over now that it was pretty damned obvious he'd lost the pastures he'd been counting on.

His index finger broke through the work-thinned leather at the tip of the glove as he pulled it on. This was turning out to be a grand day. He could only imagine what delights the north pasture held for him. And, of course, the duct tape was not in the junk drawer where it belonged. His exposed fingertip was simply going to have to take its chances.

Zach tucked his cell phone into his pocket and headed out the door where he could see his three daughters walking up the driveway to his sister-in-law, Beth Ann's, trailer. Beth Ann worked at the school as an instructional aid and gave the girls a ride every morning after Zach fed them breakfast and helped gather schoolwork, lunches and other essentials before nudging them out the door. Beth Ann was a stickler for promptness. If the girls were late, they walked the half mile to school. Simple as that.

He stopped and watched for a moment, wondering why his youngest daughter, Lizzie, was wearing his oldest daughter, Darcy's, old purple coat instead of her own new red one. He made a mental note to ask about it at dinner that night. Maybe Beth Ann had washed it. She was a bit of a clean freak, but he wasn't complaining. She was doing him a huge favor living on the ranch in the hired-hand trailer, handling the girl stuff that he, the oldest of four brothers, did not feel qualified to deal with.

Benny, Zach's young Border collie, was waiting for him at the old truck he used for beating around the ranch. The dog jumped up on the flat bed and danced excitedly, staying just out of reach in case Zach had some kind of crazy idea about not taking him.

"Don't worry," Zach muttered. "You're going." Benny, who seemed to understand every word Zach said, sat his butt down and let his tongue loll out in a canine grin.

By some miracle the ancient rig started first try and Zach headed down the lane leading toward the north hay pasture and the pump that needed to be pulled for repairs. He just hoped that he could fix it himself because if not, with cattle prices the lowest he'd seen them in three years, he'd have to cut yet another corner to make ends meet. He truly hoped that wasn't the case, because right now he was running out of corners. His cousin, Jeff, had started running some cattle with him last year and shared some of the costs, but it still wasn't enough to ease the pressure of the medical bills. All he wanted was to give his girls a comfortable life, to help compensate for losing their mom to breast cancer.

It wasn't working out so well. His daughters wore whatever Beth Ann could find on sale while he duct-taped his work gloves and prayed that the pump could be jury-rigged into lasting another year so he had the bucks to buy hay.

He needed that pasture.

TESS PUT ON a pot of coffee, checked her email, then let the dogs back inside. Two hours of sleep were not enough, but it'd be a while before she could try again. Her adrenaline was too high, her nerves too jangled by the unexpected call.

Sad, really, that an innocuous phone call from a neighbor could ruin a day.

Tess fed the dogs, dumping copious amounts of the ultra-healthy—and therefore ultraexpensive—food their former owner had fed them into two large stainless steel bowls. Mac dove in. Blossom hung back and waited for him to finish, even though she had her own dish.

"You're setting a bad precedent," Tess muttered to the dog as she went back into the bedroom to change into her work clothes, which were actually new, since she no longer fit into her old clothes.

The jeans she put on were just jeans, bought for a reasonable price online and delivered by mail. No fashionable fading, studs or strategically placed frayed areas. The T-shirt was equally plain. Long-sleeved, black and boxy with a crew neck. One hundred percent cotton without a hint of spandex. It hung loosely from her shoulders, even though she'd now gained fifteen pounds and was curvier than she'd been her entire life. The curves were part of her disguise, lame as it was, since there was no way she could disguise the scars across the left side of her face.

Her ex-lawyer and savior, William, had suggested gaining weight in addition to dying her dark red hair dark brown and buying glasses she didn't need. She'd told William that the last thing she felt like doing was eating. Actually, for the first week after the attack, she couldn't eat, but instead sipped tiny meals through a straw. And even if she did gain weight, she'd pointed out bitterly, it wasn't like she could hide the scars.

No, William had agreed in his understated way, but overly skinny people stood out almost as much as redheads and after the attack she'd become alarmingly gaunt. He was too polite to say skeletal.

So during the six weeks she'd hidden out at William's San Jose home after the attack, Tess focused on gaining weight—no easy task for a model who'd spent the past decade eating the bare minimum and feeling guilty about even that small amount. Depression and fear coupled with healing scar tissue hadn't made eating any easier, but Tess persevered. Pasta, milkshakes, ice cream. Formerly forbidden foods were now her allies and she choked them down, wishing she could enjoy finally being able to eat whatever she wanted.

By the time the LLC had been formed and William had helped her lease-option and sparsely furnish this place in the Nevada outback—a place where Eddie would stand out like a sore thumb—Tess had, for the most part, outgrown her clothes. She'd celebrated with an online shopping spree since she was too paranoid to shop in stores, and didn't care if the clothing fit right—which it didn't. Not in her experience anyway.

The tops didn't cling to her upper body, the jeans didn't hug her legs. Everything was loose and comfortable—and made her feel invisible—or as invisible as a person could be with a ruined face.

When Tess came back into the kitchen, the oversize stovetop espresso maker began to gurgle and the dogs instantly ran to the back door to wait while Tess poured coffee into a tall travel mug and added a healthy dollop of cream. She'd fallen into a routine over the past week. Coffee—regardless of what time of day she woke up—a quick breakfast of cereal and milk followed by a protein shake, then several hours in the barn sanding the old oak furniture she'd found there. Not that she knew anything about refinishing furniture, but she had instructions she'd printed off the internet and time on her hands.

Too much time. But dwelling on it made her feel even more like the prisoner she essentially was, which in turn made her determined to fill the hours so she wouldn't feel like a prisoner. Eddie had destroyed her looks and her livelihood, all because she wouldn't give him something she didn't have, something that probably no longer even existed. She wasn't going to let him destroy what was left of her life. She would hang on to what she had and make what she could of it. Then maybe, once the bastard was caught, she could slip back into the mainstream. Rejoin the land of the living.

But first he had to be caught.

ZACH RETURNED TO the house about half an hour after the girls got home from school. He'd pulled the pump and managed to fix it with the extra parts he had in his shop and then hauled the clumsy cylinder back to the well and lowered it down the hole. It had obligingly sucked up water and spit it back out through the wheel lines in the field.

Sweet victory.

When he walked into the house, the television was on and the heat was off. The three girls were in the living room wrapped in the afghans Karen had made for each of them during her illness. Emma and Lizzie were watching TV, Darcy was doing her homework at the big oak desk he'd inherited from his grandpa, the dark blue crocheted blanket draped over her shoulders. It'd been an unseasonably cold spring day and the house felt like a tomb.

"Darcy, you need to remember to turn on the heat." Zach pulled off his gloves and dropped them in the square willow basket next to the door that Lizzie called the mitten box. "I can almost see my breath."

Darcy looked at him from over the top of her glasses. "The furnace is dead and you won't let me build a fire."

Damn. He crossed the room to check the thermostat. Dead as a doornail. "You can build all the fires you want while I'm here," Zach said as he headed for the basement door.

"That doesn't do us much good when you're not here," Darcy said.

"I guess that's what afghans are for." Zach snapped on the hanging light before going down the wooden steps to battle the furnace. One of his wife's cardinal rules had been no fires, no sharp things without an adult in the house. Darcy had been nine when Karen died—old enough to use sharp things, but she hadn't. As far as he knew she still abided by the rule three years later.

He spent as much time working on the furnace as he did on the tractors and fully expected another major fight, but for once it turned out to be an easy fix. He replaced the fuse then hit the reset button and the beast roared to life. That was two relatively easy fixes in one day. But they didn't balance out losing his grazing.

"Way to go, Daddy," Lizzie said as he came up the stairs. She was still wearing Darcy's coat, which went past her knees. Zach smiled at his youngest daughter, the one with Karen's fair coloring and strawberry-blond hair. "Thanks, kiddo." He knelt in front of her, placed a big hand on each of her small shoulders and gave her an exaggerated once-over. "Where's *your* coat, Lizzie?"

The six-year-old shifted her mouth sideways. Not a good sign.

"I put it somewhere. I guess." She couldn't quite meet his eyes.

"Any idea where?"

She shook her head. Zach glanced at Darcy, who watched the action from his desk. She instantly went back to her homework. Zach sensed conspiracy.

"I want you to find it."

"What if I can't?" Lizzie asked as she twisted a button on Darcy's coat.

Excellent question. "We'll worry about that later. Right now I want you to find your coat."

Lizzie exhaled in a long-suffering way and walked out of the room, feet dragging.

"Where's Lizzie's coat?" he asked Darcy.

She met his eyes in her direct way. "Honestly, Dad, I have no idea where it is."

"She hid it," Emma said from behind him. "I don't know where."

"Why?"

"She doesn't like it. She wanted a pink coat. Tia—" aka Beth Ann "—got her the red one because it was a better price." Emma gave a philosophical shrug and then dismissively flipped one of her light brown braids over her shoulder. "You *know* how she hates red."

Actually he didn't, which kind of bothered him. It was common knowledge that Lizzie hated red?

Zach rubbed the back of his neck. "Thanks."

"What're you going to do?" Emma asked.

Consult with Beth Ann, no doubt. A new coat simply wasn't in the cards until he shipped another lot of cattle and he was trying to hold off on that until the prices jumped. He was damned tired of giving away his beef for break-even prices. Last time he sold prematurely, he'd lost money, but he'd needed the cash and had taken the financial beating.

And he'd probably have to do it again before he had all the doctors and labs and hospitals—both local and the one in Reno—paid off.

Lizzie was going to wear her coat once they found it.

As Zach walked down the hall to the kitchen where dinner simmered in a slow cooker he wondered if a red coat could be dyed a less hated color. Purple maybe?

He'd just taken the top off the Crock-Pot when the kitchen door opened and his sister-in-law came in carrying a laptop case. "Hey, Beth Ann."

"Zach." She set the computer on the counter then pushed the dark hair back from the side of her face. She looked a lot like her sister, except Karen had been fair while Beth Ann was a deep brunette.

"What's that for?"

"Darcy wants to borrow it."

"You don't need it for studying?" Beth Ann was taking online courses, trying to complete an education degree—or most of it anyway. By the time she got to the point when she would have to take regular classes, Darcy would be traveling to the high school in town, forty miles away, where the community college was located. The two of them could drive together, which would solve another problem—buying a car for Darcy.

"I can use the computer at school tonight and Darcy can take this up to her room and work in peace." Beth Ann came to stand beside him as he added salt to the stew. "Any luck with the pastures?"

"Struck out." He put the salt down and pulled the pepper out of the spice drawer, hoping Emma didn't walk in. She ate more pepper than she realized.

"Really?" Beth Ann asked. "What's she going to use them for?"

"We never got that far in the conversation."

Beth Ann cocked her head and Zach added, "The new neighbor wasn't all that friendly. Hung up on me."

"Really?" She looked shocked.

"Yep." The conversation had been over for all intents and purposes, but around here, people said goodbye before they hung up the phone.

Beth Ann took the pepper shaker from Zach when he was finished and dropped it back in the drawer while he stirred the stew. "Susan said one side of her face was bandaged when she came in to rent the post office box."

"I heard." Pretty much everyone had heard. Susan wasn't exactly shy about sharing what she knew.

Beth Ann shrugged. "Maybe she needs some time to settle in. Get used to us here."

"Maybe." Zach wasn't holding his breath. He opened the cupboard and pulled out five bowls.

"Nothing for me," Beth Ann said. "I just came to drop off the laptop and see if you needed anything from town tomorrow."

No, because he'd have to pay for it and he was saving his money for important stuff like hospital bills and equipment repairs. "I can't think of anything." He put the extra bowl back in the cupboard. "Did you know that Lizzie hates red?"

Beth Ann snorted. "I got that feeling when she pouted all the way home after I bought her a red coat."

"She, uh, *lost* the red coat."

"I think Miss Lizzie and I will have a talk," Beth Ann said flatly.

"I already had one."

"I'll add my voice to yours."

He shook his head. "I want to give Lizzie a shot at doing the right thing on her own."

"Fine." Beth Ann headed down the hall to the living room. "I'll see how the homework is going before I head on back to school."

Zach counted spoons out of the utensil drawer. His sister-in-law had been a godsend during Karen's illness and for the three years since she'd died. And despite the fact that Beth Ann was practically the antithesis of her sister in temperament, she was devoted to raising her nieces the way Karen would have wanted them raised—to the point that there were times when Zach wondered if he was taking advantage, keeping her from having a life of her own. Whenever he broached the subject, though, Beth Ann brushed him off and Zach let the matter drop.

It was a comfortable arrangement—for him anyway—and it worked.

Beth Ann came back into the kitchen with Emma behind her explaining why she had yet to start her social studies report. The beauty of Beth Ann working at the school was that she knew everything that went on in her nieces' academic lives—much to their annoyance.

"Are you sure you don't want some stew?" Zach asked as he set the bowls on the table. On the nights they used the slow cooker, it was every man for himself and then the girls cleaned up while he went into his office and ruined his night calculating finances.

Again Beth Ann shook her head.

"You need to eat, Tia," Emma said, echoing the words Beth Ann so often said when vegetables played a starring role in dinner.

"I'll eat. I do have food at my place. By the way, you'll need to find your own way home from school tomorrow." Beth Ann looked at Zach. "I have language proficiency training in town for the next three afternoons. I leave as soon as school lets out."

"We can walk home," Emma said.

"Yes, but can Lizzie?" Beth Ann asked dryly. Lizzie hated walking anywhere.

"We can take our bikes," Emma said brightly.

"Where?" Darcy asked as she came into the room.

"Tia can't bring us home tomorrow because she has a meeting in town," Emma said.

"I can take you to school and then you can walk home or your dad can pick you up," Beth Ann said.

"We'll ride our bikes," Darcy said with an air of finality. She took her position as the oldest seriously and expected to have the last word on all matters. She was a bit like Beth Ann in that regard.

"Lizzie can't ride a bike in your old coat," Zach pointed out. It wasn't difficult to imagine the outcome of a Lizzie/giant coat/bicycle spoke/gravel combination.

Emma and Darcy exchanged looks. "She'll find her coat," Darcy said. Emma nodded.

The two girls left the kitchen and Beth Ann smiled slightly. "Problem solved."

"I just hope no one cries."

"Amen to that." Beth Ann smiled a little then headed for

the door. Her hand was on the doorknob when she stopped and said, "You okay?"

Zach shrugged, hating that she could read him—but then she'd seen him in his most desperate and unguarded moments. "I'm concerned about losing the pastures." Understatement of the year.

"What are you going to do about it?"

Zach opened the fridge and pulled out half a gallon of milk, then met Beth Ann's eyes over the door. "I guess that I'm going to give it another shot."

Only this time he was going in person.

CHAPTER TWO

TESS BALANCED the coffee travel mug on top of the box of sandpaper and paint stripper that had arrived via UPS the day before, holding the top of the cup with her chin as she maneuvered the back door open on her way to the barn.

She'd yet to actually see the UPS man, who'd come to the ranch four times since she'd moved in. The first time he'd come, she'd been in the shower and had suffered a near heart attack when Blossom and Mac sounded the alarm from the living room. By the time she'd gotten out of the shower and jammed her soaking wet body into her robe and retrieved her small gun, the dogs had stilled. When she'd gotten into the living room, she saw the distinctive brown van pulling out of the driveway and a box of kitchen supplies sitting on her front porch, no signature required.

After that, Tess simply ignored the man's knock once she ascertained it was really him. The fewer people who saw her, the better...which was why the last thing she wanted to see as she rounded the corner of the house was a plume of dust coming from a pickup truck heading down her driveway.

What now?

She wasn't waiting around to find out—not out in the open. The pickup probably belonged to one of her neighbors and it no doubt looked crazy, but she turned and headed straight back around the house, the dogs on her heels. Once she was safely inside, she locked the back door and leaned against it. The front door was already locked.

She let out a shaky breath and debated. If whoever it was knocked, she could ignore it—even though she knew he'd seen her. There was no law saying she had to answer her door, but in a community like this, where the postmistress hugged the patrons, all that would do was cause talk among the neighbors.

If the guy driving the truck was a neighbor.

There's no way Eddie's found you.

The phrase was a mantra she used to soothe herself during the long hours of the night, but at the moment she was fairly certain it was true. She'd just had yet another clipped conversation with the Los Angeles detective, Tom Hiller, who was handling her assault case. She called him, once a week, for any possible updates on the case. She had a strong feeling she was bugging the hell out of him, but this was her life she was concerned about and it wouldn't kill him to take a few minutes out of his week to talk to her.

So far nothing had changed. Eddie was an exemplary parolee with a job at a car wash. He was keeping his nose clean, doing what he was supposed to do.

Tess was more concerned about him doing what he *wasn't* supposed to do.

The engine died and a minute later Tess heard footsteps on the front porch, which made her stomach clench until she thought she might throw up.

Deal with this.

Once upon a time she'd been fearless. Less than two months ago she would have described herself as savvy and streetwise. She'd had to be to survive her rugged teen years with her alleged family and their drugged-out friends. The modeling world also had its own kind of cutthroat culture. Yeah, she definitely would have called herself tough.

Looking back, though, she could see she'd been confident to the point of bravado. Confident enough to tell Eddie to take a flying leap when he'd first approached her. Confident in her abilities to stay safe right up until the guy had appeared out of nowhere as she approached her apartment building, knocked her down and slashed her face with what the doctors said was probably a piece of metal shrapnel, telling her in a low growl that Eddie was going to keep taking pieces off her until he got the money he *knew* she had. The money he'd left with her drugged-out mother before going to prison. Money she knew nothing about.

Safety had been an illusion—even to someone who thought of herself as streetwise—and she realized too late that Eddie would never believe she didn't have his dirty money stashed away somewhere. He'd keep looking until he found her.

The old-fashioned doorbell rang and Tess moistened her dry lips as both dogs growled, reminding herself that she was still tough. A survivor. Plus she had two big dogs and a gun.

She sucked in a shaky breath, then pushed off from the back door and headed for the living room. She could see her visitor—from the chest up, anyway—through the slit in the curtains that covered the window in the door. He was a guy of average height and weight—as her attacker had been. She couldn't tell what color his hair was under the beat-up cowboy hat, but guessed it was dark. He shifted his weight as he waited for her to open the door.

Tess unlocked the dead bolt and pulled the door open a crack, feeling somewhat reassured by the dogs crowding up behind her, trying to assess whether or not this guy was a threat. She kept her face tilted so he could only see the right side, the good side, but the corner of her glasses banged against the door and she had to move back slightly.

"Uh, hi," the guy said as soon as it became obvious that she wasn't opening the door any wider. The corners of his mouth tilted up slowly, as if he had to remind himself to smile, but the end result was rather breathtaking. In another time or place Tess could have appreciated a man like this. Blue eyes, incredible angles to his face, dark hair showing from under his cowboy hat.

But not at this time. She did not smile back. "Can I help you?"

"I hope so. I'm Zach Nolan. I called yesterday about the pasture."

Tess stared at him, a slight frown drawing her eyebrows together. So what was he doing here? The last thing she needed was a persistent neighbor. "Was there something about my answer yesterday that you didn't understand?"

"I thought maybe *you* didn't understand."

"Really," she said coolly, calmly adjusting her glasses, which were still slightly crooked from banging the door.

"I would pay for the use of the pasture and the cows wouldn't be anywhere near your place. Having the animals here wouldn't be much different than not having them here. They're not noisy or anything. Plus, you get the rental money."

"Would they be in that field over there?" Tess nodded toward the field on the other side of her driveway.

"That would be one of the pastures."

"And you have to do things with the cattle, right?"

"I move them around. Check on them."

Which meant someone coming and going at times she had no control over. Which meant the dogs getting used to the sounds of someone being around.

Which seemed like a good way to compromise her safety.

Tess drew herself up, her face still angled away from him, even though she felt odd looking at him with one eye. "Listen. I know this sounds cold, but no. I...I don't like cattle and I don't want to lease my pastures."

"You don't like cattle."

"Is there some reason I should?" she asked stiffly.

He gave a slow shake of his head, then peered at her from under the brim of his hat. "You might have moved to the wrong part of the country."

"I'm sorry. I'm not interested in leasing and I'd appreciate it if you'd consider this matter closed. Now if there's nothing else?" She started closing the door without waiting for an answer.

Zach Nolan stared at her in seeming disbelief as she pushed the door shut and then snapped the dead bolt in place.

Believe it, cowboy.

Tess snapped her fingers and the dogs fell in behind her as she walked through the living room back to the kitchen, wondering if Zach was still watching her through the window. A few seconds later she heard his footsteps on the porch followed a minute later by the roar of a powerful truck engine. Only then did she allow herself to sit on one of the kitchen chairs, the gun that weighed down her hoodie pocket clunking against the metal leg.

She pushed her fingers through her hair, keeping them far away from her scars and simply held them there as she breathed in and out. In and out.

ZACH GROUND THE gears as he shifted down at the end of Tess O'Neil's driveway. He tried to remember if anyone had ever closed a door in his face before.

Nope. Not once.

Definitely something off about this woman.

She'd tried hard to hide the injured side of her face as they spoke, but hadn't quite succeeded. The scars across her cheek were relatively fresh, jagged and ugly. Must have been one hell of a car wreck.

But beyond the scars, Zach had been struck by the uninjured side of her face—the wide, green, wary eyes behind the clunky-looking glasses, the full lips and high cheekbones. Practically flawless beauty juxtaposed against stark injury and inexcusable behavior.

He drove across the county road that separated his property from hers and into his own driveway, pissed that he'd hit such a brick wall. There didn't seem to be much else he could do, considering who he was dealing with, other than to take the loss of the pastures like a man and figure out how to pay for hay. Obviously there would be no dealing with a person who'd closed a door in his face.

Zach pulled the truck to a stop in front of the workshop and got out. Benny, whom he'd left at home because he didn't trust him in the good truck alone yet, came bounding out and proceeded to demonstrate exactly why he wasn't allowed out in polite company.

"Off," Zach scolded as the young collie jumped up on him, chewing and tugging at his sleeve. The teenage pup bounced backward, ready to play. "Behave or I'll turn the girls loose on you."

The pup grinned.

"Come on," Zach said, starting for the bull pen. The pup fell in beside him. Benny was going to be a good dog as soon as he got through his adolescence…and then Zach only had three more adolescences to go through after that.

Darcy would be an official teen on her next birthday.

It didn't seem possible. The years since Karen had died had in some ways crept by so slowly that Zach sometimes felt as if he'd never be able to fight his way through one day and into the next. But in other ways the time had sped by and it seemed as if he'd missed so much.

It wouldn't be long before Darcy was out of the house and on her own—probably before he had a chance to do all the things he'd wanted to do, provide all the stuff he wanted to provide.

He hadn't even taken his girls on a real vacation yet.

Zach lifted the gate latch, felt cool metal through the hole in the glove he hadn't bothered to tape up the night before. He was too young to feel this damned old.

TEN MINUTES AFTER the cowboy left, Tess collected her box of refinishing supplies and headed out to the barn. There was no reason that a neighbor's visit—business-related at that—should be so upsetting. Although, upon reflection, maybe the upsetting part was that she'd assumed when she moved to a rural area, people would leave her alone. She hadn't counted on them calling her and showing up at her door. No. That hadn't been in the game plan at all.

It was just one guy with a legitimate reason for being there.

Tess doubted the cowboy would be back. He hadn't seemed too impressed with her manners.

Once outside, the dogs barely sniffed the air before putting their heads down and investigating scents along the path to the barn, obviously at ease. Tess set the box on top of an old rabbit hutch and then rolled the heavy barn door open. It squeaked and protested until she had it wide enough to give light to her project.

The barn had electricity, but the lightbulbs were all burned out or broken, so Tess simply left the door open as she worked. She didn't really want to be closed up in the barn, peaceful as it was with the old farming implements stored along one wall and dim light filtering in through the dusty windows. She felt vulnerable closed up in a place where she couldn't lock the doors. Besides, she enjoyed the sight of the mountains rising up behind the small town on the other side of her largest field.

Tess opened the cardboard box and took out the package of dust masks. She broke open the plastic, snapped on a mask and adjusted the plastic string. She felt a bit like Darth Vader and the stiff cellulose put pressure on the tender part of her injury, but it beat sucking in sawdust.

Mac and Blossom settled outside the door in the grass, Blossom rolling over onto her back and letting her tongue loll out, looking nothing like the lethal weapon she was supposed to be. Tess picked up a piece of sandpaper, rolling it around the pencil in order to get into the nooks and crannies of the scroll work on the legs of the table.

She'd finished sanding the top and sides of the table yesterday, having eventually worked her way through four coats of different colored enamels—white, red, green and then white again—before she'd hit the gorgeous oak below.

Tess was in no hurry because once she finished, she had little to do except sketch. Sketching had been her escape since her teen years when she'd lain in her bed—shutting out the sounds of Eddie and her mother sniping at each other, or her stepbrother's overly loud music—and created beautiful people wearing beautiful clothing.

But one could only sketch so much, and Tess planned on tackling more pieces once she finished her table. In addition to the table, she'd found three grimy oak chairs and a bureau. The bureau was, quite frankly, gross, since many generations of mice had taken up residence in it, but the chairs were salvageable. They reminded her of chairs her grandmother had treasured. Chairs she'd inherited from her own mother. Jared, Tess's jerk of a stepbrother and Eddie's oldest son, had sold them after her grandmother died to settle a debt.

If only that'd been the only thing he'd done to her. It

wasn't. When Tess had moved back in with her mother and Eddie after her grandmother's death, Jared had subtly terrorized her, making sexual innuendos, brushing up against her whenever they were alone. Tess had had a buffer while Mikey, her younger stepbrother, had lived there, but after he'd left home, at the ripe old age of fifteen, Tess had been on her own.

She was still amazed she'd escaped without being sexually assaulted. But it had been a narrow escape—no thanks to her mother, who was too caught up in her drug use to notice or care.

Tess pushed the bitter thought out of her head, focused again on the rhythm of the sanding, which was oddly calming.

Eventually she would have to come up with some other way to spend her time—preferably something that allowed her to earn a living at home. She had a decent nest egg, since she'd chosen to save her money rather than party it away. No matter how steadily she worked, Tess had never ever been able to believe her modeling career would last for longer than the next contracted job, because nothing else in her life, other than her grandmother's steadfast love, had ever lasted.

How wise she'd been.

Decent as it was, though, what was left of her nest egg after leasing the ranch wouldn't last for the rest of her life.

IT WAS PAST two o'clock when Tess finally finished the first table leg and sat back on the grass to admire her handiwork. Why on earth had someone stuck such a gorgeous table in a barn?

Because someone else had painted it white, then green, then red, then white and it had been pretty ugly, that's why.

The dog closest to her sneezed, an open plea for attention and Tess reached out to ruffle Mac's ears. He lazily rolled over on his back, giving her access to his itchy belly. She patted him a few times and he sneezed again.

"Come on, guys," she said as she got to her feet. "I need to hit the shower."

She rolled the barn door shut and headed to the house, wondering if talking to her dogs as if they were people made her the canine equivalent of a crazy cat lady. Somehow crazy dog lady just didn't have the same ring.

Tess had never had a dog of her own, but had once shared a house with Demon, her grandmother's sausage-shaped Chihuahua. Demon had put her off dogs, but after the attack she'd changed her mind and told William she wanted to find a guard dog—or four—to live with her. Lethal killing machines if possible. She was a scared woman who needed protection.

William had lined up the deal for her, finding not lethal killing machines, but two retired personal protection dogs in need of a home. Tess hadn't been certain that, despite their fearsome appearance, two older dogs would fit the bill, but she'd since changed her mind. Blossom and Mac knew their jobs. They stuck to her like glue, alerted her when anything new appeared on the scene and followed her commands instantly. Plus she'd seen them attack a guy in a padded suit when she and William went to pick them up. Close enough to lethal for her.

"Who wants a snack?" she asked after locking the back door. Two canine butts instantly hit the floor. Tess gave each dog a giant rawhide chew toy and then double-checked the lock on the front door before heading toward the bathroom, pulling off her dusty clothing as she went.

She'd barely gotten into the shower when the dogs went into a barking frenzy, making her jerk so hard she hit her elbow on the faucet. And it wasn't the UPS-man-is-here-again barking. It was the this-is-something-we-aren't-familiar-with barking.

Not again...

Tess cranked off the shower and got out, heart pounding. She wrapped a towel around herself and stood for a moment on the bath rug, her hair dripping, listening.

The dogs were at the back door, not the front. Growling now instead of barking.

Crap. That wasn't good. Tess let the towel drop and yanked her robe off the hook next to the shower. She struggled into the robe and stood still again, heart hammering. And then she heard it.

Laughter.

Happy kid laughter.

The blood that had been pounding in her temples drained away, leaving her feeling oddly light-headed. Just kids.

What were kids doing on her property?

Tess tried to swallow, but it was impossible because her mouth was dry. She moved cautiously to the window. There, not fifty feet from her house, three girls walked along the path next to the overgrown creek, pushing bicycles and talking.

Tess stepped away from the window as the tallest girl, who pushed the smallest bike, looked over at the house.

Did they know they were trespassing?

Tess tightened the belt around her waist and headed for the kitchen, where the dogs scratched at the door, anxious to get out and deal with this threat.

"Nee. Af," Tess said and they both obediently dropped to their bellies. She watched the girls disappear behind the barn, then reappear on the other side. They followed the creek to the road, then pulled the bikes under the wire fence.

Tess slowly sat on a kitchen chair and rubbed her hand

over her forehead. She'd just had the crap scared out of her by children. Something had to give. She couldn't live the rest of her life like this. Afraid of little girls and cowboys.

CHAPTER THREE

"Hey, Dad?"

Zach looked up from the PVC pipe he was measuring. Darcy and Emma stood in the doorway of the shop. "Yeah?"

"Lizzie's bike got a goat head in the tire on the way home today."

Well, that explained why they were late. "Where's the bike?"

"The front yard."

"Where's Lizzie?"

"Riding my bike. Her feet can barely touch the pedals."

Zach set down the pipe, wiping his hands on a rag as he walked toward the door. "I don't think I have another repair patch." Goat heads were the round seedpod of a ground covering weed, hard as nails with a couple nasty tire-puncturing prongs sticking out. They were hell on bike tires.

"Maybe Tia can bring one home from town."

"You can text her," Zach said. Emma immediately headed off to the house. "But she may not get done with her class before the store closes," Zach called after her.

"Wal-Mart doesn't close," Darcy said.

Zach kept forgetting that. "Well, once upon a time stores *did* close," he said.

Darcy cocked her head. "And you remember those days? Man, Dad. You're old." Zach grinned as they walked toward the lawn where Lizzie's bike lay on its side.

"Yeah, and I feel it every year."

"Is that a gray hair there?" she asked.

"You should know," Zach replied. "You probably put it there."

"So how'd the pasture thing work out?" Darcy asked casually, hooking her thumbs in her front jeans pockets.

"What pasture thing?" Zach asked slowly.

"You know…the pasture across the road. The one the lady wouldn't let you rent."

"How do you know about that?"

"Tia was talking to Mrs. Bishop about it."

"Did Beth Ann or Mrs. Bishop know you were there?"

Darcy shook her head. "If they know I'm there, then I don't hear any good stuff."

Lizzie came wobbling around the corner of the house before he could answer, perched on Darcy's bike, the tips of her toes barely reaching the pedals. Benny the collie bounded alongside her.

"Don't wave," Zach said as her little hand lifted a few inches off the handlebar. She immediately clamped it back down as the bike wobbled dangerously. Both he and Darcy took a quick step forward, but Lizzie regained control and pedaled on, Benny right behind her. Zach hoped they had some Band-Aids on hand.

"She thinks she's so cool now that she's in the first grade," Darcy said.

"Yeah. I don't know anyone else who ever felt that way."

"Come on, Dad. I was a serious student. Lizzie is all about having a good time." Darcy's eyes twinkled behind her glasses as she glanced sideways at her father. He shook his head and then picked up Lizzie's bike from where it lay in the grass and tipped it upside down so he could take off the tire.

"I think this is beyond a patch kit," Zach said. "We'll have to get another tube."

"Should I text Tia again?" Emma asked, having just stepped out onto the porch.

"No. I'll get one when I go to town tomorrow." He wasn't going to have Beth Ann chasing all over Wesley looking for inner tubes when she no doubt had class work to do when she got home.

"But—" Emma started, only to be interrupted by her older sister.

"We can walk home," Darcy said.

TESS FELL ASLEEP in the chair watching television, the sound turned down so low she practically had to read lips to understand the action. She hadn't counted on sleeping at all—at least not until daybreak, which was the usual time she fell asleep. But despite the cowboy's visit, despite the shower scare, she conked out sometime in the early-morning hours, only to be startled awake sometime after sunrise by the dogs scrambling to their feet and racing for the back door.

Tess tumbled out of the chair, tripping over the fleece blanket she'd been nestled under and going down hard on her knees. And then, during a brief lull in the canine uproar in the kitchen, she heard the girls' voices.

This was ridiculous. There was no reason for those kids to cut across her property. It was, after all, hers.

She started for the back door, then stopped when she saw how far away the three girls were. She'd have to run after them if she wanted to warn them off and that smacked of crazy. She wanted to keep them off her property, not scare the daylights out of them...although that probably would keep them off her property. Something to consider.

She gripped the door frame and watched as they disappeared around a thicket of willows growing along the creek. No. She'd wait until they passed by again. From the time frame, it seemed logical that they were traveling to and from school. Yesterday they'd showed up around three. She'd make certain she wasn't in the shower at that time and if they passed by again, well, the four of them would have a chat about the meaning of private property.

ZACH LEFT THE hospital clutching a sheaf of papers. No, the accounts manager would not decrease his payment amount temporarily—even if cow prices were down. They suggested he take out a loan. Well, that was a fine idea, except that he refused to put his land, the one thing he would be able to give the girls, up for collateral.

That had been a rough enough pill to swallow, but then, on the way out of the expensive new hospital addition that he was helping to pay for, Marcela James, the hospital administrator, had collared him. He thought for one brief happy moment that perhaps she'd heard about his visit to the accounting office and was there to offer a reprieve, but no. Instead she cheerfully told him that if he wanted to sell that forty-acre parcel her husband had once approached him about, they'd still be happy to buy it.

Zach had smiled and nodded while thinking, *"When hell freezes over."*

Leave it to the Jameses to hit a guy when he was down. Zach was not parceling up his ranch. Not until he got backed into a tighter corner than he was in now—although the way things were going, that might be tomorrow.

He pressed his fist against his sternum, trying to ease the dull stress-induced ache. All he needed was to keel over from a heart attack. That'd help the girls a whole bunch.

Zach unlocked the truck, then pulled the list out of his jeans pocket and gave it a shake to straighten it out. Bike tire was at the top. Beneath that purple dye. Even though Beth Ann insisted that Lizzie was spoiled, and Zach did not disagree, Beth Ann had agreed to try to dye the coat.

Lizzie understood that she might end up with a muddy gray mess, but she was willing to take the chance. Someday Zach would have a heart-to-heart and find out why his youngest daughter hated red.

BEFORE MOVING TO the boonies, Tess had had no inkling that the simple act of sanding wood, of doing something with her hands other than sketching, could be such a sanity saver. Usually the steady rhythm soothed her, but today she sanded for less than an hour before she decided to give it up for the day and investigate possible at-home careers. The non-scam kind.

It'd been a project she'd been putting off because she was afraid of reality—as in, there probably wasn't anything she could do to make a living at home. Oh, there were jobs. Medical transcriptionist. Technical writer. Data entry. Phone surveyor. But nothing jumped out at her, mainly because she had no formal training beyond a high school diploma and an impressive modeling portfolio. She wasn't qualified for a hell of a lot, except perhaps phone surveyor.

You have time to figure this out...

But how much time? Especially if she had to train for something. She still had nearly a hundred grand in her LLC account after buying the ranch; however, simple math indicated that if she spent only the bare minimum, she could last maybe eight years. And that was if she didn't buy a newer car, had no increase in costs and was stingy with the electricity. Not exactly the way she wanted to live.

Ironically she'd given some thought to investigating second careers a few months ago. Almost ten years had passed since she'd been signed by the Dresden Modeling Agency, a near miracle which she credited to her unusual celadon-green eyes and the cheekbones she'd inherited from her Irish grandmother. Models didn't necessarily have to disappear in their late twenties anymore, but some of Tess's longtime associates had started losing work and she was not one to ignore warning signs. And then, amazingly, she'd made the short list for the Face of Savoy Cosmetics campaign and all thoughts of investigating a second career were put on hold while she waited for an answer.

Her face had been slashed before she heard.

Tess rubbed her hand over her cheek, testing to see if it still ached as much as it had yesterday. Yes. The torn muscles were slow to heal, though the stitches had probably dissolved long ago.

Her face would eventually heal, but she would never be able to make money as she had only a few months ago. Eddie had taken that away from her.

Tess tried hard not to think about that, mainly because she was afraid that if she stopped feeling numb about her career, if she let herself think about how much she'd lost, she wouldn't be able to move past the bitterness.

She turned off the computer monitor, having had enough depression for one day, then jumped a mile when Mac let out a loud bark. Blossom instantly joined in and once again they raced to the back door.

Right on schedule.

Tess walked into the kitchen just in time to see the three girls traipsing along the path by the barn, one tall and dark-haired with glasses, one just a few inches shorter with long brown braids and the last a small little thing with a short blond pixie cut.

"Stay," Tess said sharply, not being able to recall the Dutch command. But the dogs obediently held as she opened the back door and slipped outside. She'd debated about covering her injury then decided what the hell? People were eventually going to see it. Covering it only seemed to draw more attention.

"Hey," she called after the girls. They instantly stopped, whirling around with surprised looks on their faces.

Tess marched through the tall grass toward them. The littlest girl, who had a red coat bundled under her arm even though it was quite chilly, took a small step backward, her eyes fixed on Tess's scars.

"This is private property," Tess said. "You can't just cross it any time you please."

Three pairs of eyes widened then the ones behind the glasses narrowed again. "We've always used this path to go to school," the oldest girl said with a touch of indignation.

"For years," the middle girl added, nervously flipping one of her braids over her shoulder.

"Because that property owner didn't care," Tess explained matter-of-factly. "But I do."

"Why?" the oldest girl asked.

"It doesn't matter why," Tess snapped. She hadn't expected to get an argument. She'd expected to lay down the law and have the girls comply. "If you persist in using the trail, I'm going to call the police."

"Sheriff," the older girl said dryly, negating the effect Tess was aiming at.

"Whatever," Tess said. "I will contact the authorities."

The littlest girl continued to stare at Tess's face. No, she was more than staring. She was doing an in-depth study, tilting her head and wrinkling her forehead, and it made Tess feel ridiculously uncomfortable. She cleared her throat. "Of course, I don't want to do that, so please, take the road from now on."

"But—" the girl with the braids started to say before the tall girl touched her shoulder. She instantly closed her mouth.

"Is this property posted?" glasses girl asked.

Tess raised her eyebrows at the unexpected question. "Excuse me?"

The girl tilted her chin up. "Posted. If you don't have No Trespassing signs, then technically you can't accuse us of trespassing."

"I most certainly can."

The girl shook her head. "No. You can't. Look it up."

Tess let out a breath, thinking she was so not prepared to do battle with a know-it-all preadolescent when the youngest girl asked in a hushed voice, "What happened to your face?"

"I got caught trespassing." Tess grated the words out. "And trust me…you wouldn't want this to happen to you."

The little girl gasped, her eyes growing wide as she backed up until she was plastered against the older girl, who put a reassuring hand on her shoulder. The little girl's lower lip quivered, her eyes still fixed on the scars, and Tess felt bad for all of a split second. "If I were you," she said coolly, "I'd take the long way home from now on."

And then, since she'd made her point and didn't want to risk crossing verbal swords with the oldest girl again, turned on her heel and stalked through the tall grass back to her house.

ZACH PULLED TO a stop next to the shop feeling more exhausted than if he'd spent the day digging fence posts by hand. He hated going to town, and dealing with the hospital made it worse.

He was halfway to the house when the door opened and Emma and Darcy raced out.

"What happened?" he automatically asked. Neither of them had any visible injuries, but Lizzie wasn't there.

"We didn't know we were trespassing," Darcy announced from the top step.

"What?"

"Honest, Dad." Emma jumped from the top step to the sidewalk just as he got there. "We thought that anyone could take the shortcut to school. We used to take it all the time."

"Slow down and start from the beginning," Zach said, not liking the sound of this one bit.

Emma and Darcy exchanged glances and for once it was Emma who did the talking. "Tia had to leave early this morning." Translation: his daughters were late so she left without them. "We had to walk because of Lizzie's bike, so we took the trail along the creek to school this morning. On the way home that…lady…who lives there came out and yelled at us. She almost made me cry."

"More than that," Darcy said in a low voice, with a quick glance over her shoulder at the front door, "she scared poor Lizzie to death."

CHAPTER FOUR

THE ENCOUNTER with the trespassing girls had left Tess feeling edgy and unsettled. She tried to go back to her internet search, but eventually gave up and sketched, which she usually enjoyed more than being reminded of how hard it was going to be to earn a living. But today not so much. Her eye was off, the designs lackluster. She finally tossed the pad aside and told the dogs it was time for a walk. She needed to move.

Who was she kidding? Moving wouldn't solve anything. What she needed was someone to talk to, someone to pour out her mishmash of fears and concerns to. Someone to ask for advice.

But she had no one, so physical activity would have to suffice. A car on the county road slowed as she approached her field and Tess automatically froze in place, even though she recognized the car as the one driven by the dark-haired woman who lived at the ranch across the road. The wife of the cowboy who'd wanted to lease the pasture, no doubt. The rather fine-looking cowboy.

Tess touched her injured cheek, then lowered her hand, closed her fingers. There'd be no men in her immediate future—fine-looking or otherwise—and not because her face was ugly. Tess would be alone because her life was ugly.

As soon as the car turned into the driveway opposite her own, Tess climbed through the fence. Her path was always the same—across the field on the other side of her driveway, the one the cowboy had wanted to lease, and toward the mountains that flanked the west side of the valley. Once in the field, she was far enough away from the roads to feel safe, so she allowed the dogs to run. Heaven knew they spent enough time cooped up in the house with her. They needed the opportunity to stretch their legs, run and do dog stuff.

Tess walked through the knee-deep grass, the breeze at her back. The sun was starting to sink behind the mountains, casting long rays across the valley and enveloping her in golden light. A couple of months ago she might have closed her eyes and raised her face to enjoy the warmth of the rays on her skin. Let her cares go. Of course, a couple months ago she also walked fearlessly wherever she wanted, within reason. Being raised as she'd been, in a tough neighborhood where one learned to watch their back, Tess had felt as if she could handle anything.

Well, she'd been wrong. She hadn't been able to handle a surprise attack in the parking area of her apartment building.

Tess continued across her field until she came to the boundary fence. The dogs were already hunting in the field on the other side, so she lifted the top barbwire strand and eased through the fence.

The sun sank lower, deepening the gold cast of the light. Deep purple shadows stretched toward her from the base of the mountain. It would be dark soon, but Tess continued to walk until she came to the very center of the field of tall grass and there she stood, the wind ruffling her hair, and watched the last sliver of the sun disappear behind the mountains.

Was this the way her life would continue? Standing alone in the middle of nowhere? A study in solitude?

Until Eddie screwed up and went back to prison, yes.

Tess grabbed a handful of grass and yanked, twisting the blades around her hand before she turned into the wind and called the dogs to start for home. Detective Hiller didn't know Eddie like she did. Yeah, he might be working at the car wash and showing up for his meetings, but that didn't mean he didn't have someone looking for her. She'd never known Eddie to give up, but she had known him to do some sadistic things. One guy had tried to encroach on his territory shortly before she'd run away and Eddie had not only beat the crap out of him—he'd arranged to have the guy's trailer house torched while he was doing it.

Because of all the chemicals inside, the house had practically vaporized and the newspaper account had mentioned how fortunate it was that the owner hadn't been home. Tess's mouth twisted at the thought. Eddie had gotten such a kick out of that. He'd torn the article out and taped it to the fridge.

The clouds hung low and dark on the southeastern horizon, flat-bottomed and threatening as Tess headed across the field to the safety of her house. Walking toward the sunny mountains, she hadn't realized how quickly the storm had been moving in. When she reached the fence to her property she climbed through, then called the dogs again. Blossom shot past her, scooting under the wire before she stopped to grin at her, tongue lolling out the side of her mouth. Tess looked back and saw Mac hot on the trail of some small animal.

"Mac! Get over here! *Hier!*"

The dog reversed course and headed toward Tess at a dead run. Halfway to the fence he gave a startled yelp as he disappeared into the tall grass. Less than a second later he reappeared, bounding up, and continued racing toward her.

Tess crouched down as the dog approached, ruffling the

fur on either side of his neck when he obediently sat in front of her. His side was covered with moist dirt, which she brushed off. He must have fallen into a ditch or a hole hidden by the grass. Unseen danger. Exactly what she was trying to avoid.

"Let's go home," she said, and the dogs trotted ahead of her. Mac limped slightly. He kept up with Blossom, but his head bobbed up and down as he moved, making Tess wonder just how badly he'd hurt himself. The next time she walked, she'd keep the dogs closer and stay out of that part of the field.

A lightning bolt danced along the distant mountains as Tess mounted her porch steps. Another thunderstorm. Just what she needed to add to her unsettled mood.

The low rumble of thunder was followed by a gust of warm wind that lifted her hair as she unlocked the door. Once upon a time she'd loved thunderstorms.

Not so much anymore.

"COME ON, ELIZABETH. You're not afraid of thunder." Zach snapped on the light in his daughter's tiny second-story bedroom as he walked inside. It was the third time she'd called him in the past hour. The first time she'd said the thunder bothered her, but he wasn't buying it since she usually had her nose pressed to the window, watching the lightning. The second time she'd asked him to lower the blinds.

So was this an attention-getting device? Did she just want some company? Whichever it was, Zach's patience was growing thin. He was tired.

"It's not the thunder," Lizzie admitted in a small voice. A low rumble punctuated her words.

"Then what is it?" he asked softly.

"Trespassing."

"Trespassing? What about it?" He'd made it clear that

his daughters were never to cross the neighbor's property again, despite Darcy's heated protests about the land not being posted.

Lizzie twisted the edge of the blanket between her fingers. "What happens to you if you trespass?"

Zach knelt down next to the bed so they could be eye to eye. "The sheriff will warn you not to do it again."

Lizzie's forehead wrinkled. "But…her face."

"Those scars did not come from trespassing, Lizzie." He didn't know how on earth they could and he was pissed that Tess would have told his girls that.

"Then why did she say it?" Lizzie's eyes were huge.

Good question. Why scare a six-year-old? "My best guess is that she was trying to make a point. Her face didn't get hurt because she trespassed," he repeated firmly. "*Your* face will not get hurt if you trespass." He could only imagine what scenarios Lizzie had been conjuring up in her young mind. "Even though you shouldn't trespass," he added for the sake of consistency.

Lizzie sniffed. "How do you know?"

"Because that's not what happened to the lady. Her scars look like they came from a car accident, honey."

Lizzie twisted the edge of her blanket between her small hands. "She was lying?"

"In a big way." Zach reached down to smooth a few pale reddish-gold strands of hair off her forehead. In Lizzie's limited experience, adults didn't lie. She had so much to learn. "Now go to sleep, kiddo. There is absolutely nothing to worry about."

"Can Benny sleep with me?"

"Benny stinks to high heaven right now. Trust me, you don't want him in your bed or you'll smell like a ranch dog. You don't want that, do you?" A wavering smile touched his daughter's lips and she shook her head. "Benny's keeping guard on the porch," Zach said, pulling Lizzie's blankets up a little closer to her chin. "He'll bark if there's anything to worry about." Damn, he hoped the dog didn't bark. He needed some sleep.

Lizzie's smile faded away. She wrapped her arms around Zach's neck, pulling herself against him. He put a hand on her back and held her for a moment, smelling the strawberry bubble bath Emma had given her for her birthday. Then he got back to his feet and Lizzie snuggled deeper into the covers, looking so small.

"Liz, you know I'll make sure nothing happens to you. Right?"

She nodded silently and Zach smiled. "Good. Now get some sleep. Tia will drive you to school tomorrow."

Darcy's door was open and the light was on when he walked past her room a few seconds later. He paused in the doorway and she looked up from where she was reading in bed.

"If Liz yells again, I'll go," she offered.

"I think she'll be okay," Zach said. "I should just let Benny sleep with her."

"*Ewww.* Have you smelled him?"

"You guys going to wash him this weekend?"

Darcy let out a heavy sigh. "I guess."

"Just how scary was this lady?" Zach asked. The girls had poured the story out shortly after he got home but it had been jumbled, told from three different points of view. At the time Zach had brushed aside the details and got to the meat of the matter—his girls shouldn't have been on Tess O'Neil's land and they weren't to go back again. He didn't want his daughters to have anything to do with her.

"I wasn't scared." Darcy's lips twisted a little. "But I was kind of shocked. It took me a minute to realize she was being serious."

"She's serious," Zach said. And a whole lot less than friendly. Why did people like that move to small communities? "I take it you guys aren't going to use the creek path to get to school anymore? You're going to stay off her property?"

"We won't take Lizzie on the creek path. That's for sure."

"None of you will take the creek path."

"Dad, it's so much shorter..."

"And it's so her property."

"It's stupid."

"Stay away from that woman and off her land. Got it?"

Darcy let out a loud sigh—the kind he'd recently discovered only adolescents seemed to be able to make. "Fine. Got it."

"Thank you."

Zach walked down the hall to Emma's room. The door was shut, but he cracked it open and looked inside. His middle daughter was sound asleep, despite the thunder and the Lizzie drama. He smiled, wishing he had that ability. Sleepless nights were more of the norm for him and because of the uncooperative hospital accounting department, he predicted more of the same.

He opened his bedroom door and flicked on the light. For a long while after her death, he'd kept Karen's belongings out where he could see them, although Beth Ann had boxed her clothing and sent it to charity. But as time went on, he'd divided up Karen's personal treasures between his daughters. The small collection of jewelry he'd stored for later. All that remained was a photo on the nightstand and a lot of good memories.

And a lot of bad ones. Not of Karen, but of the grim months following the diagnosis. The trauma of the treatments. Meeting the needs of three little girls who were about to lose their mother. Grieving for his wife long before he'd lost her.

Zach sat on the bed and eased his boots off. The first one fell with a heavy clunk. What would Karen have done tonight after discovering what was bothering her baby? He smiled wearily. Probably marched straight over to Tess O'Neil's place and ripped into her. Karen had been sweet and peaceful, until something endangered those she loved. Beth Ann was the same way.

So was he. It was important to get along with the neighbors, but when a neighbor threatened your kids, things changed. Granted, they'd had no right to cross her land, but they were little girls, not hoodlums, following a path they'd taken for years. What the hell was she thinking trying to scare them?

Leave it. Just leave it.

Easier said than done when he was brought out of bed two hours later by a crying child. He shrugged into his flannel robe, his last gift from Karen, and he jogged upstairs to find Darcy hugging her little sister.

"It's not the lady. Honest," Lizzie said.

Like hell.

"It's okay, Dad," Darcy said. "Liz is coming to bed with me."

"You sure?"

"Yeah. But only for one night." Darcy emphasized the last words.

"One night," Lizzie agreed, making a beeline into Darcy's room.

Zach waited until the girls were in Darcy's bed, then turned off the light. Across the field, Tess O'Neil's place glowed like a beacon, every light on, even though it was almost three o'clock in the morning.

Darcy leaned out of bed and craned her neck to see what Zach was staring at out of her window. Then she shrugged.

"It's like that every night, Dad. She never shuts off her lights."

THE NIGHT BECAME still after the storm had passed, almost too still, and Tess couldn't bring herself to go upstairs to sleep. She remained in the chair, dozing fitfully and waking the next morning stiff from having finally fallen asleep in an uncomfortable position. When she pushed the blanket off her lap and got up out of the chair, Blossom shot to her feet, but Mac was slower to rise. When he finally did get to his feet, he held his injured foot a good three or four inches off the floor.

"Let's see that leg," Tess said, crouching in front of the dog. She reached out to gently touch it and Mac yelped, drawing it back, but not before Tess felt how hot it was. This was a problem.

Ten minutes later, after a short internet search, Tess called a vet in Wesley, the larger town an hour's drive to the south. As she'd feared, since Dr. Hyatt was the only vet within sixty miles, no appointments were available until the following week, but the vet tech promised to let her know if something opened up.

"His leg is hot," Tess said after receiving the bad news. "I'm afraid of infection."

"It's probably just inflammation," the tech said, "but to play it safe, I'll phone Ann at the mercantile about some medications you can give him until the doctor can see him."

"Really? The mercantile *here?*"

"Yeah. The merc is kind of our branch pharmacy."

"I had no idea. Thanks. I appreciate it."

Tess had shopped at the mercantile three times so far, and each time she'd been the only person in the store except for the tough-looking elderly woman behind the counter who'd gruffly introduced herself as Ann. Tess had not made a friend when she'd refused to offer her name in return.

When Tess parked in front of the store a half hour after talking to the vet, she was in luck again. Not a single car in the small lot. List in hand, she crossed the old wooden porch and pulled the door open, only to stop abruptly on the threshold, facing five sets of curious eyes.

Tess automatically dropped her chin, hiding her face as she quickly walked past the women who stood in a tight group near the checkout counter, and grabbed a basket off the stack at the end of the first aisle.

"Well, hello," one of the women called after her, "are you the new tenant of the Anderson place?"

"Hi," Tess replied, not answering the question and not looking back as she escaped down the aisle closest to her.

She stopped at the end of the aisle, out of sight of the group, and faced the cooler as she gathered her composure, convinced herself that this was not a big deal…just unexpected.

The mercantile was roughly the size of a large convenience store, stacked to the ceiling with a wild variety of merchandise, much of which Tess didn't recognize. Good cover until the ladies left. But the ladies started talking again and Tess soon realized that they had no intention of leaving.

Deciding she couldn't hide forever, she opened the cooler door and pulled out butter, milk and eggs before moving on to the rather sad-looking produce. If she hadn't felt cornered she might have worked at choosing the best fruit and vegetables, but as it was, she dumped carrots, oranges and apples into her basket, put three loaves of bread on top— one to eat, two to freeze. Then she peeked around the corner of a display.

The women were still there, clustered in the exact spot Tess wanted to be. Well, she couldn't hide out here forever and when Ann, the proprietress, caught sight of her and frowned, Tess sucked up her courage and headed for the checkout counter.

She was instantly surrounded by women—or so it felt.

"It's so nice to finally meet you," one of the ladies said. Tess didn't know which one because she didn't look at them. "Do you quilt?"

"No." Tess set the basket on the counter where Ann stood with a hand poised over the keys of the cash register, waiting for Tess to unload her basket. "Has Dr. Hyatt phoned in an order for me?" Tess asked her as she pulled the bread out of the basket.

"If you're Tess O'Neil he has," the woman said in a tone that told Tess she hadn't forgotten her refusal to state her name on her first visit.

"I am," Tess said in a low voice.

Ann pulled a stapled paper bag from under the counter and started ringing up the items in Tess's basket. And then the women started closing in again from behind.

"We're always looking for new members for our club," another woman, who for some reason was not taking a very blatant hint, declared from close to Tess's right shoulder. "And quilting is very easy to learn."

"Thank you very much, but I'm not interested." Tess sensed an exchange of glances as she pulled three twenties out of her very plain purse and handed them across the counter. The drawer of the old-fashioned cash register popped open as Tess quickly loaded her purchases into the recyclable tote she'd brought. A couple bucks' worth of change and she was good to go.

Except that she had to walk past the group of women and the shortest one was now studying her face with a thoroughness that unnerved her—to the point that Tess half expected her to say, "Don't I know you from somewhere?"

Maybe her disguise wasn't as good as she'd hoped. Maybe she should have gone with a wig or something. Or never left the house.

"Excuse me," she said, refusing to make eye contact as she squeezed past the women and opened the door. Okay. She was coming off as cold and rude. Tough. These ladies needed to understand that she didn't want to join their quilting bees or whatever.

"Such a *nice* young woman," she heard one of the women say sarcastically.

"I swear...I know her from somewhere."

The last words came just as the door swung shut, making Tess's blood freeze. She rushed to the car and got inside, slamming the door harder than necessary and then dumping the grocery tote on the seat beside her as the dogs nuzzled her hair. What if they figured out who she was?

CHAPTER FIVE

TESS'S HEAD pounded with a stress-induced headache by
the time she turned her car into her long driveway. Realistically, what were the chances that the inquisitive ladies in the mercantile would connect her, a scarred woman
with dark brown bobbed hair and horn-rimmed glasses, to
photoshopped magazine ads featuring a redheaded model?
Slim. Very slim.

But she still felt ill.

After putting away her few groceries, Tess tricked Mac
into taking an antibiotic pill by wrapping it in cheese, then
went out to the barn to put the final coat of finish on the
oak table.

She swept the barn floor in the area around the table,
trying not to think about the women. Trying not to obsess.

There was no breeze to stir the dust she hadn't been able
to bring up out of the rough floorboards, so Tess left the
barn door rolled open. The dogs soon settled in the sun outside the door and Tess began applying the clear finish over
the golden oak stain, focusing on her brushstrokes, trying
to make the finish as perfect as possible.

She was in the zone, done with the top and crouched
down to start a leg, when a fracas outside the barn door
brought her bolt upright. A split second later Mac and Blossom shot into the barn, tumbling over each other and knocking down the garden tools leaning against the far wall in
their frenzy to do...what?

The brush fell out of Tess's hand as she stumbled backward, instinctively heading for cover—until she heard a frantic squeaking and realized the dogs were after a small animal, now hiding behind an old mower.

"Leave it alone! *Foei! Zit!*"

Blossom instantly fell back at the Dutch commands, which meant business, then slowly sank down onto her haunches, her sharp gaze still zeroed in on whatever had hidden behind the tools. Mac was slower to obey, but then he, too, sat with his injured leg held out slightly, as if pointing to his prey.

Tess pressed her hand to her hammering heart then walked over to gingerly pick up the brush from where it had fallen on the still tacky tabletop. The finish was ruined, marred from the brush and the dust the dogs had carried in with them in their frenzy to get whatever furry little beast had raced into the barn ahead of them.

Her fault. She should have closed the door, but this was no big deal to someone with a lot of time on her hands. She'd simply wipe it down and start over.

But Tess's very logical assessment began to disintegrate as she stared down at the marred table. The dogs continued to hold, waiting for her to release them, and the critter, whatever it might be, stayed huddled where it was. For a brief moment everything in the barn was still, and then Tess felt tears start to well. Stupid tears that rolled down her cheeks—not because of her ruined work, but because of her still hammering heart. Because of the fear reactions she didn't seem able to control.

Something had to give.

"Let's go," she said to the dogs, motioning to the door. Once the dogs were out, Tess rolled the door most of the way shut, leaving a crack big enough—she hoped—for the furry little beast to escape through.

Hands shaking, she made a cup of tea to calm her nerves and forced herself to drink it before pulling out her cell phone and calling Detective Hiller.

It took two tries and several minutes on hold before the detective answered by stating his name in a clipped tone. Tess identified herself and asked if there was any news on Eddie or the guy who slashed her. Despite the tea, her voice still shook.

"Nothing new," he said in his usual brusque tone, indicating without saying a word that he had bigger, more urgent problems than an essentially cold case—her case—and he undoubtedly did. How many new and possibly urgent cases had he started working on since her assault? She was old news.

"Thank you," Tess muttered flatly, ready to hang up. She hated feeling like she was bugging the hell out of him, but she had no one else. He was it.

"Hey," he said just as she was about to say goodbye. "Is everything okay?"

Was that a grudging hint of empathy in his voice?

"No." She blurted the word, and it felt great to say it out loud, even to this guy who obviously had better things to do than talk to her. No. Everything was not all right.

"What's wrong?"

"I can't shake the nerves," Tess said, her voice low and intense. "I'm scared. All of the time." She was in the middle of nowhere, as hidden away from Eddie as she could be and she still felt like a target.

The detective pulled in a breath. "Are you in contact with anyone you know? Anyone Eddie might know?"

"Just you." She'd wanted to contact William, just to have someone to talk to, but hadn't.

"I don't count," he said. "Would Eddie have any reason to suspect you've gone to where you are now? Any connection between the place you're living and your past that he would know about?"

"Not much." Did one visit when she was twelve count? Her grandmother had taken her to see a friend in Barlow Ridge, who'd long since passed away. Her younger step-brother, Mikey, had been with them, but the stop had been part of a longer trip to Salt Lake City. It'd been a short over-night visit, but the isolation of Barlow Ridge had struck Tess, stuck with her. She'd felt so far away from her prob-lems there. So protected from the reality of her life—not her life with her grandmother, but the reality of her mother's life. It had been no accident that when she started to look for places to hide, she'd checked Barlow Ridge. Finding the An-derson Ranch for lease had seemed like a sign. A godsend.

"We passed through here once sixteen years ago on our way to another city," Tess said, walking over to the win-dow and staring out without actually seeing anything. She was too focused on Detective Hiller and his questions. His ultimate conclusion.

"No connections there?"

"No." And still none.

"What specifically is making you nervous?"

"I'm afraid of someone recognizing me and word get-ting out that the slashed model lives here." It sounded lame when she said it out loud, as if she was overestimating her importance and how much people thought about her, but the story of the slashing had made the news. Being recog-nized was not out of the realm of possibility—which was why she was here in the first place.

"How would they recognize you?" the detective asked. "Not to be blunt…" *When wasn't he blunt?* "But I've seen you before and after the attack. You look nothing like your old self."

Tess hadn't expected the remark to sting, but it did. Her

career, her looks, had given her an identity, made her more than a runaway and a survivor. She was back to being a survivor.

Tess took a moment, trying to find the words to explain why her fear of Eddie was so pervasive. Finally she settled on, "I know what a sadistic bastard Eddie is. I can't help worrying about him finding me, because if he does…" She swallowed to keep her throat from closing, remembering how the guy who cut her face had said that Eddie would keep taking pieces off her until he got what he wanted. She reached out with her free hand to stroke Blossom. The dog leaned into her leg.

"I understand your concern," the detective said as if he was reading a script. Not exactly reassuring.

"He's done some awful things to people," Tess said. She hated how defensive she sounded.

"Let's look at this logically. Would he be able to hang out in your community without being noticed?"

"Not easily."

"Is there a drug culture?"

Tess almost laughed. Yes. A huge cowboy drug culture. "If there is, it's really small and private." But she saw where he was going with this. Was there anyone who might know someone who knew someone who knew Eddie? But thinking of the people she'd met so far in Barlow Ridge…unlikely. "I don't think there's a bunch of trafficking through this particular community, but I don't know about the closest town. It's…larger."

There was a brief silence then the detective said, "You've been assaulted. Your fear is normal, but my gut says the chances of your stepfather running you down are remote if everything you've said is true. But you have to follow *your* gut."

"All right," Tess said quietly. The detective was basically

telling her that she had nothing to worry about, then adding a disclaimer in case he was wrong. Again, less than reassuring, but somehow Tess did feel reassured. A little anyway. Her fear was normal. She knew that, but it felt good having someone say it out loud.

"I'll call if we get any new information on the case, but for right now all I can tell you is that your stepfather has made every parole meeting and as far as I know, hasn't missed a day of work. I'll call you if that changes or we get any new information."

There didn't seem much to say after the detective's summation, so Tess simply said, "Thank you."

"If there's nothing else…?"

"No."

"Then have a good day." The line went dead before she could say goodbye.

Tess hung up the phone and then walked over to the window to stare out across the sunny fields behind her house. What the detective said made sense. Eddie really had no way to track her here. If someone recognized her, what would they do? Contact the media? It wasn't like she was missing and the authorities were looking for her. If people thought they recognized her, they might talk among themselves. Wonder.

And maybe someone Eddie knew would get wind of it…

What were the chances? She was eight hundred miles away from Eddie.

Tess leaned forward until her forehead touched the glass. What she needed was perspective—to look at things without filtering them through the residual feelings of trauma left by the attack.

Just because she'd been a victim didn't mean she had to remain one. All she had to do was figure out how to get a grip…and separate reality from paranoia.

She let out a breath that briefly fogged the window. That was going to take a whole lot of practice.

ZACH WAS IN the kitchen when Beth Ann and Emma came into the house. The bills sat in a stack next to the phone, stamped and ready to go. The bank account was drained and he'd had to call Jeff, his cousin and ranching partner, to set up a time to discuss selling cows earlier than planned. He was so damned tired of hanging on by a thread.

"Lizzie and Darcy thought they saw a late calf and went to check," Beth Ann said as she dumped two backpacks onto a kitchen chair. "And Emma has news."

"We're going to 4-H horse camp. Both Darcy *and* me this year." Emma grinned widely before opening the fridge and pulling out the milk. She poured half a glass and then put the top back on the plastic bottle and shoved it back inside the fridge.

"We haven't filled out the forms yet. Or paid," Zach said, not quite certain how to take this happy news.

"We got scholarships," Emma said. "Irv stopped by the school and told the class who'd won scholarships. It was me and Darcy and Luke."

"Scholarships?" Zach met Beth Ann's eyes over the top of his daughter's head. Every year the volunteer firemen gave scholarships to various camps and the graduating seniors for college.

"Yes. This year Emma and Darcy got the scholarships. You didn't know?"

No, he didn't know, and he was a fireman. When had the guys decided that his family would receive the charity this year?

"Isn't it great, Dad?" Emma said, doing a happy twirl that came close to slopping the milk out of her glass.

"Well," Zach started before he caught Beth Ann's eye

again where he read "leave it for now." Fine. He'd leave it, but he was going to pay for this camp. "I don't know what Lizzie and I are going to do without you guys around for a week."

"You'll manage," Emma said. "I can't believe *I* get to go this year!" She skipped out of the kitchen, happy as can be, leaving Zach and Beth Ann and a whole lot of tension in the air.

"I didn't know the girls put in for scholarships."

"Everyone in the 4-H club puts in for a scholarship," Beth Ann said.

"There are kids who need the money more than Emma and Darcy."

"Can you really afford to have both of them go this year?"

He could barely afford having Darcy go alone last year. The camp, which was near Boise and associated with the university there, ended up costing almost nine hundred dollars per kid for travel, a week's worth of food and the instructors, who were always top-notch.

"I can figure something out."

"Damn it, Zach. What's more important here? Your pride or both girls getting to go to camp?"

"There's got to be a way other than charity."

"Scholarships are not charity. They're awarded to deserving kids, regardless of need."

"Bull. I've been in on enough selection meetings that I know exactly how they're awarded." Because pretty much every kid in the local 4-H club was deserving. Need was the number one factor used when the firemen selected their scholarship recipients.

Darcy came in through the back door just then, smiling widely. "You have a new bull calf, but the mama isn't going to let anyone near it. Did Emma tell you about horse camp?"

"Yes, she did."

"Isn't it great?" Darcy asked as she pulled her backpack out from under Lizzie's pink one. "Now I can use the hundred dollars I saved for something else!"

"Yeah," Zach said, forcing a smile that he hoped looked halfway genuine. "It's good to have a windfall like that. Where's your little sister?"

"Lizzie thought she heard something in the barn."

"Like…what?"

"Like her imagination," Darcy said. "I couldn't hear anything, but you know how she loves to find baby barn cats. She'll be in pretty soon." She hefted her backpack and headed out of the kitchen toward the living room.

"I know you hate this, Zach, but you're thinking about this the wrong way," Beth Ann said once Darcy was hopefully out of hearing range.

Zach chose not to answer, because no matter how he thought about it, it stung. Maybe it wouldn't have stung so much if he could have afforded to send both girls and this was a happy surprise, but that wasn't what it was. His fellow firemen were giving him charity in the one way he wouldn't be able to say no.

"Now you can use that eighteen hundred dollars for something else," Beth Ann pointed out, echoing Darcy.

"I guess," Zach said. Hard to argue since that money would take a bite out of the medical bills. "Staying for dinner? We're having another slow-cooker delight."

"No. I think I'll head home and hit the books." She touched his upper arm, patting lightly. Zach met her eyes. Smiled a little.

"See you later," he said.

TESS STAYED AWAKE until daybreak. She'd read and drawn and even conducted a late-night job search. She went over and over her conversation with Detective Hiller, told herself that he was right, but as soon as it was dark outside she found herself with all the lights on, listening for anything out of the ordinary. There was no storm that night, which may have been why she could hear so much more than she had the previous few nights. Rattling windows, creaking boards. The noises of an old house, but enough to keep her on edge.

This is normal. You've been assaulted. Of course you're on edge.

Why was it so damned hard to put this all into perspective? It'd been three months since she'd been slashed and she'd expected once she got out of California and deep into the wilds of Nevada that the fear would fade faster than it was.

Maybe that was part of her problem. The fear wasn't going to simply fade away after a trauma. She had to work at overcoming it and thus far all she'd been doing was reacting to it.

Finally, after the sun came up, she let the dogs out, then crawled back into bed, meaning only to close her eyes for ten or fifteen minutes before she let the dogs back in. She woke up with a start, realizing the dogs were still outside and that somehow she'd fallen asleep.

She grabbed the clock which was facing the wall and turned it around. One-thirty?

She'd slept for eight hours straight. A record. She didn't know whether to be happy or disturbed. She'd been unconscious, oblivious to danger for eight long hours.

But nothing had happened.

Pushing the rumpled hair back from her face, she walked into the bathroom, grimaced when she saw the crease marks on her face from sleeping so hard.

Tess pushed aside the bathroom window curtains to see the dogs sleeping in the shade under the big elm tree in the backyard, the sunlight that filtered through the branches dappling their coats as they snoozed. They looked so peaceful. Everything seemed so...dare she say it, think it? Everything seemed so normal.

And then the phone rang, scaring the bejeezus out of her.

She scooped it up on the second ring, answered it after taking a deep breath so that her voice sounded normal.

"Ms. O'Neil? We have a cancellation this afternoon at four. Could you bring your dog in then?"

Could she? Tess pushed her hair back, leaving her hand on top of her head as she calculated. Almost two. She could be ready by two-thirty. An hour's drive to Wesley...

"Ms. O'Neil?"

"Uh, yes. I can make it."

"Great. We'll see you and Mac at four."

Half an hour later, she loaded the dogs into the backseat of her car. It was the first time she'd left Barlow Ridge since arriving. The first time she'd ventured out into the world at large to risk being recognized.

But somehow getting sleep, real sleep, not her usual pattern of sleeping for half an hour and then waking, made her feel better. Stronger. Able to tackle this mission.

Or maybe the logic of Detective Hiller's assessment had finally sunk in to the point that she could work on believing it. She didn't care which it was as long as she could start easing herself back into a more normal existence— or as normal as it could be living in the middle of nowhere under a false name.

The vet office was easy to find and little more than an hour after she'd left the ranch she was there, sitting in the car, summoning the courage to go inside.

Tess touched her cheek, which she'd left uncovered, having decided that a white bandage caught the eye more than unsightly scars. Instead she'd worn a light blue knit cloche hat that flattened her hair down onto her cheeks, partially covering the injury, and sunglasses to hide the drooping corner of her left eye.

"Hello," the vet tech, a young woman with a reddish-brown braid down her back, called brightly as Tess and Mac entered the waiting room.

"Hi." Tess smiled briefly and then pushed her glasses up to the bridge of her nose as they started to slide down. There were no other people in the office, but a lot of barking in the back.

"I need you to fill this out," the girl said, coming around the counter and handing Tess a clipboard. "New in town?" she asked before kneeling in front of Mac who obligingly held his bad leg out.

The question made Tess's stomach knot. "I've been here for a while," she said as she took the pen and started filling out the information. When she was done, the only truthful information was her phone number and Mac's vitals. Everything else was a fabrication. Her entire life was a fabrication.

Tess brought the clipboard back to the counter just as a tall broad man with blond hair opened the door leading to the clinic. "Hey," he said with an easy smile. "I'm Dr. Hyatt—Sam." His eyes traveled over her injured cheek, making her stomach tighten even more, and then he focused on Mac. "What happened?"

Tess gave him a quick rundown and then the vet said, "I'll have to x-ray." He cocked one eyebrow as if waiting for Tess to ask a question. It took her a moment to realize he was waiting for her to ask how much an X-ray would cost.

"Whatever it takes."

"I'll keep the cost down as low as I can."

"You'd never survive in Beverly Hills," Tess said with a half smile, trying her best to act nonchalant. Normal.

"Are you from Southern Cal?" Sam asked shooting her a quick glance as he ran a hand over Mac's head.

"No." The word came out too quickly and sounded very much like the lie it was. Tess faked a smile. "Um, how long will this take? I have a couple errands I need to run."

Dr. Hyatt frowned slightly before he said, "An hour. Tops."

"Okay. Thanks. I'll see you in an hour."

Tess made her escape, pulling in a deep breath of crisp air as the door closed behind her. It did nothing to clear her head. She had no errands. She simply needed to get away from the vet and his cute chatty receptionist before she made more mistakes—or her stomach turned inside out from stress.

Blossom whined and nosed her cheek when she got into the car.

"I know the feeling," Tess said, ruffling the dog's fur before she started the car. She'd been in town for all of twenty minutes and she felt like she'd been put through an emotional wringer. So much for normal. But it was her first outing. Surely things would get easier with practice.

The town was small, about ten thousand people, and it didn't take long to drive the length of the main street. There were the usual chain businesses and fast food establishments, as well as a few smaller stores. A Western supply store, a coffee shop, a bakery. She needed a grocery store and found one in a small strip mall at the very edge of town, where the trees disappeared and the desert began.

Tess pulled into a parking spot in front of a tiny clothing store and sat in her car for a moment, gathering strength. The dress hanging in the window in front of her caught her eye. It was simple. Stylish. Something she would have worn not that long ago. Not that long, but in some ways a lifetime.

Tess touched her cheek, hesitated for a brief moment,

then pulled the keys out of the ignition and got out of the car, automatically pulling the cloche down. People walked in and out of the store as she approached, her sunglasses still on, her eyes down. *They don't care about you.*

Half an hour later she wheeled an overloaded cart out to her car and opened the trunk. No one had given her more than a passing glance, but she felt emotionally drained. She also had another half hour to kill. Tess slammed the trunk down and was about to get into her car, when she decided that instead she'd check out the hobby shop next to the clothing store where she was parked.

There were only two people in the store, an elderly man and woman looking at yarn, but Tess immediately went down an aisle. Jewelry-making supplies. She stopped for a moment, studying the long strings of bead of various colors. This had possibilities.

And then she spotted the bolts of fabric on long tables at the back of the store. One of the lengths of fabric matched the dress she'd seen in the clothing store window next door. Tess reached out and ran her hand over the geometric-printed jersey.

"That's lovely fabric," a woman said from behind her. Tess turned toward the woman standing a table away, tidying up the bolts. "Can I help you find anything in particular?"

"Uh, no," Tess said. Now that the woman was looking at her, she felt the usual urge to run. "I'm just checking out possible crafts."

"We have a lovely hobby kit section up front," she said.

"Thank you. I'll take a look."

The lady went back to her folding and Tess returned to the front of the store. She spent a few minutes looking over the kits, none of which appealed to her the way the fabric had, and then quietly left the store for the safety of her car. Enough dillydallying around. She headed back to the vet clinic.

"No fracture," Dr. Hyatt said after the tech ushered Tess back into the clinic area where Mac was lying on a table obviously woozy from a sedative. His front leg was wrapped with gauze and covered with some kind of pink stretchy wrap.

"Then…"

"It's a soft tissue injury and perhaps a pulled tendon. I wrapped his leg so he stays off it."

Sam gave her instructions on how to care for Mac's leg, told her to give the wrap at least a week before taking it off, although, he warned, Mac may remove it himself. Sam wanted to see the dog again in two weeks if he didn't improve.

Tess thanked him, paid cash for the visit and then waited for the receipt the girl insisted on writing while Sam carried the still woozy dog out to her car.

Wind whipped her hair as she left the clinic and walked over to her car where Blossom was now riding shotgun. Low dark clouds hung on the horizon in the direction she'd be driving. Another storm. Great. Tess was beginning to hate storms.

Despite the clouds, this one seemed to be mainly wind, which buffeted her car for most of the drive home, finally easing up about ten miles from Barlow Ridge. Tess's knuckles ached from clutching the steering wheel so tightly. It had been one hell of a nerve-racking day—to the point that she might actually sleep tonight from sheer mental exhaustion.

It was close to seven when she crossed the cattle guard that marked the city limit of Barlow Ridge. When she stopped at the first of the two four-way stops, she noticed an odd orange glow on the far side of town, like a sunset on the wrong side of the valley. Tess frowned as she stopped at the second four-way, then her stomach tightened as she realized just what that glow was.

Fire.

CHAPTER SIX

"DAD!" Emma skidded into the office where Zach was tallying up the monthly expenses. "The mean lady's barn is on fire!"

Both Zach's pager and his phone went off before she'd finished speaking. He automatically turned off the pager as he picked up the phone, which showed the number of Irv Barnes, the rural fire chief.

"The Anderson barn is on fire," Irv said as Zach brought the phone to his ear. "Can you get over there and make sure the home owner isn't doing anything stupid while we gear up?"

"Okay. See you in a few." Zach pocketed the phone without another word and headed through the living room.

"It was the lightning, don't you think?" Emma said, still trailing behind Zach as he went to the enclosed porch to put on his fire gear, which consisted of most of his regular gear and his oldest boots.

"Probably," he said, tugging at the laces of his left boot to tighten them before tying the knot. A storm had passed over. There'd been some thunder, but he hadn't seen any lightning.

"Dad, there's a fire!" Lizzie said as she clattered down the stairs to the living room.

"He knows," Emma answered impatiently.

Zach left the house with both girls following him. Emma

wanted desperately to be a firefighter and he knew what was coming next.

"Dad...?"

"Sorry, Em."

"But I can sit in the truck. I just want to *watch*."

"No." Zach pulled on his coat as he headed out the door. Benny wanted in on the action, too, and Zach had to kick him out of the back of the truck before he left. He could see the collie sitting forlornly in the road, with Emma beside him, one hand on top of the dog's head. Zach pulled his phone out of his pocket and dialed Beth Ann.

"What's up, Zach?" She sounded distracted and he figured she'd probably been studying or she would have noticed the black smoke billowing up from across the road.

"There's a fire at the Anderson place," Zach said as he drove by her trailer house. "Would you please make sure Emma doesn't drift down the driveway too far?"

"What's on fire? The house?"

"Barn. Gotta go."

Flames shot out of the top of the old wooden structure as Zach's truck bounced across the county road and onto Tess O'Neil's driveway. Was she home? Fighting the fire with a garden hose? He knew from his trainings that too many people got injured fighting their own fires or trying to rescue things from a burning building. Not that Tess would have much to rescue from the old barn unless she'd stored her own belongings in there, which seemed unlikely considering the size of the house.

Zach pulled his truck off the side of the driveway, in the grassy median between gravel and fence line, leaving plenty of room for the fire trucks to pass. The windows of the house were dark—however, it was likely she'd already lost power, since the lines ran to the barn and then the house.

The headlights of the first fire truck appeared on the

county road about a half mile away as Zach ran from his truck to the house and pounded on the door. No answer, but according to Len, the UPS man, this woman rarely answered her door—although she'd opened it for him the time he'd come to talk about the pasture lease, and then shut it in his face—which still pissed him off.

The killer dogs weren't barking, though, and who in their right mind didn't answer the door when their barn was on fire? Unless she was sleeping. Or not in her right mind. Something was very off about Tess O'Neil.

The fire truck pulled into the driveway and Irv jumped out. Wes Crane and Tom McKirk parked their pickups behind Zach's, and then the second engine turned the corner into the driveway. And right on the tail of the second engine was the small car that Zach recognized as Tess O'Neil's. At least they now knew where she was.

"That's the property owner," Zach told Irv.

"Talk to her," Irv said as he started connecting the couplings.

"Sure," Zach replied, so looking forward to the prospect.

The car stopped dead in the center of the road, but Tess didn't get out of it. One of the dogs was with her, sitting in the passenger seat, and as Zach approached the car the other dog sat up in the backseat. Damn but they were fierce-looking beasts.

Tess hadn't noticed him as he'd walked around the back of her car and she jumped a mile when he knocked on her window. Even in the dim dashboard light he could make out the look of utter terror on her face as she jerked around to meet his eyes through the glass. Shit. He hoped she didn't go into shock.

He had to knock again before she rolled down the window. She wore a hat, which pushed her dark hair down onto her cheeks, but because her left side was closest to him, Zach could still see parts of the jagged scar extending from her eye to her jawline, marring the beautiful lines of her face. But beauty, he reminded himself, was only skin deep, a tenet this woman seemed very intent on proving.

"How'd it start?" Her voice was hoarse, as if she'd been breathing the smoke.

"Lightning is my best guess."

Tess's chin jerked up. "I didn't see any lightning while driving home." Her words sounded like an accusation and Zach wasn't in the mood for more craziness.

"That doesn't mean there wasn't any." He glanced at the flames over the top of her car. "It'd be best if you weren't here while we deal with this."

She blinked at him. "Where can I go?"

If it was anyone else, he would have sent them to his place. But not her. Not the woman who'd purposely frightened his kid.

"The café. It's almost closing time, but they'll let you stay there. The fire chief's wife runs the place."

She didn't seem to grasp what he was saying, or so he assumed from the slow way she shook her head as she stared at the flames again. "Will the house catch fire?"

"The wind isn't bad, so hopefully not." Not unless a spark or two floated over to that dry cedar shake roof.

Her face grew incredibly pale and again he wondered about shock. "Can I get some stuff?"

"No."

Her mouth fell open. "But—"

Come on, lady. "No."

"Fine." She snapped the word out, reaching for the gear-shift. Zach stepped back, assuming she'd peel out or do something equally dramatic, but instead she rolled forward and carefully executed a three-point turn a few yards up the road.

Zach jogged back across the road toward the fire engine but shot a glance toward the end of the driveway in time to see that Tess had turned her car toward the mountain instead of toward town.

What was with this woman?

LIGHTNING.

If she'd been in any other situation, if she hadn't known about Eddie torching at least one house as a warning, Tess would have had less of a problem believing her barn had been struck by lightning. But right now she didn't know what to think. Hell, she barely *could* think, which sucked after she'd spent the afternoon consciously trying to look at her situation rationally instead of through the filter of fear.

Tess drove about half a mile up the county road toward the mountain, then turned around and parked. She wasn't going to sit in a café and wonder what was happening at her place. She was going to sit on the opposite side of the field and watch.

Was Eddie, or one of his cronies, also watching?

Stop it...

Not every bad thing in her life was caused by Eddie. Just a lot of them.

Tess gritted her teeth as she turned off the lights and the ignition. And then she hit the automatic door lock.

Now that she was a distance away, she could understand why her neighbor hadn't wanted her to go in the house. As the wind picked up, the flames licked closer and the dark smoke billowed directly over the two-story frame structure. A few sparks on that shake roof and her house would be a goner, too.

Please don't let that happen.

Tess closed her eyes for a brief moment as she said a prayer, letting her head rest against the back of the seat.

So was this just a run of bad luck? A lightning strike? A warning?

There was no way she was going to find out tonight.

Mac sat up in the backseat and Tess realized she probably should let the dogs out to do their business. Cautiously she checked her surroundings, even though it was impossible to see much in the dark, then unlocked the doors and got out of her vehicle. She stood for a moment in the road, watching the fire trucks spray water on her house and barn, before opening the back door. Mac jumped out, landing awkwardly due to his wrapped front leg. Blossom scrambled over the seat and joined him in the road. For a moment all three of them stood facing the fire, then the dogs went to the edge of the road, snuffled around a bit, peed. When they finished, Tess opened the door and they got back into the car without her saying a word. She followed, once again locking the doors, and then she sat. Watched and waited. Almost an hour later, when one of the fire trucks finally pulled away from the orange glowing heap that had once been her barn, Tess started the car and slowly drove back to her place.

When she pulled to the side of the road into one of the spots vacated by a large pickup that was just leaving, Zach Nolan once again approached her car, crossing the road with long, easy strides.

He must have been put in charge of her, Tess thought darkly as she opened the door and got out of her car, wrinkling her nose as the smell of acrid smoke hit her nostrils.

"I'm not leaving," she said as soon as he was a few feet away. He had dark smears of greasy dirt across his cheek and forehead, and his eyes were red-rimmed from smoke. She could only imagine what his clothes were going to smell like when he got home.

"Do what you want." He spoke indifferently, his expression cold and distant. His attitude shouldn't have stung, but it did.

Well, what did she expect after the way she'd treated him? A big hug?

Tess ran a hand over her upper arm. "I can go into my house?" Because she needed to be in her house. Now. Locked away and safe. Not that she'd sleep, but she'd have some walls around her.

"I'm not going to stop you," he said. "Someone will stay here until morning to keep an eye on things. There were a bunch of old tires stored in the barn and they're going to smolder for a while."

"Will it be you?" she asked. "Staying, I mean."

A spark flashed in his eyes, belying his cold tone when he said, "Should it be?"

"No." She had no idea why she'd asked. Maybe because they'd actually spoken a few times and she didn't know the other men who might stay. "It's just that…you live close."

"It won't be me." He started toward his truck without another word.

"Excuse me, Ms. O'Neil." Tess jumped at the unexpected voice from behind her, then turned to find a husky gray-haired man ten or fifteen years older than Zach approaching her. "I'm Irv Barnes, the fire chief." He wiped his hand on his pants, took a look at his grimy palm, then dropped it back to his side without offering it to her.

The fire chief—someone who could possibly give her some answers. Tess gave a brief nod of acknowledgment, then said, "Do *you* think the fire was caused by lightning?"

Irv's eyebrows moved a fraction of an inch closer at her brusque question. "We don't know yet."

"Zach said it was lightning."

Irv nodded slowly, but he didn't say that he agreed. "The fire marshal will come out tomorrow and take a look."

"So until then—"

"We don't know," he said.

Tess hesitated very briefly before she asked, "Could it have been set on purpose?"

"We don't know," Irv repeated.

Tess didn't like the way he was looking at her. "No theories?"

"None I care to share. After the fire marshal makes his report, you can contact your insurance company and send a copy in order to make a claim for both the barn and the damage to the house."

"The house?" That was when Tess noticed the dark singe marks up the side of her house, illuminated by the headlights of the small yellow fire engine. Damn. Maybe it had been a good thing her neighbor hadn't let her go inside. "I almost lost my home," she said.

"It was a bit dicey for a few minutes." He shifted his weight, still eyeing her in a less than friendly way, and Tess suddenly realized why. He thought she'd started the fire. Because of her questions.

What now? Protest innocence?

That'd do her a lot of good. Zach Nolan drove by at that moment and she glanced at his truck, wondering if he thought the same—that she was an arsonist.

"You're going to be without electricity," the fire chief said, pulling her attention away from Zach and back to him. "You'll need to call the company tomorrow, but even so, it might be a day or two before they can get it fixed."

"Thank you," Tess said automatically, though she didn't think she had a lot to be thankful for. A fire of undetermined cause, which this guy thought she might be responsible for, and possibly days in a dark house.

"I, uh, could lend you a flashlight, if you need it," the fire chief said brusquely.

"No, thanks. I have a good one in the car."

"Someone will be here through the night, so you don't have to worry about flare-ups."

"Good to know," Tess said, trying to work a note of politeness into her voice, but it was so damned hard. "I, uh, appreciate all you've done."

"I'm sure you do," Irv said on a rough note of irony before he turned and walked back to his fire engine, leaving Tess staring after him for a moment.

Her barn was a smoldering mess. The table she'd spent so many hours on was gone. The fire chief thought she was an arsonist and she still didn't know how the fire had been caused.

Would it not be the ultimate irony if someone else had started the fire and she ended up going to jail because of it?

BY THE TIME Zach got home, it was close to 2:00 a.m. He left his smoky clothes, more rank than usual because of the burning tires, in a pile on the bathroom floor, showered and fell into bed. He felt like he'd slept for all of five minutes when he heard a knock on his door frame. He pried one eye open to see Emma standing there.

"Everything okay?" he mumbled.

"Yes. I just wanted you to know that we're leaving."

"Thanks."

"Darcy and I fed Benny and the leppy calves."

He smiled a little. "Thanks, kiddo."

She gave a nod and left. Zach closed his eyes, but it was no use. He was awake now and he had more hungry mouths to feed. He waited until he heard the kitchen door shut and the sound of his daughters' voices as they headed down the driveway toward Beth Ann's trailer. Darcy and Emma were arguing about something.

He rolled out of bed and sat on the edge, hands loosely

clasped between his knees. The sheets stank of smoke despite the quick shower he'd taken and there were still streaks of black greasy residue up his arms. Zach stood up and automatically started stripping the sheets off the bed when the phone rang.

"Hey, Zach. Irv."

"Yeah."

"Do me a favor, would you?"

"Sure."

"Head over to your neighbor's and take one last look at those tires sometime this morning." *Oh, joy.* "Wes has to go home and feed his livestock and I want to make sure those tires don't cause any problems."

"Sure." Maybe Tess would stay holed up in her house.

"Jeff will be out later today with the fire marshal to make an official report."

"What for?" Zach asked.

"Insurance."

Of course. Had to be certain it wasn't arson.

"Yeah." Try as he might, he couldn't put any enthusiasm into his answer. He didn't bother showering again, but instead dressed in old jeans and a sweatshirt and headed out the door to feed the cows that were already gathered near the gate since he was running late this morning. Benny shot down the driveway from Beth Ann's house, ready to go to work as Zach went into the barn to start the tractor.

Maybe he'd get lucky and the fire marshal would make it out early—before he had to go check on those damned tires.

JUST AS IRV, the fire chief, had promised, a fireman had hung around outside Tess's house until morning. She checked on him from her bedroom window every now and then, since she had nothing to do except sit in the dark. Every time she looked, he was in the cab of his truck, watching the smoldering tires and wood. Finally around 3:00 a.m. she lay down on her fully made bed and fell sound asleep.

A knock on the back door four hours later brought her rearing up out of a deep sleep, still dazed, the result of exhaustion and her reaction to the fire. Both dogs jumped to their feet and scrambled out of the bedroom, Mac holding his pink wrapped leg out in front of him as he awkwardly followed Blossom down the stairs.

Mac's tail had just disappeared from sight when the tentative knock sounded again and Tess realized that it had to be the fireman. She could hear the dogs growling in the kitchen below her as she walked to the window and opened it.

"Yes?" she called to the man standing on her back step, staring dubiously at the door that separated him from Blossom and Mac. He looked up and then took a few steps back so he could see her better.

"I have to go home now," he called. "Somebody else will be stopping by in an hour or two to check on things. Uh—" he pointed at the door with one hand as he shielded his eyes from the glare of the rising sun with the other "—you might want to keep your dogs inside."

"I will. Thanks."

"And if you see anything that resembles a fire, call Irv. He gave you his card, right?"

"No."

"I'll just write his number down and slip it into the screen door."

"Thank you." Tess moved back and shut the window, then ran a hand over her hair. It felt grimy, even though she hadn't spent that much time in the actual smoke—or at least it hadn't seemed like she had. She sniffed at a hank and then dropped it. Damn—did she dare take a shower? She hated the thought of being that vulnerable until she found out whether her barn fire was an accident or arson.

She could shower when the new fire guy came...except
that she had no electricity to pump the water. Tess's temples
began to throb as she walked downstairs. The dogs were
still standing at the door, waiting to get out and eat a fireman, no doubt.

"He's gone," Tess said wearily, but she took a quick look
outside just in case. No truck. Just a whole lot of smoldering ruin.

The note the fireman had written fluttered to the ground
as she opened the door and stepped outside to survey the
damage firsthand. She picked up the note and surveyed
the scene.

Not only was the barn gone, but her furniture, too. The
beautiful table she'd poured so many hours into. Gone.

The sense of loss was overwhelming.

"Just a barn and some old furniture," she muttered to herself. But it was more than that. The furniture had kept her
busy, given her a bit of purpose. Now she had no idea how
she was going to fill her hours—or even if she was. If this
fire had been set on purpose, she had to leave. Immediately.

The wonderful epiphany she'd had yesterday about over-
thinking and overreacting due to the trauma was long gone.
Now, she was firmly back to *what if?*

What if Eddie had found her? Was showing her he meant
business before confronting her and demanding his money?

What if he hadn't found her and she was making herself
a miserable wreck?

Tess sank down on the step then jumped back to her feet
as the dogs headed toward the stretch of cyclone fence the
firemen had knocked down to make room for their equipment.

"Af!"

The dogs obediently turned and came back, but she could
see that their paws were covered with mud. At least she'd

stopped them before they'd hit the black stuff that seemed to be everywhere on the far side of the flattened fence.

A few minutes later Tess had had enough of the acrid odors and depressing scenery behind her house. She called the dogs and, after cleaning their paws as much as possible with a wad of paper towels, went back inside, where she tried to put on the teakettle, only to remember that her stove wasn't going to be working for a while.

Cold, dark and hungry. She needed to call the power company and remedy that—if she had a phone.

To Tess's surprise, a healthy dial tone hummed in her ear when she picked up the receiver. She held the phone on her shoulder as she thumbed through the Wesley phone book for the number, and had just started to dial when the dogs jumped up and raced for the front door. Less than a second later she heard a firm knock. The fireman?

Tess hung up the phone and silently walked into the living room to the window where she could get a slanted view of the porch without being seen. Not the fireman.

Two ladies stood there, in front of her door, unaware that she was peeking at them, and they were carrying... food? Each had a foil-covered bowl in her hand. And one of them was the woman from the mercantile who'd thought Tess looked familiar.

Crap.

Tess turned away from the window and leaned back against the wall, putting a palm to her forehead and closing her eyes. Food. Just what she needed when she had no electricity. No way to keep it cold or heat it up. And no desire to eat.

Another knock. Tess stayed still right where she was with her back plastered against the wall, feeling like a fugitive in her own home. Yes, she should answer the door. Greet the neighbors, take the food. Even though she looked like hell.

The thing was, she didn't want to encourage them.

The other thing was they weren't showing signs of giving up. They were still on the porch...weren't they?

She gave another peek and then quickly ducked back. *Had they spotted her that time?*

One more knock. This one firmer, more determined.

With a heavy sigh she pushed off from the wall and side-stepped the dogs to open the door a crack, just as she had with Zach a few days ago, only this time she didn't knock her glasses off her face—because she'd forgotten to put them on. Damn.

She didn't say a word as she met first the eyes of the inquisitive quilting lady from the mercantile and then a benignly smiling white-haired woman.

"Hello," the quilt lady said briskly, holding out the foil covered casserole. "Since you're without electricity, I've brought you a meal."

"That's very...kind," Tess said. But from the way the woman was angling her head, trying to get a look at the injured side of her face, Tess wasn't sure kindness was the true motivation. For a moment they faced off, Tess leaving the door right where it was, shielding her injury and the woman standing with the casserole at chest level. Tess gave in first. "I'm not decent. Not to be rude, but would it be possible to leave it on the porch, and I'll get it as soon as I am?"

"I'd be happy to wait while you...get decent," the woman said. The older woman nodded from behind her, still smiling.

"Thank you, but it might take me a little while to get decent. I don't have any water. I'm sure you understand."

"Of course," the woman said with a sniff. "You can leave the bowl in the post office. Mrs. Stratford will be by later today with another meal to help tide you over until they get the electricity turned back on."

"Oh, please no." Not more people traipsing to her door unannounced.

"No?" The white-haired woman's smile faded as she spoke for the first time. "But we organized—"

"No," Tess said adamantly. "I appreciate the thought, but…no."

The quilt lady inhaled deeply. "Well…I…I…"

Never?

Tess realized that she was so exhausted she was shaking. All she wanted was for this nosy woman to leave and to take the sweet-looking grandmother with her. Along with the casserole if possible.

"No offense intended. I just want to be left alone. I…I—" she lifted her chin, being careful to keep her face angled away from them "—value my privacy."

"Obviously. Well—" the woman hugged the casserole close to her body as she turned to go "—sorry to have wasted your time. We need to go, Melba."

"It's nothing personal," Tess muttered as the women tromped down the steps. And then she closed the door before she could hear anything she didn't want to hear.

She went back into the kitchen, needing caffeine in the worst way, but since she couldn't make coffee or tea she sank down at the kitchen table and rested her head on her arms. Her intention upon moving here was to disappear. Ignore her neighbors so that they would ignore her. It was the way it'd worked in every city she'd ever lived in. Unfortunately she'd never lived in a rural area and hadn't realized that the rules might be different.

No doubt the neighbors would leave her alone now, but they wouldn't forget her. What with her barn burning down and refusing casseroles she was nowhere near flying under the radar.

Tess's eyes drifted shut then flashed open again as the

dogs started barking. A split second later someone else pounded on her door.

It had to be the fireman, but that didn't keep her heart from knocking against her ribs as she went into the living room and looked out the window to see Zach Nolan standing on her porch.

Feeling relieved that it was at least someone she was vaguely familiar with and that he wasn't carrying food, Tess opened the door a few inches.

"I have to check the remains of the fire and I wanted to let you know." He sounded utterly ticked.

"Thank you," Tess said. What else could she say?

He didn't respond. Didn't move, didn't do anything except stare her down with cold blue eyes. Tess shifted uncomfortably and was about to close the door in his face again when he said, "What's wrong with you?"

"Pardon me?" she asked, startled. Was he asking about her face? Which she thought she was keeping out of sight.

"I said, what's wrong with you?" He planted a hand against the wall and leaned closer to the open crack between the door and the jamb, so close that she could feel the warmth of his body. Or was it her imagination? "Have you always been like this?"

"Like what?" *Scarred?*

"Like what?" he asked on a disbelieving note. "Like being a person who slams doors in people's faces, chases away grandmothers with food and scares little girls."

Tess pulled back at the unexpected attack. "I just want to be left alone."

"That shouldn't be a problem, lady." He pushed off from the door frame and started down the porch steps, reaching the sidewalk before he muttered a few words she probably wasn't meant to hear.

Well, she had heard—or at least thought she'd heard. Regardless of the words, there was no mistaking the tone. Tess stepped out onto the porch, no longer caring about hiding her injury from him. She had been through hell last night. No, make that *more* hell. Who was he to judge?

"I don't see how my interactions with other people in this community is any business of yours," she called loudly.

Zach came to a dead stop, and then he turned toward her. "Oh, it's my business."

His certainty perplexed her. "How so?" she demanded. "Because I won't let your ruddy cows onto my land?"

"No. Because the little girl you scared happens to be my youngest daughter."

Tess simply stared at him for a moment. The girls she'd threatened two days ago were *his* kids? *Oh, excellent.*

But she'd been well within her rights and she was not backing down. "Your youngest daughter was where she shouldn't be."

"*I* know that," Zach said with an edge of heavy sarcasm. "But they didn't. They'd followed that path to school for years."

Tess lifted her chin, once again tilting her face so he couldn't see her scars. "Well, now they do know."

"Tell me about it," he growled, once again stalking away.

What the hell did that mean? It sounded like he'd dealt with some repercussions.

"I'm sorry if your kid was frightened by my face," she shouted after him, totally angry that she was the bad guy.

Once again he stopped. "It wasn't your face," Zach said. "Not entirely anyway."

Honesty. She had to appreciate that, even if she hated the fact that her face could scare children. "Then what?"

He shifted his weight, giving her a clinical once-over. "You haven't spent much time around six-year-olds, have you?"

Tess hesitated before she answered, wondering where this was going. "Can't say I've had the pleasure."

"Then you probably wouldn't understand how telling her that your face got injured trespassing would scare the hell out of a kid with an imagination."

"How?" Tess asked, baffled. "Did she think I was going to come after her?"

"I don't know what she thought, but I spent half a sleepless night trying to calm her down. You gave the kid nightmares."

Nightmares? How was she supposed to respond to that?

"All I want," she said coldly, "is to be left alone." Why did no one in this stupid valley understand that?

"You already mentioned that," Zach said. "And I mentioned why you were going to get your wish."

Tess watched him leave her cracked sidewalk and start walking toward the devastation that was once her barn, wanting very much to tell him she had a pretty damned good reason for being the way she was. But instead she yelled, "I'm *sorry* I scared your kid," at his retreating back. She'd meant for it to sound sarcastic, but somehow it didn't. It sounded almost like an actual apology.

CHAPTER SEVEN

ZACH STOPPED at the unexpected apology, turned, met the woman's gaze. He had no idea how to respond. *"Oh, that's okay,"* wasn't appropriate, because it wasn't okay.

She stood staring at him, facing him full-on from the porch. She wasn't wearing the glasses today, but he could no longer see the injured side of her face, since she had it tilted away from him. Zach studied her for a moment as he debated, allowing his gaze to travel over her face, taking in the wide green eyes, the high cheekbones, the pale skin.

What was it about her that seemed so oddly familiar? Who did he know that looked like her?

She was dressed, as always, in baggy jeans and a T-shirt, but there was no hiding the rather spectacular lines of her body. If she cared to be, Tess O'Neil could be stunning even with scars. Apparently she didn't care to be.

She shifted her weight, uncomfortable under his scrutiny. "I take it my apology is not accepted."

"Would it matter to you if it wasn't?" Zach asked.

"Touché," she said softly. "Well—" her full lips curved up slightly as she stepped back into her lair "—it's been nice talking to you."

"Can't wait for the next time," Zach replied. "I'll be out back, you know, helping out a neighbor in need." He touched his hat in a mocking salute, knowing he was being a total jerk. Not that she hadn't been asking for it, but his mom had really hammered in that lesson about two wrongs not making a right.

Well, his mother didn't need to know.

A WAVE OF shame washed over Tess as she leaned back against the kitchen counter, out of sight of the window—she hoped—and watched Zach shovel dirt at the edge of the burned area. Muscles flexing, expression taut, he worked, *helping a neighbor in need.* Despite the fact that he had every reason to consider her a cold bitch.

She'd closed the door in his face when he'd come over to discuss a business deal. Shortly after that, she'd chased his daughters off the path they took to school, and then, in a masterful coup de grâce, she'd managed to give his youngest daughter nightmares.

And he'd done *what* to her?

Not one thing.

Tess brought her half-finished bottle of water up to her forehead and pressed it against her aching head, wishing it was cooler, but she had no refrigeration. The power was off and would remain off until the electric company sent a repair person.

This isn't how I want to live my life. This isn't how I want to behave.

The thought struck her hard and she immediately rallied against it. This was how she *had* to live her life. Thanks to Eddie. Thanks to the attack.

She hated it, but that didn't change things.

Tess set the bottle down on the counter and abruptly left the kitchen. She didn't want to watch her neighbor be…well, neighborly…despite her poor behavior. And she didn't like the way her thoughts kept drifting toward how damned attractive he was. A married man. Children.

Had she no shame?

Obviously not, judging from her recent behavior.

Zach stayed in her backyard for almost an hour before he walked back around the house and got into his truck without bothering to tell her he was leaving.

And then she was alone. Again. But for how long?

The power company had a troubleshooter coming by late that afternoon. She had no idea when the fire marshal was going to show up and either exonerate her and Eddie, or make her worst nightmare come true. As far as she was concerned, he couldn't come soon enough. She needed answers. Now.

Tess sank down into her recliner and once again felt very much like crying. She was getting tired of her fear of Eddie coloring everything in her life.

Was it stupid and paranoid to think that her stepfather was responsible for the barn? If he was, then what would he do next?

Catch her unawares and then…?

Tess got up out of the chair and walked into the kitchen, where she dialed Detective Hiller's number and extension from memory. After he answered, it didn't take long to realize that she should have waited for the fire marshal's assessment before calling.

He listened without interrupting as she told him how her barn had burned and then described how Eddie had once burned the house of someone who'd crossed him.

"You think *Eddie* started the fire?" He didn't try to hide his incredulity. So much for the detective understanding her fears. He did not know Eddie like she did.

"He's done stuff like this before," she explained.

"Consider his resources," the detective said, giving Tess the feeling that he wanted to reach out and shake her. "Your stepfather works in a car wash. He's been out of the drug business for a decade. How many loyal associates could he have?"

"He was able to get someone to slash my face."

"Allegedly slash your face…"

Tess felt as if she'd been slapped. "The guy said—"

"I know," the detective replied in a weary voice. "Trust me, I'm not belittling what happened to you. It was heinous. But you're a long way from L.A. A long way from your stepfather. If the fire marshal comes up with anything suspicious, give me a call. If he doesn't…"

"What?"

"You need to get on with your life, Terry."

Her old name sounded so harsh, as did his statement.

"Get on with my life?"

"I'm not trying to be flippant, but you're not doing yourself any favors jumping at shadows." He paused and his voice sounded slightly more gentle when he said, "You have continued counseling in your new locale, right?"

"Counseling?" *Continued?*

"You *were* offered counseling services after the attack, right?"

Maybe. She couldn't remember. As soon as she'd been released from the hospital and finished talking to the police, she'd headed from L.A. to San Jose and holed up with William. That had been her way of dealing with the trauma of being slashed.

"I never saw a counselor," she said. "I was in hiding." There was no way she would have seen a counselor under those circumstances. She hadn't even left the house until she moved to Nevada. Not once.

The detective cursed, softly but still audibly. "Post-traumatic stress is nothing to mess around with," he said sternly.

Post-traumatic stress? She didn't have post-traumatic

stress. She was just trying to keep from being assaulted again. She was suffering from fear of something happening *now* or in the near future, not fear of something that had happened before.

"Find a counselor," he repeated when Tess didn't respond. "I'll contact you if I feel you have any reason to be—"

Tess abruptly hung up the phone without a goodbye and then stood with her arms around her middle, staring at the kitchen floor. She wasn't seeing a counselor.

Post-traumatic stress. She let out a small snort at the thought. That was his way of explaining why she was nervous about things like her barn burning down.

She was frightened, yes, but that was a normal and realistic reaction to being assaulted. It wasn't like she had nightmares or woke up in a sweat…because she didn't sleep, but again, that was a reaction to the here and now.

Get on with your life.

Only three months had passed since the attack. She didn't even have time to develop post-traumatic stress. Did she?

Tess put the flat of her palm against her cheek, pressing until she felt the pain. *Get on with your life.* Easy for him to say. His face was whole and his barn hadn't been burned down.

The fact that he could so blithely give her such bullshit advice pissed her off.

ZACH'S COUSIN, Jeff, local deputy sheriff and known beer mooch, stopped by the ranch after going over the remains of Tess O'Neil's barn with the fire marshal. He caught Zach as he came out of the barn, sweaty and tired after an afternoon searching for cattle that had strayed from the grazing land he leased from the government. Even though it was early May, it had been an unseasonably hot day.

"Verdict?" Zach asked as Jeff handed him a beer that had

come out of his own fridge. They had to talk about shipping cattle, but right now he was more interested in whether or not Tess O'Neil was an arsonist as Irv had hinted when they'd talked a few hours ago.

"The fire marshal says lightning. I thought it was a no-brainer what with all the storms blowing through, but apparently Ms. O'Neil asked Irv how he thought the fire started, and he began to wonder if maybe she'd started it."

"But she didn't." Zach sat down on the porch steps and Jeff leaned against the railing.

"Not according to the burn pattern." Jeff gestured with his beer. "So what the hell you think happened to her face?"

Zach shrugged. "Maybe you should ask her."

"No, I don't think I'll do that," Jeff said. "She doesn't seem like the friendly type."

"So definitely not arson," Zach said.

"You sound disappointed."

"Maybe a little," Zach answered with a half smile. He wouldn't mind having a new neighbor. One that he understood.

Jeff laughed. "I heard she sent sweet Melba Morrison and her casserole packing this morning."

"I was there for the aftermath."

"Interesting woman."

"*Interesting* isn't the word I would use."

Jeff turned to him with a mock serious expression. "What word would you use?" When Zach didn't answer, because he couldn't think of just one word, Jeff's face relaxed into a smile and he shifted his gaze back to the ranch across the road. "She probably has good reason for acting the way she does. Most people do."

"And the rest of us have good reason to stay away," Zach said before taking a long drink. Why couldn't someone more...normal...have leased the Anderson Ranch?

The door opened behind them and Beth Ann came out on the porch, carrying her laptop, which Darcy had borrowed the day before. "Everything okay across the road?" she asked Jeff.

"The barn's gone."

Beth Ann smirked at Jeff and then turned to Zach. "Do you know what she did to Melba?"

"I showed up just as Melba and Elaine were getting into their car."

"You're kidding." Beth Ann sat on the porch between the two men. "So you can tell me if she really told Melba to get off the property and never come back?"

"I don't know what she said. I arrived after the showdown."

"Damn." Beth Ann practically radiated disappointment.

"Does it matter?" Zach asked with a slight frown.

"To most of the gossips in town, it matters. I want to be accurate," she said with a smile.

Zach simply shook his head and stared into the distance. He wasn't getting sucked into the fray.

"Interesting woman," Beth Ann said darkly.

"That's not the word Zach would use," Jeff added helpfully.

"What word would you use?" Beth Ann asked.

Zach simply shook his head, staring off into the distance. He was still working on Jeff's good reason remark. Of course Tess had a reason for acting the way she did, but what made a person that rude and personally defensive?

Anger. Bitterness.

Fear.

Zach turned his attention back to his cousin. "We need to talk about the cattle," he said. "Now or after dinner?"

"Now," Jeff said. Beth Ann got to her feet.

"I'll leave you two to it," she said. "I'll be back after dinner to help with math." She headed back to her trailer, leaving Zach to ponder the irony of her being the math tutor when he was the one who spent most of his time dealing with numbers.

ANGER HELPED. Being totally pissed at Detective Hiller got Tess through the days after the barn burned and in an odd way gave her a sense of purpose. She needed to be angry and she needed to digest what he'd told her. After the anger finally started to fade, she'd had enough time to understand how crazy it must have sounded for her to suspect Eddie of starting the barn fire. Eddie, who never missed a day of work.

Her stepfather was nowhere near Barlow Ridge, nor were any of his minions—if he even had minions. She *was* suffering from post-traumatic stress, just as Hiller had said, and because of it, jumping at shadows.

At least she'd finally identified the problem, thanks to the brusque detective, and had started to realize how overblown some of her fears were. No, she didn't want anyone to recognize her, was still afraid of the off chance that if her identity leaked out, the media might pick it up as a human interest story. Slashed model makes new life in rural community. Was that as crazy as believing Eddie had ways of finding her?

Maybe. But she was working on deciphering what was a reasonable danger, what was not. She had a very long, slow road ahead of her, but at least she'd started the journey.

Tess did not believe for one second that Eddie had fully given up on her. As long as he thought she had money that belonged to him, she'd be on his radar, but at least she was far away from where he was so industriously working in the car wash. And how long was that going to last? Eddie hated physical labor. He'd be looking for an easier way to make money and one of these days he'd screw up—hopefully—go back to prison and maybe then she could have a normal life. A less lonely life.

For the first time since the attack, she was starting to miss human companionship. Because of her talk with Detective Hiller?

Or was it the fact that she was effectively being shunned? When she'd gone to the mercantile yesterday, Ann did little more than grunt at her, and the pleasant postmistress became very busy behind the counter when she'd checked her mail. The surly postmistress, who had also been there, made eye contact, but it was not of the friendly variety.

You asked to be left alone and now you've gotten your wish...

From now on she was going to be more careful about what she wished for. And she wouldn't kick grandmothers bearing casseroles off her property.

Her sketch pad lay on the table, every page covered—she'd filled the last half of it since the barn had burned, drawing the dogs, still life and the mountains, in addition to the Art Deco-ish figures she loved. Drawing helped her cope—it always had—but after refinishing the table, Tess had come to realize that she also wanted to create more practical items. Something she could use instead of hanging on a wall. Refinishing furniture was out. She had no old furniture and she had no place to work, since the barn had been the only outbuilding on the property.

So what could she, who'd never made anything in her life, make? What craft could she learn all by herself?

Tess had been thinking about the bolts of beautiful fabric in the hobby store, the dress that had been displayed in the clothing store window. Maybe she could make a dress. What a kick that would be.

She'd had a roommate in the early days of her career

who'd designed and draped dresses, selling them to a boutique. Tess had been fascinated—and certain that she could never do anything like that. When one had spent most of their early life in an environment where people simply did not create, the idea of making something from scratch seemed as if it were a magical ability or something.

But it wasn't—she had refinished a table using instructions on the internet and, what's more, she had done a reasonable job turning a hideous piece of painted wood into what was supposed to have been a gorgeous addition to her nearly empty living room.

The more she considered the idea, the more she liked it. Making a dress might not be the answer to her career problems, or post-traumatic stress, but it could be a remedy for long empty hours. Fabric and sewing supplies she could get online—she wouldn't even have to go out in public.

There was only one small problem.

Tess didn't know one end of a needle from the other.

How hard could it be to learn? The quilting lady had said it was easy to quilt, so it was probably fairly easy to sew. Just a matter of getting a machine and following seam lines.

"Crazy talk," she muttered to Mac, who snuggled up on her other side, his injured leg still wrapped in pink vet wrap. But Tess felt a twinge of excitement.

Now all she had to do was find a sewing machine.

"Dad, have you seen Misty?"

"Not lately." The last time he'd seen Emma's cat, she'd been curled up with Benny on the porch.

"I can't find her. It's feeding time and she didn't show up."

"She's probably hunting," Zach said. "She's disappeared before for a day or two."

"I'm." Emma placed her hands on her hips. "Worried."

"I. Know." Emma worried too much. Which at times worried Zach. "Give her a little time."

Emma had lost her first cat shortly after Karen had died, when she needed a pet to cling to. She hadn't allowed herself to get attached to another until orphan Misty had appeared at the school last year.

"You don't think she got hurt in that fire?"

"Unlikely."

"But she could easily have traveled over there."

"Yes, but Misty isn't stupid. She would have been out of the barn the second it caught fire." Zach pushed his hat back. "I'm sure she'll turn up soon."

"All right." Emma pressed her lips together and went back into the house, long braids bouncing as she ran up the porch steps. Damn but he hoped nothing had happened to the cat. Since Karen's death it had been an ongoing battle to not try to protect his daughters from every other hurt in the world. As he well knew, a person couldn't control everything…but they could damn well kill themselves trying.

"Hey, Dad?" Darcy called from the porch. "Irv's on the phone. He wants to know if you can stop by the firehouse today."

"Tell him no. I'm going up on the mountain." Three of his cows had ended up on the neighboring feed allotment and he needed to find how they were getting out. Darcy disappeared back into the house and Zach continued saddling Roscoe.

A few minutes later he whistled for Benny and set out for what was probably going to be a long day.

"Hey, Dad?" Darcy stood on the porch again. He stopped Roscoe and turned back, wondering what Irv wanted now. "Have you seen Misty?"

"Em already asked. No."

Her thin shoulders slumped and she went back into the house, his caretaker child. Sometimes he wished Darcy didn't feel the need to solve all problems for her sisters, but he knew where she got the inclination. He'd given up trying to convince her that she didn't need to mother her sisters.

Once he turned onto the county road, he urged Roscoe into a trot to take some of the kinks out. It'd been a couple weeks since they rode and the horse was feeling his oats. Roscoe was an excellent horse in many ways—he had incredible endurance and good cow sense, but he also had a propensity for shying when he wasn't in the mood to work. And the more time he spent in the pasture with the cows, the less he felt like working. Zach was not in the mood to put up with any nonsense today. He had fences to fix.

The county road made a T about half a mile from his place, the road running along the base of the mountain, but Zach continued straight ahead, through the Murray Ranch's open gate and down a rutted track of a road that led up the side of Lone Summit. After he gained some altitude, he stopped and looked back over the valley, his gaze immediately drawn to the Anderson place, where there was now a blackened smear of ash and cinders where the large barn once stood.

What was his neighbor going to do about the remains? Hire someone to clean it up? Leave it? He could have given her the names of a couple of people who would clean up the mess at a very reasonable price, but he wasn't going to go out of his way to do that. He didn't like her attitude and it still pissed him off that she'd been cranky with his kids, even if they were in the wrong. They were kids, damn it, and had been using that path for most of their lives. Jim Anderson certainly hadn't cared.

But she did.

Maybe she had reason.

Jeff's words drifted into his mind and Zach firmly shoved them aside as he pulled Roscoe's head around to start back up the trail. Stewing about the neighbor wasn't going to find his cattle and the hole they'd escaped from.

And neither was looking for them, it turned out. After easily finding the section of downed fence and repairing it, he scoured the mountain for almost five hours before coming to the conclusion that his missing ladies must have crossed to the other side. People tended to underestimate the mobility of cattle. He'd seen cows jump a five-foot fence from a standing start and he'd found them traversing craggy passes that he wouldn't ride his horse over.

Zach pushed back his hat, wiping the back of his sleeve over his forehead. He'd make some calls once he got home, put the word out and hopefully someone would find his cows in their herd.

The trip down the mountain was much faster than the trip up, despite the fact that riding downhill was harder on the horse. Roscoe was in a hurry to get home and Zach gave him his head for the most part. They traveled down into a small valley behind the foothill and then topped the last rise before home, when Zach pulled the horse up. Below them, in Murray's field, he could see a lone figure and two brown dogs ambling along.

It had to be Tess. No one else had two wolflike dogs.

Zach should have rode on by, kept his distance and tended to his own business. Should have. He didn't.

Once Zach hit Murray's field, he turned to the left, despite Roscoe's head-tossing protestations that home was straight ahead, and rode toward Tess. She slowed to a halt when she saw him coming. The dogs stopped hunting and instantly returned to her side.

Even from a distance he could read her body language,

saw her fighting the urge to turn and simply walk away—
or perhaps run away. But today there was no door to shut
in his face. Just the two of them in a field that neither one
of them owned, but that he had permission to cross when
necessary. Did she?

She wore sunglasses instead of her regular glasses and
for the first time Zach was able to get a good look at the
reddish, relatively fresh scars extending from the area covered by her oversize sunglasses to the edge of her mouth.
Another shorter scar started at her temple and met the long
scar midcheek, forming a rough Y-shape. Tess's hand went
up to her cheek as he continued to stare and then she lowered
it again. In the harsh light of day, the scars were impressive. Whatever had cut her face had been jagged, reinforc-
ing his theory that she'd been in one hell of a car accident.
Did a car accident explain her attitude?

Perhaps she was bitter about having her face ruined. Who
wouldn't be? But she didn't need to take it out on him and
his family, or whoever else happened to be near.

Or perhaps she was damned afraid of something.

But she didn't look afraid. She looked defiant as she
stood with her chin up, as if daring him to ask about her injuries. He didn't, but he did have another matter he wanted
to discuss—for his girls' sake.

"You do realize you're trespassing, don't you?"

She had the grace to blush, which surprised him. A lot.
"Is this your property?" she asked. He was tempted to say
yes, as she so obviously expected him to.

"No."

She put her hands on her hips, pulling the ugly T-shirt
taut, outlining the curves of her breasts. Which Zach was
taking pains not to notice.

"Then aren't you trespassing, too?"

"I have permission."

Tess glanced down at the ground for a moment, then back up at him, her sunglasses reflecting the mountain behind him. "There's no house here," she finally said. "I'm not disturbing anyone's privacy."

"Oh." He held her eyes for a moment—or assumed he did, since her glasses were so dark he couldn't see her eyes. "So, that's the criteria for trespassing? A residence? And here for all these years I thought it'd been a matter of posting the place." He pointed at a sign on a fence post near the road.

She let out a breath. He could see her chest fall when she did so. There was no defense. He'd caught her dead to rights, and now that his point had been made, he was done. He nodded at her and reined Roscoe to the right, intending to take the shortcut through the field to his back pasture.

He'd barely taken two steps when Tess suddenly called from behind him, "Be careful."

Pulling the bay to a stop, he looked back over his shoulder with a perplexed frown at the imperative note in her voice. What the hell?

Tess gestured as if embarrassed at her outburst. "There's a hole…somewhere over there. My dog fell into it and hurt himself. I wouldn't want your horse…" She abruptly shut her mouth, as if she'd said too much.

"So that's what happened to your dog. I'd wondered."

"Why didn't you just ask?"

They both knew why he didn't just ask, but he answered anyway. "You aren't that easy to talk to."

"Maybe I have a reason for that," she said darkly, unknowingly echoing Jeff's words. She turned then and started walking back toward the boundary fence for her own property, her strides long, her eyes focused on her house as if it was a target.

Zach watched her go with a slight frown. The last thing he'd expected after purposely going out of his way to give her a hard time was for her to warn him about prospective danger—even if she was only thinking of his horse.

"Hey," Zach called after her. She stopped, hunching her shoulders a bit, as if she'd been desperate to escape and had just been caught, which didn't read at all as bitterness or anger.

"Can you show me where this hole is?" he asked.

CHAPTER EIGHT

IT WAS on the tip of Tess's tongue to say, "I think you can find the hole without me," but she didn't. She wasn't certain how she knew—maybe it was just the slight change in his tone of voice, or the what-the-hell-am-I-doing? look on his face—but Zach was making a peace offering. Maybe not a full armistice, but a token, and after everything that had happened between them, she was going to be reasonable about it. She had enough issues without continuing to fight on all fronts.

But she couldn't bring herself to say yes. Instead she nodded and then called the dogs, telling them to stay close. She didn't want another vet visit.

Zach dismounted as she approached and she almost turned back around. Tess hadn't expected him to walk with her, to wait next to his tall bay horse for her to reach him.

And she hadn't expected every nerve in her body to go on high alert once she was close to him. He was taller than she remembered, or maybe she was just way more aware of him out here in the field, where she had no place to escape. And he smelled good.

Married man. Children.

"It's, uh, this way," she said as she pointed, her voice ridiculously husky. "I think."

They walked slowly through the tall grass, the horse reaching out for a mouthful every now and then as he trailed behind Zach, who was focused on what he could see of the ground in front of them. And she was focused on Zach—out of the corner of her eye. He was wearing jeans that were nearly worn out from work, not from processing and chemicals. His brown leather boots were scuffed and scarred and the pocket of his shirt was ripped so that it flapped slightly as he walked. Working clothes on a working man. And why was she so focused on his clothes?

Because it kept her from focusing on the fact that she hadn't been this aware of a man in a long, long time. It was only because they'd had a nasty argument the last time she'd seen him and now they were making peace. Because she was secretly grateful not to be fighting.

But he was still too close for comfort.

"You can probably see better from horseback," she pointed out.

"So if the horse goes into the hole, I go in, too?" he asked.

"That was my plan," she said without looking at him.

He gave a soft snort, which may have been a laugh, but when she glanced over at him, he wasn't smiling. He had lines, though, at the corners of his eyes, that hinted that he was a man who smiled and laughed. Or had been. There was an air about him, sadness maybe, or resignation. She couldn't decide.

"Your dogs are well behaved," he commented after a few silent seconds.

"They had a good trainer," she replied.

He kept his gaze straight ahead as he said, "You?"

It was her turn to snort. "No. Hardly. They were trained when I got them."

"You adopted them?" Now he did look at her and once she met his eyes, it was hard to look away again, but she did.

"You could say that."

He cut her a sidelong glance when she didn't elaborate, but kept walking. A few seconds later he stopped as a deep narrow ditch came into sight through the tall grass only a few feet in front of them.

"Diversion ditch," he said, parting the grass and moving closer. "I didn't realize Murray had put one in. Must have been last year."

He'd barely gotten the words out when his horse bumped his shoulder with his nose, pushing him forward. Zach stumbled, almost fell into the ditch, then rounded on the animal, an irritated expression on his face.

"If you knock me in this ditch, you're going to be sorry," he said. The horse, looking patently insulted at Zach's harsh tone, took a few steps back.

Tess pressed her lips together to hold back a laugh. Damn, how long had it been since she'd laughed? When she looked back at Zach she lost the struggle and smiled.

"What?" he asked, straightening his shirt with one hand. There was grassy horse slobber on his shoulder.

Tess cleared her throat, trying not to laugh. "Your horse seems very unrepentant."

"He is. This animal is shameless." Zach shook his head with a half smile and Tess felt the undeniable pull of attraction and it had nothing to do with making peace. This was one hot guy. With a family. "But I don't want him falling into ditches," he said directly at the horse, before bringing his attention back to Tess. "Thanks for the warning."

"No problem," Tess said, taking a casual step back and folding her arms across her midsection, closing herself off. "I'm glad I know where it is now, so I can avoid it next time I trespass."

"Will that be soon?"

"Probably not now that I know how easy it is to catch me."

He smiled again, wider this time, his expression surprisingly open for all of a heartbeat.

"You could call Murray and ask permission."

She smiled politely, knowing she wasn't going to be calling anyone. She'd simply stay out of this field. Zach gave his head a slight shake. "You know, Tess, this isn't a bad community."

"Meaning?" she asked, hating the defensive note that crept into her voice.

"Just what I said. We're not a bad bunch here. You might just…lower the shields a little. Get to know people. I think you'll like them."

"I'll keep that in mind," she said, sounding less than convincing, even to her own ears.

He rubbed a hand over the back of his neck, as if acknowledging he'd taken on a losing battle. "We didn't start off well, you and I."

"I'd say that's correct."

"But we are neighbors."

Tess nodded, her heart beating a bit faster as she wondered where he was going with this.

"I'm not asking to be friends or anything," he continued, "but…well…maybe we could be…less adversarial? For the good of everyone involved?"

He was a couple feet away from her, but it seemed like he was closer. Much closer. She dropped her gaze down to his boots, but somehow it traveled up the worn denim of his jeans to his belt buckle, where it lingered for a few seconds, then up over his chambray shirt to his very blue eyes. His incredibly gorgeous very blue eyes.

Tess needed to get out of there, to head back to the safety of her house. Safety that had nothing to do with post-traumatic stress and everything to do with being attracted to a man who had a wife and family.

She forced a smile and pushed her hair back like she used to do, before her face was ruined, gave him her serene

model look—a look she hadn't used in a long, long time.
"I'll try," she said. "I need to go now."

Zach nodded. "See you around. I guess."

"Likewise," she said. But by the time the words had left
her lips she and the dogs were already heading in the opposite direction. Toward safety.

TESS'S SEWING MACHINE arrived less than a week after she'd
ordered it. The UPS man never bothered knocking anymore,
so she found the sewing machine box on the porch early
Friday morning, along with another box from an online
sewing site containing two how-to-sew DVDs—chosen at
random from the zillions available since her internet was
too slow to watch online tutorials—a book, a couple dress
patterns—"very easy" according to the label—scissors,
needles, pins, fabric and thread.

Now it was all here on her porch and she had to figure
out what to do with everything.

With a happy sense of anticipation, Tess lugged the boxes
into the house and started unpacking. It didn't take long to
remove all the components and set them on the portable
table she'd bought at the mercantile expressly for her sewing. After shoving all the packing material back into the
box, she sat back and admired the cream-colored machine.

There were unidentified buttons and knobs and wheels—
seemingly dozens of them. She touched a lever and the metal
foot dropped down with a clack. *All right*...

Slowly she turned the wheel on the side of the machine
and watched as the mechanism above the foot rose and fell,
rose and fell.

Tess blew out a breath and sat back, feeling a flutter of
excitement mixed with trepidation. The upside was that
she had nothing but time on her hands to learn to use this
thing and no one would see her mistakes. The downside

was that she had no one to turn to for advice. Picking up one of the DVDs, she slit the cellophane seal and popped open the case.

After watching the DVD—twice—Tess had a distinct in-over-her-head feeling. Had she just wasted close to a thousand dollars on the machine and various accoutrements?

Tess turned off the TV and sat for a moment studying her inscrutable nemesis.

Then she sat down in the chair in front of the machine and tried to do what the lady on the DVD had done so easily. She tried to sew two squares of fabric together. And then she tried again.

It took some time to get the hang of controlling the fabric as it sailed through the machine at breakneck speed, but as she learned to control the amount of pressure she put on the foot pedal, she learned to control the direction the seams took—for the most part. Holding the fabric taut helped. In fact, the tauter she held it, the straighter the seam.

"Nothing to this," she said to Blossom. A split second later there was an odd pop and the machine jammed. It took a second for her to realize that the needle had broken.

Back to the instruction booklet. Tess changed the needle then spent a good ten minutes taking out the seam before she tried again. Success. She carefully backstitched, held up the two pieces of fabric she had joined, testing the strength of the seam.

"Look," she said to the dogs, who both ignored her. "Fine. Don't look."

She reached for the next two pieces and started feeding them through the machine. Less than a minute later the needle broke.

What the…?

Tess changed the needle, consulted the instruction manual. The needle size was correct, but after two more seams she broke another needle. And another.

Noting that she had only two needles left, Tess rested her head on the machine. What was going on? Why was her beautiful new machine pulverizing needles right and left? And where would she get new ones?

The mercantile. The store had everything from hog chow to embroidery hoops to portable tables. Surely there were sewing machine needles. She hadn't been out for groceries in over a week. It was time.

And thankfully the mercantile was empty except for Ann.

"How's that dog of yours?" she asked after Tess had found the needles, stocked up on bread, eggs, milk and apples and set them all on the counter.

"Limping, but better."

"What happened to him?"

"He fell in a hole."

Ann lifted an eyebrow then shot her an ironic look when she rang up the needles. "Taken up quilting, have you?"

"Uh, no." Tess bit her lip then took a chance since Ann seemed moderately friendly today. "Do you happen to know anything about sewing machines?"

The old lady laughed and shook her head. "You'd have to talk to someone from the quilting club."

"I can't see that happening."

"Neither can I. You should have taken the casserole," Ann said, pushing the bag closer to Tess.

"Yeah," Tess said with a sigh. "Live and learn." To her surprise, Ann laughed.

"Doesn't pay to piss off the queen bees around here," she said.

Tess smiled a little. "Thanks."

"Good luck," Ann called after her.

Tess skipped the post office and drove straight back to the ranch, where she unpacked her groceries and then sat down to sew again.

Five minutes later the needle broke. Tess was seriously considering beating her head on the sewing machine when the dogs scrambled to their feet and headed to the living room, scaring the bejeezus out of her. A second later there was a knock on the door.

Tess slipped into the living room, checked out the window, taking care not to be seen, and then let out the breath she'd been holding and went to the door. Glasses girl, Zach's daughter, was on the porch.

"I'm not supposed to talk to you," the girl said as soon as Tess opened the door.

"But you are," Tess said.

"It's important. My sister's cat is missing. This is what she looks like…" The girl held out a photo of a black cat with a white face and front paws. "My sister is very attached to her."

"The little sister?" *First I scare her to death? And now she's lost her cat?*

"No. My other sister." The girl tucked the photo away. "Have you seen the cat?" she asked with a touch of impatience that reminded Tess of her father, and then she glanced furtively over her shoulder at her own house.

"No," Tess said. "But if I do, I'll call."

"Thanks." The girl once again looked at her place as if ascertaining that the coast was clear before starting for the steps.

"Did you sneak over here or something?"

"Or something," she agreed. "I'm on my way to quilt club. I didn't think anyone would notice if I took a detour, but you never know."

Tess wasn't certain how to take that. The kid was forbidden from going near her, to the point of being afraid of being caught? How did this tie into the neighborliness her father had mentioned? Maybe it didn't extend to his kids... or maybe it was because she'd kicked his daughters off her property. That actually made sense, but this kid was here anyway. The middle sister must be pretty attached to the cat.

And then it struck her. Quilt club...

"Do you sew?"

The girl lifted her tote bag instead of replying.

"You made that?" Tess asked, impressed.

"Yeah."

"All of it?"

The girl scowled at Tess's comment before glancing at her house again. She turned back and opened her mouth, but Tess cut her off. "If your father doesn't want you over here, maybe you'd better go."

"It's just because you scared my little sister."

Bad move, that. "I'm sorry I scared your little sister."

"Then why'd you do it?"

"I didn't realize she'd take me literally. I was trying to make a point." Tess reached up to lightly touch her scars.

"That's what Dad spent two days trying to convince her of. Well, more like a night and breakfast the next morning. Six-year-olds have wild imaginations."

Tess almost smiled. "And you're...?"

"Twelve. My imagination has slowed down."

Somehow Tess didn't think so, and she didn't want her tenuous peace with her neighbor to be disrupted by his daughter sneaking over to see her. "If I see the cat, I'll call."

"Why'd you want to know about my bag?"

"I'm trying to learn to sew."

"Guess you should have joined quilt club when you had the chance." The girl was in the position of power. She seemed quite at home there. "What kind of help do you need?"

"I keep breaking needles."

The girl frowned. "Look. I have to get to quilt club. If you let me use the creek path, I'll come back that way and maybe help."

"What about your folks?"

"It'll be fine." The kid spoke with such authority that Tess almost believed her.

Tess gave a quick glance in the direction of Zach Nolan's house trying to tamp down her conscience. Zach had forbidden his daughter from seeing her and she was not going to encourage the kid to break the rules. As much as she'd like help, it wasn't right.

"You can use the path, but just go straight home, okay?"

The girl nodded and started down the porch steps, the tote bag bouncing against her hip.

"Hey…what's your name?" Tess asked as the girl reached the bottom step.

"Darcy." She adjusted the tote bag's shoulder strap. "I've gotta go." A second later the girl disappeared around the corner of the house.

DARCY NOLAN SHOWED up on Tess's porch two hours after she'd left.

"Hi," she said as soon as Tess opened the door, nudging the dogs back with her leg. "I'm back."

"So I see." Tess liked this kid's direct manner because it made it easier to be equally direct. "It's not right for you to be here when your parents told you not to come over here."

The girl appeared unfazed by Tess's declaration. "Parent," she corrected. "I only have a dad, and he didn't say I couldn't be here. He just told me not to trespass."

Only a dad? Tess felt like her heart had just stopped.

Then who was the woman who drove in and out of Zach's ranch? Did he have a live-in girlfriend?

Tess cleared her throat, which seemed unusually tight. "I thought he told you not to talk to me."

"Well, specifically, when I asked if I could call round to the neighbors to see if they'd seen Misty, he told me not to talk to you."

"I don't know—"

"But I do."

Tess frowned. "You know what?"

"The answer to your needle problem." The girl dug into her pocket and pulled out a folded sheet of white paper. She flipped it open and read, "Needles can break because they're put into the machine wrong, they're threaded wrong, the size is wrong, or there's too much tension while sewing." Darcy looked up from the paper. "Could any of those be the problem?"

"Maybe...?" Tess said.

"Why don't you let me watch you sew? I can tell you if you're doing it right."

Yeah. She could let the kid into her house and then go through all kinds of hell when her father found out.

"My dad will understand," Darcy said, accurately reading Tess's thoughts. "I'll confess I helped you sew when I get home if it makes you feel better."

"What if I say no?"

"I'll leave and you'll keep breaking needles."

Good point. "Fine." She stood back and Darcy walked into the house, pausing to pet first Blossom and then Mac, who wagged their tails and pushed each other aside trying to claim all of the girl's attention.

"Nice dogs. What happened to him?" Darcy asked.

"He fell in a hole and sprained his leg. He's getting better," Tess said. Darcy gave the dogs one last pat, then crossed the room to the sewing machine set up on the portable table next to the window where Tess got the best light.

Darcy reached out and tested the table's stability. It wobbled beneath her hand. "You might want to get something better." Tess agreed wholeheartedly. The portable table vibrated like a jackhammer when she sewed.

"I had something better, but it burned up," she said.

"Yeah. That's too bad," Darcy said as she leaned closer to the sewing machine, inspecting the dials. "I bet you're glad the fire marshal cleared up that deal about how the fire started." Tess frowned. How did this kid know about her worries on that front?

"Glad how?" Tess asked cautiously, having a strong feeling she wasn't going to like the answer.

Darcy glanced up at her, her expression candid. "Glad that they decided you didn't start it. Irv said you asked a lot of questions that arsonists ask."

Tess fought an upwelling of anger. Was nothing private in this valley? "I just wanted to know how it started. I hadn't seen any lightning so it was hard to believe that was the cause." And she couldn't believe she was defending herself to a twelve-year-old.

"Sometimes there are spontaneous strikes," Darcy said as she gestured for Tess to sit down. Tess slowly sat. "We learned about it in science. There's a lot of weird stuff about lightning. Ball lighting, St. Elmo's fire. It's not all forked stuff."

"Interesting." And how ironic that all Tess had wanted to do was to disappear here and instead she'd briefly become an arson suspect. That wouldn't make her stick in people's minds or anything.

"Show me what you do," Darcy said. Tess complied. The sooner she got this over with, the sooner she could shoo the girl back home where she belonged. She took two pieces of cloth from a pile of practice squares she already had pinned together and carefully fed the fabric through the machine, holding it taut as it moved under the needle.

"Too tight?" she asked when the seam was finished, even though the needle was still intact.

"Yeah," Darcy said. "I think so. What size needle are you using?"

Tess reached for the packet in the basket on the floor next to her. "Eleven?"

"No wonder. Too small. You need a thicker one if you're going to pull like that. You're bending the needle and it's hitting the hole in the faceplate."

"I see…"

"You won't be able to bend a size sixteen, but it's kind of big for cotton. Maybe you shouldn't pull so much."

"The seams go crooked."

"Practice," the girl said in a way that made Tess think she's heard the word a time or two herself.

"Okay. I'll practice."

Darcy picked up a pair of pinned squares off Tess's stack, rubbing her thumb over the top of the fabric. "You need to get some cheap sale fabric. This stuff is too nice to practice on."

"You learned all this in quilt club?"

"And 4-H. Tia made me, but now I like it."

Tess wasn't going to ask who Tia was. She may well be the nosy lady who'd come to her door with the casserole-bearing grandmother.

"You could learn a lot in quilt club, but I don't know if you can join. Now."

"Probably not," Tess agreed.

Darcy picked up her tote bag. "I can stop by every now and then and see how you're doing," she said. And then, before Tess could respond, she added, "And maybe in return you could let us take the path along the creek to school."

Tess was searching for a way to explain that it wasn't that she really had anything against the girls taking the path, but rather that she was trying to avoid any kind of false alarm setting the dogs off, when Darcy added, "Honestly, since you ticked off the quilt club, you aren't going to get help from anyone else."

"I have a book," Tess countered.

Darcy shook her dark head. "Nothing takes the place of a real person. Trust me on this—you can't believe how many things can go wrong when you're trying to learn to sew."

She did look as if she knew what she was talking about.

Tess shifted her jaw sideways, the movement pulling on the scar tissue. What was the worst that could happen if she let the girls use the path? Her dogs would bark and scare her, at least until they recognized the girls and accepted them as part of the daily routine. If they ever did.

Did she want to jump out of her skin whenever the girls took a shortcut to school?

On the other hand, did she want to move toward having a more normal life?

"Are you all right?" Darcy asked with a slight frown.

"Wonderful," Tess said dryly. "If I let you use the creek path, I want a note from your parents…uh, your dad… saying he knows about this deal and that you have permission to come over here."

The girl's eyes narrowed thoughtfully behind her glasses and Tess felt a vague sense of satisfaction. Score one for her. She really didn't want to give up learning to sew before she started out of sheer frustration, but she didn't want to be accused of kidnapping or contributing to the delinquency of a minor, either.

"Do you think that'd be a problem?" Tess asked.

Darcy cast her a sideways glance. "Maybe not if you also let him use the pasture for his cows."

"What?" Tess demanded. Did this kid never stop?

"He needs that pasture."

"Why?"

Darcy's rolled her eyes. "Economics?" There was a lot of preadolescent sarcasm in the one word.

"I meant why *my* pasture?"

"Because the other pasture land in the valley is all leased right now and if he can graze his cattle, he has less hay to buy. Everything our family has depends on the price of cattle and hay." Darcy shifted her weight. "You don't know much about ranch life, do you?"

"Absolutely nothing."

"Then why did you move here?"

Tess had a sudden and deep understanding of the term "deer in the headlights" because at that moment she felt exactly like one. "I, uh…" *Don't have a quick answer here.* An obvious question for a kid to ask and she should have prepared a pat answer in advance, but hadn't. So she did the only thing she could and redirected the conversation. "So you'll help me with the ins and outs of sewing and all I have to do is give your family free access to my place?"

Darcy considered then said, "Pretty much."

"I don't want to sew that much."

"Suit yourself," the girl said lightly, as if she hadn't just poured her heart into negotiations. She picked up her tote bag and inside Tess could see purple and orange fabric stitched together in an intricate pattern. A twelve-year-old could do that and she couldn't sew more than a dozen seams without breaking a needle.

Darcy headed to the door, the dogs trailing after her. They sat as she opened it. "By the way," she said, standing with the doorknob in one hand, "my sisters and I don't need to take the creek path to school…but my dad really does need that pasture."

The last words were uttered with surprising intensity before Darcy slipped out the door and shut it behind her without waiting for Tess's response. As if she had one.

Well, crap.

Tess watched Darcy for a moment out the front window, then crossed the room to sink down in her recliner, letting out a long, slow breath as she let her head fall back to stare up at the ceiling.

Paths and pastures and one persistent kid.

There were many, many reasons not to get involved with this family, but the truth was that for the few minutes Darcy had been there, Tess had felt almost human again. And now that the girl was gone, the house felt empty. Lonely.

Because she was lonely.

"You what?" Zach pulled his head out from under the hood of the truck where he'd been refilling the power steering fluid.

Darcy folded her arms over her middle as she walked around Benny, who was sleeping next to the truck. "I went to ask Tess, or Ms. O'Neil, or whatever you want me to call her, if she'd seen Misty and then she needed some help sewing, so I helped her. I told her that I would tell you that I'd been there." Darcy shoved her hands into the back pockets of her jeans. "She kind of insisted."

Great. "You know I had reason for asking you not to go over there."

"I thought that was all about the trespassing," Darcy said. "But I wasn't trespassing. I was on my way to quilt club and I wanted to make sure that Misty hadn't shown up there and Tess—Ms. O'Neil—hadn't thought she was a stray and adopted her. Remember how that happened to

Jessica McKirk's cat when those new people moved across the field from them?"

"No, I wasn't aware of Jessica's cat problem," Zach said. "But I do remember telling you to keep off her property."

"It's Misty, Dad, and Em cries at night sometimes. I had to make sure."

"Don't do it again," he said.

"Well," Darcy said slowly, "I kind of want to go back and help her learn to sew. If she'll let me. I don't know if she will."

Zach set the empty power steering fluid bottle on the work bench, frowning as he faced his daughter. "Why do you want to help her sew?"

Darcy gave a quick shrug. "She needs the help and since she ticked off the quilting club, she isn't going to get any help from them."

"Maybe she should buy a book."

"You can't learn to sew from a book, Dad," she said impatiently. "Besides, if I help her, then we can use the creek path again."

Now he was getting to the bottom of things. "Whose idea was that?" he asked, even though he was fairly certain of the answer. Darcy was the negotiator of the family.

"My idea, Dad, even though she said no this time, I think she'll say yes next time. She was wavering. But she wants a note from you if I go back to her place. Saying you know where I am and it's all right."

"I don't want you bugging her," Zach said as he dropped the hood and it shut with a bang that echoed through the barn. "Do you have homework?"

"Yeah," Darcy said, obviously sensing it was time to drop the matter—for now, "but I want to wait for Beth Ann. I need some help with my math."

"Why don't I help you?"

"Beth Ann knows how Ms. Bishop wants it done."

"Glad to know I'm useless," Zach said musingly as he tossed the plastic bottle into the trash and then wiped his hands.

Darcy laughed. "Good old useless Dad. We just keep you around because you're good company." She patted his arm consolingly just as Benny jumped to his feet. They turned in unison to see a woman walking down the driveway, hands shoved deeply into her pockets.

Tess had come to visit.

CHAPTER NINE

ZACH AND Darcy stood side by side in front of the barn as Tess walked toward them. The collie scampered up to welcome her, but neither Zach nor Darcy moved. In fact, Darcy appeared alarmed to see her.

"Hi." Tess shoved her hands deeper into her coat pockets. She wore the blue cloche hat and her sunglasses—the armor she needed to get through this mission. "I came to talk about the pasture."

Zach shot a quick look at his daughter, who carefully kept her profile to him, and then, when he looked back at Tess, he asked simply, "Why?"

Why?

"Because…" Tess's voice faltered as Darcy caught her eye and gave an almost indiscernible shake of her head. "I've rethought the matter."

Zach's mouth twisted sideways as if he were giving the matter careful consideration, which was not the reaction Tess expected when she'd come here to make her offer. Darcy tried to catch her attention again, but Tess ignored her.

"Do you want the pasture?" she asked Zach. She'd spent almost an hour mentally gearing up for this trip after making her decision and now this guy was screwing with her?

Zach looked down at Darcy and gestured toward the house with a jerk of his head. Darcy sighed deeply and then headed across the driveway, but not before giving Tess one more quick warning glance over her shoulder. When she was almost to the front door Zach turned back to Tess, who didn't think it was possible to shove her hands any deeper into her pockets, but she tried anyway.

"I'd really like to know what made you change your mind," he said.

"Does it matter?"

"Yeah. It does."

Her shoulders stiffened. If he was going to make this difficult, then he could just go to hell. She'd thought she'd come here to do a good thing and in return she was getting grilled. What about "we're a decent bunch," as he'd told her in the field?

"Never mind," she said. "Sorry to bother you."

She turned on her heel and started stalking down the driveway, totally pissed off.

"I want the pasture."

The words barely slowed her down.

"The offer is rescinded," she said without looking back.

"Wait." She heard the sound of his boots on gravel and felt the urge to run, but instead forced herself to stop and turn back.

He continued toward her, stopping a few feet away, somehow knowing the point where she would start backing up if he got any closer. Damn, those eyes.

"Look," he said, hooking a thumb in his front pocket as one corner of his mouth tightened briefly, "Darcy didn't happen to say anything when she was at your place today, did she?"

It wasn't hard to read the self-consciousness of his stance, or to figure that he would not appreciate his kid being so blunt about his economic situation. She knew about being in economic straits—knew more about it than she cared to—

and how embarrassing it could be. But she couldn't flat-out lie to him, so she sidestepped the question.

"It finally occurred to me, after Darcy's visit, that you probably wouldn't have asked to rent the pasture if you didn't need it." She sounded like she was reciting lines, which was what she got for role-playing the encounter—which had gone nothing like any of her mental scenarios—before she got there. "I really don't have any reason to keep you from it."

Then why did you?

Tess could easily read the question in the way he raised his dark eyebrows at her. The lines of this guy's face were incredible. Jonas, her favorite photographer, would have had a heyday with Zach.

And she needed to get back home.

Tess summed up by saying, "Look…you can have the pasture if you want it."

"Deal's back on the table?" he asked with such an off-hand tone that she almost missed the relief in his eyes.

"It is," she said, keeping her tone formal, business-like, not wanting to be drawn to this man—physically or otherwise—especially now that she knew he wasn't married. "And I need to get home. I left the dogs in the house." So much for not lying.

"Do you want to have someone draw up a contract for us or go with the standard contract I used with Jim?"

"I'm good with a handshake deal," she said. The fewer people involved the better.

Zach shook his head. "I'll jot down a few terms and we can go over them together. Just to make sure we're on the same page."

"That makes sense," Tess agreed, already taking a few slow backward steps toward home.

"I'll stop by when I get it written up. Tomorrow probably."

"Fine." Tess turned and started back down the driveway, feeling an overwhelming need to return to the safety of her house.

"Tess?" She glanced over her shoulder. He hadn't moved, but he was smiling. A little. "Thanks."

"No problem," she called as she started to walk. "See you later."

But still probably sooner than she was comfortable with.

ZACH COULDN'T BELIEVE he'd almost lost the pasture out of sheer pride and stubbornness. But the thought of Darcy negotiating a deal with Tess bothered him.

"So what happened?" Darcy asked a little too innocently as soon as he walked in the door.

"You heard most of what there was to hear."

"Then why'd you send me back inside?"

"In case there was more," Zach said as he headed for his office, where he had a copy of the contract he and Anderson had used on the computer. He'd update it, take it to Tess tomorrow. If all went well, he'd have some of his cattle on pasture by the weekend.

"What more could there have been?" Darcy asked from the doorway.

"I wonder?" Zach asked, giving his daughter a long look that had telltale color rising in her cheeks. If Darcy had brokered a deal on his behalf, did he really want to know?

Not especially, but he also didn't want her to do it again.

"Look, Darcy, I don't know exactly what went on with you and Ms. O'Neil, but in the future, don't make any deals with anyone without involving me."

"I didn't exactly make a deal. I just mentioned that we'd *always* used the pasture."

"And that's all."

"And that economically we were better off with the pasture than without."

Zach opened his mouth to tell Darcy that he didn't want her discussing their finances with anyone, but the wounded look on her face stopped him. She'd been trying to help.

He was damned embarrassed at how broke he was, had thought he'd done a pretty good job of hiding it from the girls, but Darcy was old enough to understand the reality of the situation. To see the medical bills still rolling in. Plus she had excellent hearing and had probably heard him discuss matters with various people over the phone. He let out a long breath and pulled her into a quick hug. "You aren't the ranch manager yet. Please include me in your plans."

He could feel Darcy smile against his sleeve. "All right."

"Beth Ann isn't home yet?"

Darcy stepped back out of his embrace and smiled up at him. "Nope. Must have gotten hung up in town."

"Better start your math."

"Already on it," Darcy said as she started toward the door. Before she disappeared into the hall he saw her blow out a quick breath of relief. He felt like doing the same.

No, he didn't like the way he'd gotten the pasture, didn't like Tess knowing his circumstances, but in spite of that, he kind of felt like smiling. He had his pasture back.

WAS THERE NO end to this black crud that showed up in Tess's house, her yard, on her dogs, her shoes, everywhere?

Probably not as long as there was a huge source on the other side of her inadequately propped-up cedar fence.

Tess pulled a lawn rake through the grass in her backyard, trying to collect the windblown cinders and ash into a pile before she shoveled them into a garbage bag. The only reason she had a rake was that it had been leaning against the side of the house when the barn had burned. The shovel was the folding emergency kind from her car trunk. Realistically there was no way she was going to be able to keep cleaning up this never-ending lawn mess with a rake and an emergency shovel—although at the moment it was a better use of her time than trying to figure out that Very Easy sewing pattern.

Very easy her ass. It seemed that one either needed an engineering degree or deep familiarity with garment construction to understand those very easy directions. But she wasn't giving up. She wanted to make a dress. And then another. Fill her hours.

When she was finally done raking and stuffing, Tess wiped the hair off her forehead with the back of her hand and regarded the sad remains of the barn, wondering what she was going to do. Was she destined to months and months of the dogs tracking greasy, black stuff into the house? Would grass ever grow over the blackened material? She didn't see how.

The dogs, who'd been sleeping on the small back porch while Tess worked off her sewing frustrations, perked up at the sound of an engine then sprang into action. Cautiously Tess propped the rake against the porch and went where she could see the county road.

Zach. On an all-terrain vehicle. The engine noise grew louder as he crossed the road and started up her driveway.

"House!" she shouted, calling the dogs back and then opening the back door to put them inside. They were not yet aware that they could knock the propped-up parts of the fence down if they so desired, and she didn't want them to figure it out.

Once the dogs were inside, she walked around the house to the front yard, where she waited near the gate, trying to ignore the fact that her heart beat faster and for once it wasn't because of fear. Well, not the kind of fear she'd been dealing with for the past few months.

So what was she going to get paid for renting her pasture? She had no idea if it was five dollars or five hundred, monthly or yearly. She was going to lease the pasture to Zach regardless—mainly because she believed Darcy— the family needed the pasture for economic reasons. Kids didn't make up stuff like that; they parroted what their parents said. Also, she sensed that a guy like Zach was going to be fair…or did she just want to believe that because she found him so very attractive?

Tess shook off the thought as Zach pulled to a stop and she realized that since it was cloudy outside she didn't have sunglasses, a hat or a door between herself and Zach this time. How ugly was she?

Apparently not too ugly, because Zach didn't recoil or anything. Instead he said, "No glasses." But when his gaze traveled over her face, he didn't look as if he was put off or that he was trying to place her, the two things that sent her into defensive mode.

"I left them in the house," she said as casually as possible.

He held up the papers again. "This is the standard contract I used with Jim Anderson," he said. "It's year to year and everything is spelled out very plainly. You still might want to have your lawyer take a look."

She nodded as if that was a good idea, but she had every intention of simply reading it over and signing it, unless it had something that appeared suspicious. Right now, though, looking directly into Zach Nolan's blue eyes, she didn't think there'd be anything shady in this contract. The guy seemed like too much of a straight shooter. There'd been times in the past when Tess had been wrong about people, but for the most part, she was excellent at reading them. It'd been a survival skill honed by years of practice while living first with her mother and Eddie and Jared and all their whacked-out acquaintances, and then at the halfway house after she'd run away.

"It needs a notary," she said after a brief glance at the signature page.

"Irv's wife, Mary, at the café, is a notary, and so is Ann McKirk."

"How handy." Tess creased the contract back into thirds with quick movements of her fingers. She couldn't wait to go see Ann again.

Zach smiled a little, making her wonder if he knew what she was thinking. "I'm going to check the fence line," he said, tilting his ball cap back a bit to see her better. His eyes didn't settle on her scars and hold, but he didn't avoid looking at them, either. Instead his gaze kind of passed over her face like it was a normal face. Not beautiful, as it'd once been, or ugly, but just…regular. And she liked that.

"I thought cowboys rode horses," she said, not quite ready to be all alone again.

He smiled, the corners of his mouth tilting up in an interesting way that had her nerves humming and made her want to smile back. "Generally we ride whatever will get the job done fastest." He put a hand on his thigh and she fought not to follow the movement. "I should have asked this sooner, but your dogs won't chase cattle, will they?"

Tess rubbed a hand over her upper arm. "They never leave the yard."

"What about your walks across the field?"

She gave a soft snort. As if she was going to walk across a field with cows in it. No, thank you. "I'll find another way to get my exercise," she said.

He seemed satisfied with that and reached for the ignition key. Tess turned to go back into the house as he started the engine, then paused on the porch to look back and watch him drive through the open gate and start riding along the fence line, the ATV bumping and bouncing along. It looked like fun.

Tess opened the door and retreated into her sanctuary.

WHEN TESS O'NEIL relaxed, dropped her shields, she seemed to transform into a different person, giving Zach a glimpse of what she might have once been like before whatever had driven her here to Barlow Ridge. Not that she'd relaxed all that much while talking to him, but she'd been less defensive than before. And when she'd fought that smile, he'd found himself wanting to tell her to go with it. Ease up a little.

A half hour after Zach had driven through the gate, he drove back out again. He'd made two minor repairs, but all in all, the fence was in good shape. He left the gate open, since his cattle knew exactly where they were going when he started them down Tess's driveway, and then rode back to Tess's house to give her a time frame for keeping her dogs in the house. The last thing he needed was a wreck involving Tess's urban dogs, Benny and a bunch of mama cows hell-bent on protecting their calves.

And speak of the devils... The dogs tore around the house when Zach parked the ATV, jumping up on the gate, barking wildly.

"Afliggen!" Tess yelled as she came around the corner of the house. The dogs instantly dropped to their bellies, obviously waiting for another command.

Impressive and telling. He knew from Jeff's experience with K-9 that protection dogs were often given commands in a foreign language.

"Sorry about that," Tess said, coming through the gate.

"Let me know when you've gone over the contract and if it's agreeable, I'll move the cows," Zach said, keeping his eyes on the dogs, who were now grinning and wagging their tails, but still on their bellies as Tess had commanded.

"Sure." Tess nodded as she bent down to stroke the injured dog.

"How safe is it for my daughter to be around those dogs?"

"Totally safe," Tess said with a lift of her eyebrows. "They put on a big show, but don't do anything."

"Unless told?" he guessed. Tess cocked her head at him, her eyes narrowing slightly. "They act like guard dogs."

"They're retired."

"You have retired guard dogs for pets?"

Her barriers started sliding back up again. "Actually they're personal protection dogs, not K-9s or anything, and yes, they are my pets. They had to go somewhere when their owner no longer wanted them."

That sounded reasonable, unless you added in their current owner's scars, desire for isolation and defensiveness.

"What brought you here, Tess?" he said softly. It was a reasonable question if his girls were going to be in contact with her.

Tess stood up, her fingers clutching the edge of her plain black T-shirt. "I needed a break from my old life."

His gaze settled on her scars, but he let her get away with the half-truth. And now that her glasses were not obscuring her eyes, he could see they were a shade of green he'd never seen before. Green like the Depression glass his mother used to collect.

"How long have *you* been here?" she asked, apparently trying to make it seem as if they were having a normal conversation. They weren't. Too many undercurrents.

"I was born here," he said. "The ranch belonged to my parents. Shortly after I got married, they moved to Colorado where my dad was raised, so my wife and I bought the place from them." She didn't flicker an eyelash at his announcement, which told him that she knew about Karen.

"Generational ranch, then?" she said.

"Yours was a generational ranch, too, right up until old Jim Anderson got put into the home. He tried to sell it to pay for his care. Ended up leasing when no one bought."

"He had no family?"

"None that wanted to buy a ranch."

"Good for me, I guess." She pressed her lips together and glanced down at her shoes. Her hair fell forward, hiding the scars, making Zach want to gently brush it back, find out if it felt as silky as it looked, shining in the sun.

The reaction startled him.

It was time to go.

TESS WATCHED ZACH ride down her driveway, barely visible in the cloud of dust the ATV kicked up. The next time he stopped by, she was sticking to hi and bye. No lingering chitchat, because she didn't want him asking more questions.

Why had she moved here?

You don't want to know, Zach.

Maybe she would have been better off if she hadn't leased the property. Things had been simpler when it was just her and the dogs, living her isolated life…and she hadn't been thinking about a guy she couldn't have.

Tess read the contract as she drank a glass of wine later that afternoon—the first alcohol she'd touched since moving to the ranch because she hadn't wanted anything to dull her senses, make her slower to react. Today she indulged. Today something other than Eddie was keeping her on edge. Zach.

The contract was simple and to the point, just as she'd assumed it would be. Either party could end the agreement with thirty days' notice. She got paid monthly and the terms of the contract would be reviewed for renewal every twelve months. Good enough. She smiled a little when she read the part about her being allowed access to her own land during the lease period.

He'd taken care of the potential trespass issues.

CHAPTER TEN

ZACH WAS saddling Roscoe for the morning mountain ride when he heard the crunch of gravel behind him. Tess. It had to be. He finished pulling up the cinch, then dropped the stirrup. By the time he was done, Tess was only a few feet away. She stopped as soon as he looked at her, leaving a good stretch of gravel between them.

She held up a folded paper. "Did I come at a bad time?"

"Not at all," he said, untying Roscoe and walking a few steps toward her. He had a strong feeling that she wanted to cut and run, as she always did when she wasn't on home turf, but she held her ground as he approached.

"I take it you had no problems with the terms?" he said, taking the paper she held out to him.

Tess shrugged. "It's very straightforward."

"That's the way I like things," he said, folding the paper again and slipping it into his shirt pocket, making a mental note to take it out before he did laundry. "No convoluted language, no bullshit."

"You wouldn't have made a very good lawyer," Tess said, putting her hands into her pockets.

"Which is probably why I'm here wearing jeans instead of gabardine."

"I don't think lawyers wear gabardine," Tess replied with a half smile. A breakthrough. Zach wanted to see if he could get more.

"See how ill prepared I would be for that profession? I wouldn't even be able to dress properly."

As he'd hoped, her smile widened. Even with the scar pulling at the left corner of her mouth, it was something. And gone too soon.

"Going out to do…cowboy stuff?" she asked, nodding at Roscoe.

"Yeah," Zach said. "I'm going out to ride the range, round up some doggies." He wondered if she knew that a doggie with a long *o* was a calf.

"What do you really do?" she asked, once again fighting a smile. This was the Tess that intrigued him, the Tess he wanted to get to know.

"Look for holes in the fence, try to find the cows that got out through those holes and put them back where they belong."

"I'd hate to keep you from that," she said with another ghost of a smile.

"I'll walk with you to the road."

"I don't want to slow you down." Tess took a step backward as she spoke, her heel catching on the low curb of concrete next to the barn, and Zach put a hand to her elbow, to both steady her and stop her from retreating so fast. Her breath caught as he made contact, her eyes flashing up to his in an instantaneous fear reaction. *Fight or flight.* Zach let go of her arm.

She's been assaulted.

The thought hit him from out of nowhere. He could be wrong, but he didn't think so. Not judging by the way fear had flashed in her eyes at his unexpected touch. And suddenly a whole lot of stuff made sense and he felt like a jerk for not considering this possibility earlier. No. He'd assumed she'd been in a car wreck.

An assault may not have anything to do with the scars…
but he was pretty sure it did.

Zach stepped back, bumping into Roscoe as he gave Tess
space, and she let out the breath she'd been holding once he
was a good two feet away from her. For a long moment she
solemnly held his eyes as if silently asking him to forget
what had just happened. He wouldn't forget, but he wouldn't
ask any questions, either. Yet.

"You can walk with me," she said, as if nothing had
happened.

"Let's go."

They started down the driveway in a not very easy silence, and then Tess pointed to his boots. "How comfortable are those things?"

"I've put in miles and miles in these *things*," he said, glad
she was making an effort at conversation. Glad she hadn't
hightailed it home after he'd touched her. "Almost five miles
once when Roscoe here abandoned me up on the mountain."

"He what?" Her eyebrows went up comically.

"Not his fault." That time. "I was working on the fence,
spooked a buck and when the deer jumped out of the un-
derbrush, Roscoe took off."

"Didn't the girls worry when he came home without
you?"

"They were at school. We all got home about the same
time, except that I had blisters and they didn't."

Tess laughed, and though she didn't look at him when he
glanced over at her a few seconds later, a smile still played
on her lips.

Satisfied, Zach left it at that. They walked the rest of the
way down his long driveway to the county road and stood
for a moment regarding Tess's long driveway. The houses
were both about a quarter mile from the road, so they sat

a mere half mile apart—practically on top of each other in this country.

"What are you going to do about your barn?" he asked. The place still looked odd without the huge old wooden structure.

"What barn?" Tess asked innocently.

Zach smiled. In her effort to sidetrack him from her earlier reaction, she was dropping more barriers than usual. And Zach liked what he was seeing. "I guess I mean what's left of the barn."

Her forehead creased. "To tell you the truth...I'm not sure."

"I can contact a guy I know and get an estimate for a cleanup."

"Which involves...?"

"Bringing in a loader and a truck and hauling the debris away."

Tess brushed her hair back from the injured side of her face, without seeming to realize what she was doing. The still-red edges of the healing scars stood out against her pale skin.

The scars made him angry. Who'd done that to her?

He had to be careful about jumping to conclusions. The scars could still be the result of some other kind of accident. But he didn't think so.

"Well," she said, "it would be kind of nice not to have the dogs tracking black crud into the house every time they went outside. And I'll have to do something about the propped-up fence before you put the cattle on the property. My dogs are natural shepherds, I hear, and they may want to shepherd your cows."

"I can come by tomorrow morning before I move the cows and put it back up for you."

"Oh, no." She flushed. That pale skin again. "I wasn't trying to get you to do that."

"I know," he said simply.

She pressed her lips together briefly and he wondered if he'd stepped over the line, offered to help just a little too much. But then she gave a small nod and said, "If you want to."

"I do." He pushed his hat back. "We're neighbors, after all, even if we did get off to a rocky start."

"You mentioned that once before. Neighbors. The rocky start."

"Maybe it was so rocky, it merits mentioning twice."

The corners of her mouth tilted up. "Yes. Maybe." The smile faded way too soon.

He wanted to touch her, reassure her that he was a good guy who meant her no harm, but knew that was the last thing she wanted. So instead he said, "I, uh, guess I'll see you tomorrow morning."

"Yeah, I guess." She tilted her chin up. "Tomorrow morning, then."

She gave a brief, cool smile, then started walking down her stretch of driveway. Zach watched her for a moment, appreciating the way the sweatshirt curved over her butt and emphasized the sway of her hips, thanks to her hands being jammed so deeply in her pockets. He finally tore his eyes away and mounted Roscoe, turning the horse toward the mountain.

He glanced back over his shoulder at the exact instant Roscoe chose to shy violently at the horse-eating rock in the ditch.

"You son of a bitch," Zach muttered as he regained his seat. He reined the horse around and made him approach the rock that he'd used as an excuse to shy. Roscoe blew through his nostrils as if terrified—a blatant ruse, since

Zach had ridden him down this road about two zillion times without the rock attacking even once—and then touched his nose on the stone.

"Keep it up," Zach said to the horse, "and I'll sell you to those junior rodeo kids on the other side of the valley." Even though he knew it'd be a long time before he found another horse with as much endurance and cow sense. Sometimes enough was enough.

As soon as she walked into her house, Tess closed the door and leaned against it as the dogs joyously celebrated her safe return by dancing in front of her, poking their noses at her. Then she blew out a breath that lifted her bangs.

She ran her hand over her injured cheek, then abruptly pushed off the door and headed to the bathroom, dogs close on her heels, where she leaned over the sink and studied her face, first full on, and then tilted to either side.

Good side.

Bad side.

Pretty side.

Ugly side.

She studied the way the corner of her left eye was pulled down. The nasty jagged red lines, the upward tilt of that side of her mouth from the healing scar tissue. Things could be done, eventually, to mitigate some of the damage to her face, but it would take time. That wasn't what was bothering her.

Why was Zach flirting with her? Or if not flirting, then being so very nice? It couldn't be because he wanted something. She'd given him the pasture.

Tess turned away from the mirror and went back to the lonely living room where her sewing machine sat with fabric draped over it.

She didn't want to think about why he was being so nice, because Tess did not want to get knocked on her ass again—

especially since she was so damned attracted to him and didn't totally trust herself.

And she wasn't even going to think about whether or not he'd noticed her knee-jerk reaction when he'd reached out to touch her earlier. Of course he'd noticed—but that didn't mean he'd interpreted her response correctly. How could he have?

He may have just thought she was reacting to nearly falling.

Yes. *That* was what she was going to believe.

BETH ANN PULLED into the driveway shortly before Zach crossed the ditch and rode through the side gate leading into his property. The girls piled out of the car as Zach rode to Beth Ann's trailer, Lizzie running up to pet Roscoe on the shoulder after Zach dismounted. The big horse put his nose on top of the girl's head.

"Careful," Beth Ann called. "He'll snot you."

"He will not," Lizzie said indignantly, but she put a hand on top of her head and backed away. "Are all the calves gone now, Daddy?"

"Tomorrow, but I'm not taking the two leppies. You and Emma still have to take care of them." Orphan calves that he wasn't able to graft onto a new mother took a lot of care. He handled the brunt of it, but the girls were a big help. In return for raising the calves, they got to keep them.

"They're going to miss their friends," Emma said, slipping her backpack onto her shoulders.

"I don't think they had that much contact with their friends," Zach pointed out. The leppies had their own corral.

"They talked over the fence," Emma stated matter-of-factly before starting down the road toward their house.

"Can I have a ride to the house?" Lizzie asked hopefully.

"Roscoe's being a butt today. You can ride Snippy later if you want."

"Okay." Lizzie took off after Emma, her bright pink backpack bouncing on top of her grayish-lavender coat—a color she didn't seem to mind one bit because it wasn't red, which Lizzie had recently explained to him was a *boy* color. Lizzie didn't do boy colors.

That left Darcy and Beth Ann, who was unloading her laptop and box of supplies from the trunk.

"Everything go okay?" Darcy asked.

"Fine," Zach said, wondering what could have possibly gone wrong other than Roscoe leaving him on the mountain again. Darcy sent a quick look at Beth Ann, then swung her backpack up onto one shoulder and followed her sisters.

"So she gave you the pasture," Beth Ann said as soon as Darcy was out of hearing range, although sometimes Zach wondered if Darcy was ever out of range. She seemed to hear everything.

"Tess is leasing it to me, yeah."

"That's good. I guess."

"Why 'you guess'? I think it's just plain good."

"Something about her bothers me," Beth Ann said, settling the edge of the box on her hip and looking upward with a frown as if trying to recall some illusive detail. "Oh, yeah," she said, bringing her eyes back to meet his. "I know what it is. She's acted like a wacko ever since she moved here."

Maybe she has reason. "She gets better the more time you spend with her." Beth Ann's eyebrows shot up in a way that surprised him, as if he'd just said the last thing she'd wanted to hear. Then she pressed her lips together and reached down with her free hand to pick up the handle of the laptop case.

"If you say so."

"You want some help?" Zach asked after reaching out to shut the trunk lid for her.

"No."

"Dinner tonight?"

She shook her head. "I have to work on one of my ridiculous college assignments that has nothing to do with real life education of children, but I'll do it to get that piece of paper that allows me to teach."

A familiar rant and not unjustified, since in a small rural school the aids sometimes did almost as much instruction as the actual teacher. But there was something else bothering her. Tess?

Beth Ann and Karen had been very different, despite being close. Karen had been the easier going of the two, tactful and nonconfrontational—unless something threatened someone she loved. Then the gloves came off and she took care of business. Beth Ann tended to skip the tactful phase of negotiations and took care of business from the get go.

"I'll come to the house later to help Darcy with her math and make sure Emma's doing her social studies project."

"Lizzie's in the clear?"

"Finished her spelling during class, so yes."

"Come to dinner. You need to eat," Zach said.

Beth Ann hesitated, then her shoulders drooped a little and when she looked up at him, she made an effort to smile. "Did you make anything in the slow cooker?"

"Just another stew." About all he had time for in the spring.

"Well," she said, "maybe you *can* set me a place. It wouldn't kill me to take a break before starting this stupid assignment."

"Will do, Beth Ann. See you then."

TESS WAS UP and dressed in her usual less than flattering outfit of loose jeans and T-shirt when Zach knocked on her door at 8:00 a.m. The dogs did their tough act at the sound of the knock, but it lacked conviction, telling her that they already knew Zach, knew he wasn't a threat. In fact, when she opened the door, they both fell back and slowly started wagging their tails.

"Just thought I'd let you know I was here," he said, tilting his ball cap back so she could see his eyes. As usual, she found them utterly fascinating and also found herself wishing she wasn't dressed so poorly, even if she had done it on purpose.

Tess did not want to be attracted to this man, but she was, so she'd put on some ugly armor and hoped it would remind her of all the reasons she needed to stay sane.

"I brought some fence posts to replace the ones that Irv knocked over. It looked like they had some rot."

"I'll pay you for those," Tess said. "How much—"

"No need." He smiled slightly. "Maybe you could just come out and keep me company while I work."

Tess's stomach flip-flopped, which in turn irritated her. She was not sixteen and Zach was not the cute guy next door. Well, he was, but she was definitely beyond sixteen.

"Sure," she said with a casual shrug.

"Maybe we could leave Cujo and the missus in here?" he suggested, nodding at the dogs.

"Package deal," she said. "All or none."

"Fine. Bring the wolf pack," he said with an easy smile. "Meet you out back?"

"Yeah."

Zach had already knocked down the parts of the fence that Tess had propped up using old weathered 2x4s she'd found stacked near one end of the house in deep grass.

"You want to grab the posthole digger?" he asked when she came down the steps, Blossom and Mac close behind her.

"Sure," Tess said. "Go lie down," she told the dogs, who trotted to the middle of the lawn and dropped into the grass. Blossom started to roll, a blissful expression on her face.

"They're bilingual?" Zach asked as he started knocking a panel free of the old fence post with a few blows of a hammer. He seemed to know exactly what he was doing, working without a wasted motion. "German and English?" he added.

"Dutch," she said as she walked over to his pickup, which had several posts and various tools in the bed. "I give them the Dutch commands—the ones I can remember—when I mean business. The rest of the time I just talk to them and they seem to know what I mean." She moved a shovel aside to get at what had to be the posthole digger, since the only other tool in the truck was a long steel bar. "They're really remarkably smart."

Zach knocked another panel free, then examined the post and set it aside.

"Is the rest of my fence going to fall over from rotted posts?" It didn't seem damp enough here for anything to rot.

"I think you have several years left on these posts, but the alkaline soil tends to eat them, so there's no sense putting the old posts back if they're not one hundred percent."

"At least part of my fence will be standing in a few years?"

"We can hope," he said, taking the diggers from her, their hands brushing in the process. And because she'd expected his touch, Tess did not react. Visibly, anyway.

The posts Zach had brought were longer than the ones the cedar panels had been attached to, so he needed to deepen the holes. On the one hand, Tess didn't feel totally comfortable with him doing all this work for no recompense, but on the other, it was rather fascinating to watch him do it.

He stabbed the diggers into one of the holes, then opened the handles and pulled the tool back out, dumping the damp earth in the grass at the side of the hole.

"Your grass is getting long," he said.

"Going to offer to mow my lawn?" she asked wryly.

"I can put a few cows back here. They mow and fertilize."

She laughed. "Actually I have a new lawn mower coming. I ordered it a few days after the barn burned." Another stab of the diggers, another ripple of muscle under his cotton shirt. "Before that I was going to see what could be done with the old ones stored in the barn, but I never got the chance."

"Are you familiar with engine repair?" he asked.

"No," she said with a smile. "But I actually got one started before it turned to toast."

"Then you *must* be familiar with engine repair," Zach replied dryly. "I've seen Anderson's mowers."

"Not really, but I am familiar with starter fluid and checking the oil. I used to help the caretaker with the gardening where I lived."

"Caretaker?" Zach pulled the diggers out of the hole and then leaned on them, holding her gaze with a slight frown. "As in your family had a groundskeeper?"

Tess made a face. Oh, yeah. Right. The closest they'd come to groundskeeping was when Eddie tended the pot plants, and they were inside the house. No grounds involved.

"Nothing like that," she said. "I stayed in a home for kids for a while when I was growing up and they had a caretaker. We took turns helping with the upkeep of the house. Learned some practical stuff."

She didn't know why she'd given him that little tidbit of personal history. Maybe to put another wall between them,

since the one she usually depended on, rude and distant behavior, had crumbled days ago. If he asked why she was
in a home, she was simply going to tell him her family life
had sucked and she didn't talk about it.

He didn't ask. Instead he started digging again—the best
possible move he could have made. After he finished one
hole and started on the next, he asked, "What kind of stuff
did you learn?"

Tess answered, even though she wasn't certain she
wanted to. "I learned about maintaining—and starting—
lawn mowers and weed whackers and stuff like that." She
shrugged. "A little about cars." Even though they weren't
allowed to have cars. "The caretaker was always working
on hers and I watched when I had nothing better to do."

She hadn't thought about how much she'd enjoyed that
in a long time. It wasn't the engines—she didn't have the
fascination with mechanics that some people had—it was
the meticulous order of things. The slow step-by-step process that didn't change.

In other words, the antithesis of what her life had been
before landing in the home. And maybe that was why she
was trying to learn to sew. To follow a process and end up
with something usable.

"Caretaker was a lady?"

"A very competent woman," Tess said. "A survivor. She
told me not to be afraid to follow dreams, because if I didn't,
I'd regret it. So I did follow my dreams for quite a while."
She smiled with a hint of sadness. "I tried to contact her to
thank her for the advice a few years ago, but she'd moved
on."

"What were your dreams, Tess?"

She stilled then said, "A career in advertising." Not really
a lie. "I worked at it for several years."

"But gave it up?"

Tess shrugged, starting to feel uncomfortable. She hadn't realized how badly she had wanted to simply talk about herself, to lighten the burden she carried, but this was getting dangerous. Her mouth was getting away from her and she was dropping way too many hints about who she was. Zach must have noticed her shift in mood because he asked no more questions, but instead focused on deepening the fence holes. Tess tried very hard not to focus on him. She failed.

The sun rose higher as Zach dumped the five fence posts, one after another, into the new and improved holes.

"Can you give me a hand here?" he asked after setting the last one and tamping the earth around it with his foot.

Together the two of them lifted the panel of cedar planks and Tess held it in place while Zach attached it to the post using a drill and massive screws. When he was done, Tess had a stretch of superbly sturdy fence.

"I really appreciate this," Tess said as Zach loaded his tools. She wished she had lemonade or tea or something to offer him, but all she had was water and Zach had brought his own.

"No problem," he said as he picked up the shovel. He met her eyes and she could see that he was about to say something, but wasn't certain how to go about it. Which in turn made her think she did not want to hear it. She was about to say something—anything—to sidetrack him when he said, "You know, Tess, if—" he paused, as if searching for the right words, and her stomach tightened "—you have concerns, I'm just across the road."

"What kind of concerns?" Tess asked, her voice suddenly brittle.

"The kind that makes a person nervous."

Damn.

She'd figured that he was sharp, that he had to know

something was up after she'd jerked away from him that day, but she hadn't expected an offer of assistance.

Brain racing, she was working on forming some kind of a sane nondefensive reply when he said abruptly, "That's okay." He tossed the shovel into the bed of the truck with a loud clatter and then slammed the tailgate shut. "None of my business. I'll move the cattle tomorrow morning, if that works for you."

"Works just fine," Tess said, trying very hard for a normal tone. She appreciated his offer. Really she did.

She simply couldn't accept it without telling him the score, and she was not going to do that.

HE COULD HAVE been a little smoother in delivery, Zach thought as he unloaded the tools from his truck and stored them in the barn. But at least now Tess knew that he was there, willing to help if she needed him. The big question was whether or not she'd take him up on his offer.

The phone rang in his office as he approached the house and Zach jogged up the steps, half hoping it might be Tess.

But it wasn't. Bradley James, self-proclaimed gentleman rancher and husband of the hospital administrator, identified himself after a quick hello.

"Bradley, how are you?" Zach said cautiously. He did not like the feel of this.

"Fine, fine. You may have guessed that I'm calling about that parcel."

"Uh—"

"It's been a year," Bradley barreled on, cutting Zach off, "and I just wanted to touch base again. Let you know I'm still interested if you *ever* decide to sell."

"Well…thanks," Zach said. And that was all he said, because he'd made his position very clear the first time Bradley had approached him about buying forty acres. He wasn't parceling off the ranch.

There was a few seconds of dead air and then Bradley cleared his throat. "I'll let you go," he said on a congenial note. "Good talking to you."

"Likewise," Zach lied.

The bait tossed out, the hint dropped, Bradley hung up. Now he was probably retreating to his lair to wait for Zach to get out his budget books and realize how much better off he'd be if he sold the forty. It would pay off most of the remaining medical bills—but so would another two years of paying the way he was…and hoping that no emergency situations cropped up.

He'd go with hope and a prayer.

CHAPTER ELEVEN

How did one move cattle?

Tess envisioned a big truck backing up to her pasture gate and cows stepping out of the back, but instead, at about ten the next morning, she looked out her upper-story window—after the dogs had begun some serious barking—to see a herd of cattle ambling down her driveway. There were at least fifty animals, maybe more, most with babies at their sides. Zach rode behind them, and trotting alongside the herd, keeping a close eye on the animals, was Zach's black-and-white collie.

Since Zach was at the back of the herd, Tess wondered if the dog would be able to stop the cattle from continuing up the driveway to her house and onto her lawn.

But the dog didn't have to do anything, because the first cow made a beeline for the open gate and all of the other animals followed her inside, where they immediately spread out and started eating. A few of the calves lay down, perhaps tired after the excitement of the trip from one home to another, and the rest hugged up close to their mothers, surveying their new environment.

Tess held the curtain and leaned forward to see what Zach was doing. He closed the gate from horseback, then wheeled the animal around and looked straight at her. Tess stepped back despite knowing he couldn't possibly see her in the glare of the sun. At least she hoped he couldn't.

The cows were delivered. Now the cowboy could go

home and she could get on with her day. But she'd be think-ing about him.

She was getting better, wasn't nearly as jumpy as she had been, didn't think about Eddie every waking minute of the day, but he was still out there. Regardless of De-tective Hiller's admonition to get on with her life—or the fact that he'd been right about post-traumatic stress—Tess knew it'd be foolish to think that she was home free. Not if Eddie thought she had money. He might wait a year. Maybe two. Maybe until he was off parole, but he'd come look-ing for her.

There was no way she would ever be able to totally drop her guard, develop anything lasting with anyone.

But if she enjoyed a few minutes here and there with an attractive guy…well, there was nothing wrong with that. As long as she left it at that.

TESS YAWNED LAZILY as she crossed the kitchen to the back door. The first few nights after Zach had put the cattle on her pasture had been less than restful as the occasional bo-vine bellow had woken her, but she solved that by staying up late and sewing until she couldn't see straight. And then she'd go to bed. It worked—to the point that she was over-sleeping. She opened the back door, following the dogs out onto the sunny porch, the warm wood feeling good under her bare feet.

Both dogs stopped dead at the top step.

Tess instantly froze, a deep chill of terror running through her when, with a nerve-rattling growl, a noise Tess had never heard either dog make before, Blossom shot off the porch, her toenails raking the wood. Mac followed a split second later and Tess nearly tripped over herself in her hurry to get back into the house.

She slammed the door, twisted the dead bolt, shot one

last look out the window before racing back upstairs to get her gun...

And then stopped.

Blossom had thrown herself on her side and was furiously digging at the bottom of the fence with both front feet. Mac stood with his good front foot planted on the fence, balancing himself, whining and giving high sharp yips.

Not protection mode.

Prey mode.

Tess pressed her fingertips to her forehead, feeling almost physically ill from fright. And here she'd thought she was getting better.

After waiting a few seconds for her heart rate to slow, Tess let herself out the back door and forced herself to approach the fence where the dogs were digging. There had to be a rabbit or some other small animal on the other side that for some kamikaze reason had not run away at the sound of a hundred and fifty combined pounds of canine muscle and teeth.

Tess rose up on her toes and peered over the fence. A black calf stood on the edge of her lawn, across the driveway from the pasture where he should have been. Tess lowered herself back to earth.

She'd almost had a heart attack over a baby cow.

"Knock it off," she said to the dogs, who stopped digging and went down to their bellies, mistaking "off" for *af,* the Dutch command to lie down, giving her looks that clearly said, "Are you kidding? Do you realize what's on the other side of this fence?"

Yes. A baby with no mama in sight—which was probably a good thing. Cows were big and possibly dangerous.

So what now?

Did she try to put the calf back into the pasture? No. Because there was a group of cows down by the gate. Even if she could manage to push him along in the right direction, the second she opened the gate she did not doubt for one minute that either a) the cows would run out, or b) they would attack her for handling one of their babies. Tess had seen her share of nature documentaries and did not want to become a cow casualty.

Leaving the dogs to snuffle along the bottom of the fence, she went into the house to find Zach's phone number, remembering how the last time she'd called him, she'd hung up when he answered. Maybe someday she'd tell him about that. Maybe.

"Hello?" The phone had barely rang before he answered.

"Hi. This is Tess." She gripped the phone tighter, still recovering from her scare. It had nothing to do with talking to Zach. "A calf is out."

"Just one?"

"Yes." Thankfully.

"Be right over."

He hung up without saying goodbye and Tess put the receiver back into the old-fashioned cradle. She wanted to go to the bathroom and check her face, which was ridiculous because she knew what it looked like. Clean and makeup-free with a nasty crisscrossed scar on one side that pulled her eye down. Nothing that makeup was going to fix.

ZACH WAS GLAD he'd forgotten his fencing pliers on the kitchen counter and had gone back inside to get them before heading up on the mountain. Otherwise he would have missed Tess's call. One escaped calf wasn't that big of a deal—nine times out of ten it would have figured out how to slip back through the fence to get to its mother. But there was always the chance that mom would jump the fence or come through it if she thought her baby needed her. He was just glad that Tess had called him instead of handling it on her own. She did not strike him as a cow-savvy woman.

Roscoe was waiting next to the porch when he exited through the back door, as was Benny. Roscoe's ears twitched when Zach mounted, and he tossed his head as they started down the driveway.

Zach nudged the horse forward, and Benny gave a sharp yip as they headed across the county road and down Tess's driveway, happy to have some action at last. Zach slowed to a walk as he approached the house, thinking again how odd it looked without the barn that had stood behind the house since before he'd been born. Hell, before his father had been born.

Zach stopped at the gate and dismounted. He shot his usual glance at the upper window, where Tess often stood watching—when she wasn't in the lilac bushes or the lower window—but she wasn't there. Call made. Duty done. So why did he feel vaguely disappointed?

"Get the calf," he told Benny, who shot off down the driveway. It didn't take long for Benny to send the calf trotting his way and the mother cow, who'd been grazing a good distance away, to raise her head and start for her baby. Zach swung the gate open, Benny pushed the calf through and he closed it again. Moments later the calf was mothered-up and the two set off across the field.

So did he check the fence now for the hole where the calf got out? Or later, after he was done on the mountain, dead tired and wanting nothing more than a cold beer and a shower?

Now.

Both for the obvious reason that he didn't want another escape and for the less obvious reason that he was making up reasons to come back.

He rode the perimeter of the fence starting at the gate

and heading toward the county road, then turning toward the mountain. As he'd expected from where Tess had found the calf, he didn't find the hole until he was once again approaching her house twenty minutes later. It wasn't huge, but definitely big enough for another calf to escape. Roscoe tossed his head crankily when Zach dismounted.

"Deal with it," he muttered to the horse as he tightened the wires. Roscoe stamped his foot in reply.

A few minutes later Zach dropped the pliers into his saddlebags and mounted the bay. Benny, who'd been lying on his belly in the grass, jumped to his feet ready for action.

And action he got.

Roscoe barely went fifty yards before Tess's dogs leaped up from behind her fence and the horse shied violently, hitting his ribs hard against a fence post in the process. After that, Zach lost track of events.

The next thing he knew he was sitting on his butt in the middle of the driveway and Tess's front door was flying open.

"ARE YOU ALL right?" Tess skidded to a stop a few feet away from him.

Fine. Just fine. Zach refused to meet her eyes as he stood and watched Roscoe cross the county road, heading for home. Zach cursed under his breath. He'd been okay until the horse hit the post. That had scared the shit out of the bay and after that, well…yeah.

Zach blew out a breath and reached down to pick up his hat, which he slapped against his leg before jamming it back on his head.

"You…want a ride home?"

He shot Tess a look. "I'll walk." He brushed the dust off his butt, adjusted the leather chinks he wore over his jeans and started walking. He really didn't have much to say to his new neighbor right now.

"Don't be embarrassed," she called after him.

Zach stopped. "Why on earth would I be embarrassed?" he asked.

She didn't answer, which made him feel like he needed to say something.

"This doesn't usually happen."

"Happened today," she pointed out. She didn't smile, but he could see that she wanted to, which almost made the humiliation worthwhile. Almost.

"Yeah. Sometimes Roscoe catches me unaware."

Her eyebrows lifted. "You make it sound like he does this on purpose."

"He does," Zach answered matter-of-factly. "He hates working and leaving his buddies."

"Well, he's back with them now."

Zach smiled in spite of himself. "I imagine so." He cocked his head. "Do *you* ride?"

Her expression immediately shifted, as if he'd encroached on forbidden territory now that he was asking her questions, instead of the other way around.

"I, uh, no...that is, once I really wanted to learn, but it didn't work out."

"Why not?"

"Because my stepbrother wrecked the family car and the money mom had said she'd give me for lessons went to buy another beater."

So she had a stepbrother. "Those things happen."

"Yeah." The single word came out bitterly and the open expression was long gone, as was the moment.

"Well, if you have any more escapees, give me a call." He tried another smile. "But I can't promise you a rodeo every time."

A polite answering smile played on Tess's lips, but it didn't come close to reaching her eyes. "I'll remember that. Thanks."

Zach, feeling the growing awkwardness between them, turned and followed his asshole horse back to the ranch.

"Hey, Zach?" Tess called a few seconds later.

"Yeah?" He turned to find her closer than expected. She held out a closed fist. Automatically Zach extended his hand to receive whatever it was she held.

With a slight smile she opened her hand and pressed a dusty jackknife—the knife he'd had since he was ten—into his palm. Her hand was warm and smooth and soft…and she didn't remove it from his immediately.

"You lost this," she said. Then she turned and headed back to her house.

THE KNOCK ON the door startled both Tess and the dogs, who'd been sleeping. The dogs leaped up and ripped across the room, but by the time they reached the door their tails were wagging. Darcy Nolan stood on the porch.

Tess opened the door, wondering why the girl was there—a new negotiation perhaps?

"Break any needles lately?" Darcy asked.

Tess smiled. "No. Oddly I've discovered a way to keep them whole." And she'd also discovered how to keep her seams straight. Not panicking when the machine took off seemed to be the key. "I didn't expect you to come back."

"Deal's a deal," Darcy said as she came inside.

"We didn't make a deal per se."

"No…but I don't think you would have offered my dad the pasture if we hadn't talked. And thanks for that, by the way."

Tess wasn't going to tell the girl that her decision hadn't been based so much on "the deal" as it had been trying to put the feeling of normality back in her life and doing the right thing. "And for not telling your dad why I offered it?"

"Dad doesn't like charity," Darcy affirmed in a serious tone. "After Mom died, all these people kept dropping stuff off and Dad had to take it, because it's rude not to." She cast Tess a quick glance, as if she'd just realized that she'd put her foot in it.

Zach was widowed, not divorced. She'd wondered about custody of the kids. Now she knew.

"I don't like charity that much myself," Tess finally said, since Darcy was obviously waiting for a response.

"So you can understand that if he knew I told you he *needed* the pasture then he'd be pretty hot about it." Darcy shifted her weight and confessed, "But he knows now. I don't keep much from him, even if sometimes I take my time telling him."

Tess had kept plenty of secrets from her mom and stepfather, but it'd been in the name of self-preservation. They didn't need to know where she was, how she was keeping herself safe from Jared, her nasty stepbrother, and whoever else was staying at their run-down house, leering at her. Her skin crawled at the memory.

"So you're pretty tight, you and your dad?" she asked, trying to shake off the creeped-out feeling she always got thinking of her stepbrother.

"He's all I have," Darcy said simply. "Well, other than my aunt, Beth Ann, and my sisters. Mom died three years ago of breast cancer, but I miss her a lot."

"I know what you mean." Sometimes Tess remembered her mom, how she was before she'd gotten deeply into drugs and quit caring about anything other than helping Eddie keep his business afloat. Tess missed that woman—even if *that woman* had disappeared around the time Tess had entered grade school. What would it be like to have lost a mother that you truly loved and needed at such a young age?

Come to think of it, in a way she had.

"Did you have a mom?" Darcy asked, keying in on her comment.

"Not really," Tess muttered. She smiled a little when she said, "But I had a grandmother who I lived with until I was thirteen."

"Then what?"

"I moved in with other relatives," Tess said, vaguely realizing the story didn't exactly match the one she'd told Zach. And three years later she had run away, eventually landing in the halfway house where she found life so much more tolerable than it'd been in her own home. Her time with "relatives" was minimal.

"What're you working on?" Darcy asked, moving over to the sewing table where Tess had strips of fabric pinned together.

"I'm practicing my seaming like you told me to. Over and over and over."

Darcy laughed. "I know that feeling. Tia was heartless about that. I couldn't move on until I could sew straight. But it was worth it. Now I sew really straight, which is important when you're quilting."

"Who's Tia?" Tess hated that she had to ask that question, but…well, she had to, since Tia came up in the conversation so often.

Darcy looked surprised. "My aunt, Beth Ann." She smiled. "A lot of us Basque call their aunts Tia."

"You're Basque?"

"Only a quarter," Darcy admitted. "My grandma is Basque. My grandpa isn't. But that's enough to belong to the Basque club."

"Good for you," Tess said. She liked talking to this kid.

"On your way to quilt club now?" she said, pointing at the girl's tote bag.

The girl shook her head. "Coming back. We're making a quilt to raffle off at the Father's Day picnic. It's a pretty good moneymaker for us."

"What do you use the money for?"

Darcy shrugged. "We donate it to the community. They put it in a pot for whenever someone needs help. Things happen," she said matter-of-factly. "Kind of like your barn burning down."

"Right," Tess said. "So you're just here for a visit?"

Darcy looked surprised. "No. We made a deal and I'm here to see if you need any help sewing."

"Darcy...there really isn't a deal. I offered the pasture because it was the right thing to do."

"And you'll let us use the creek path for the same reason?" she asked.

Tess cocked her head. "What kind of grades do you get?"

"Straight As."

"No doubt." Tess folded her arms over her chest. "I do have a few questions about some sewing issues, but I still want an okay from your dad. Just so there's no misunderstanding about where you are or why." Because she didn't want to ruin their tenuously friendly relationship...no matter how many times she told herself she should leave things alone.

"I'll get a note from Dad," Darcy said wearily. "Then maybe we could stop by on our way home from school."

"Meaning you and your sisters?" When Darcy nodded, Tess said, "Even the little one?"

"Lizzie? She'll come round." Darcy squinted at Tess's scars. "Maybe you could tell her the real way you got hurt."

Tess shook her head. "That would be even more upsetting." The wrong thing to say because it was obvious from the way Darcy perked up that she'd piqued her interest.

"And you don't want to talk about it."

"Not one bit."

"Dad says it was probably a car wreck." Darcy waited for either a yay or nay, but Tess disappointed her. "All right," she said, correctly realizing Tess wasn't going to talk about it. "Emma and I have already told Lizzie not to ask if she sees you again, but if she does, don't say anything that scares her again, okay?"

"I'll do my best."

"Thanks." Darcy opened the door before pausing and looking back over her shoulder. "They really don't look that bad. The scars, I mean."

Yes, they did, and both of them knew it, but Tess was touched by Darcy's white lie.

"Good to know. Thanks."

Darcy smiled and walked out onto the porch. "See ya," she said before bouncing down the stairs to the sidewalk.

Tess shut the door, then went to the window and leaned her shoulder against the wall, watching the girl walk down the long driveway.

Don't let yourself get too drawn into this. You can't tell the truth about yourself. You may have to pull up stakes and move tomorrow. Do not allow yourself to get connected.

Especially when she hadn't sorted out how much of this connection was because she enjoyed talking to Darcy, or how much was because she was attracted to the father.

DARCY GOT HOME late from quilting and it wasn't hard for Zach to guess why. She'd stopped at Tess's house again. Probably checking on Misty the cat, who hadn't yet shown up. Emma was beside herself and there was nothing he could do about it. The best he could do was promise Emma a new house cat if Misty never returned.

"Hey, Dad," Darcy said as she came into the kitchen. She dropped her tote on the table and pulled out two finished purple and orange squares. Actually, with the black background, they weren't quite as heinous as he'd first thought they'd be when he'd seen the fabric she'd chosen, but he wondered how many raffle tickets were going to sell this year.

"Very purple and orange," he said.

Darcy snorted. "It's cool-looking."

"Indeed."

"Don't patronize."

"Where'd you learn that?" Zach asked.

"One of this week's vocabulary words. I'm supposed to use it three times."

Great. "Did you stop at Tess's place on the way home?"

"Yeah. I didn't think you'd care, since you didn't tell me not to stop there after the pasture deal. *But,*" she said just as Zach was about to answer, "she wants me to tell you whenever we go over there. *And—*" Darcy hesitated for that split second that told him something was coming she wasn't quite sure of "—tomorrow Emma and Lizzie and I are going to stop by on our way home from school."

"Lizzie?"

"Unless she's afraid. If she is, then we'll come straight home." Darcy lifted her shoulders. "I told Tess if she told Lizzie how she really hurt her face then Lizzie might come around. But she just said it was a lot scarier than the trespassing story and that Lizzie shouldn't hear it."

"Well, she should know."

"Don't you wonder, Dad?"

"I do," he said. All the time.

"And when you see the side of her face that isn't messed

up, it's like really pretty, you know?" Zach didn't answer, but he'd noticed.

"I told her about Mom," Darcy said, staring down at her hands with a slight frown, "because I thought it'd help her see that we all have something bad in our lives, but…" She shrugged again and met his eyes.

"Um, you know, Darcy, you need to be careful not to stick your nose too far into a stranger's business…or to tell her too much of ours." Especially when Zach was still working out exactly how he wanted to proceed with Tess. Did he pursue the attraction? Would it affect his daughters if he did, and if so, how? He didn't want Darcy in the middle as he figured this stuff out, but forbidding her to see Tess wasn't going to fly, either.

"I'm not doing that," Darcy said earnestly. "I just didn't want her to think she was alone in having trouble. You know how Grandma always talks about how bad her life is whenever something bad happens to someone else? I thought maybe it'd help her get…"

She gestured and Zach said, "Perspective?"

"Yeah. That's it."

"It's not your job to help Tess get perspective."

Darcy carefully folded the quilt squares into fourths. "I think she's lonely."

"She's not a stray kitten."

"I know. But she is lonely and I like talking to her."

TESS DIDN'T KNOW how many of Zach's daughters would stop by after school, if any, but when she answered the door at 3:15 all three girls stood on her porch. One of them looked very unhappy. Tess tamped down the stab of guilt and stepped back.

"Come on in." She held the door open and the middle girl

stepped inside, followed by the youngest girl, after Darcy had given the tiny blonde a firm nudge in the lower back.

"Thanks for coming," Tess said, feeling ridiculously awkward.

"No problem," Darcy said. "I thought maybe you could show us what you want to do and then I can help you do it?"

"Sure."

The little girl stared at the floor.

"It's okay," Tess said to her. "You can look at my face. I'm sorry for what I said about trespassing."

"Dad says you were lying to me." The girl's gaze remained glued to the floorboards.

"I exaggerated," Tess said, wondering if this had come from one of those late-night talks Zach had said he'd had. "I shouldn't have done that."

The girl's lips pursed together and then she said, "Can I wait on the porch?"

"Lizzie—" the middle girl started to say, but Tess cut her off with a quick lift of her hand.

"Do you want the dogs to come with you? They need some exercise." *Please don't be afraid of dogs.*

"No, thank you," Lizzie said politely as she walked to the door. Tess and the other two girls stood silently as Lizzie slipped outside.

Lizzie was going to be a hard sell.

Lizzie? Darcy? She turned to the middle girl. "I don't think we've been introduced."

"Emma," the girl said, pushing one long braid back over her shoulder and then she and Darcy said simultaneously, "We know."

Tess smiled. "Your parents must be die-hard Jane Austen fans."

"Only Mom," Emma said. "Dad didn't even know."

"Does he now?"

"Somebody told him after Lizzie was born," Darcy said as she picked up the evil Very Easy pattern Tess was still trying to figure out. "Dad doesn't read much. He's more of a music guy."

"Have you read any Austen books?" Tess asked.

"Not yet," Darcy said. "Tia—Aunt Beth—says they'll be more fun when we're older."

"She's probably right," Tess said, still smiling.

"Greg—one of the high schoolers—had to read it for a class," Emma said, "and he said it's all mushy, so I don't know if I even want to read it."

Tess gave a serious nod. Emma looked to be about nine years old, so yeah, mushy probably wasn't going to float her boat.

"This isn't that hard," Darcy said, looking up from the pattern instructions she'd been reading. "Usually I need Tia to translate, but even I can figure out these directions. Most of them anyway."

"Great," Tess said, feeling a wee bit stupid.

"I told Dad we'd be home by four-thirty," Darcy said, "so let's lay out your fabric and I can show you how to pin it. Then we can come back tomorrow and help with the next steps."

Tess was pretty certain she could do the pinning part with no assistance, but if Darcy wanted to help, she wasn't going to send her home. "Will Lizzie be all right out there?"

"Her choice," Emma said. "I sew a little, but I'm too young for quilt club."

"Well, ladies," Tess said. "Let's do it."

"First we have to make sure your grain is straight," Darcy said, picking up the length of fabric Tess had draped over the back of her sewing chair.

"Isn't that only for cotton?" Emma said.

Darcy gave her a superior look. "*All* grains have to be straight."

"What's the grain?" Tess knew the answer to that from her DVD, but wanted to hear Darcy's answer.

"The way the threads run. Do you want to cut it out here on the floor?"

"Can't think of a better place," Tess said.

"Tia makes us mop first when we use the floor," Emma said, crouching down as Darcy flipped the fabric out.

Tia sounds like a lot of fun. And Tess still wondered why she lived on Zach's ranch. She hoped it was to take care of her nieces, even though she didn't want to admit that to herself.

"The floor's clean," Tess said. Fairly clean. She'd swept that morning, but having two dogs in the house did tend to generate dust bunnies.

The girls helped her fold the fabric in two, making certain the grain lines were straight, and then Darcy patiently showed her how to use the guide in the pattern to lay out her pieces, matching the arrows on the pattern pieces to the grain.

"If the arrows are crooked, then whatever you're sewing won't hang right."

Tess noticed that Lizzie had begun to pace on the porch. Her blond head passed by the window like a soldier on watch. "Should we check on her?" Tess asked at one point, but Darcy waved off the question.

When they finished half an hour later, Tess hadn't learned anything she hadn't already gleaned from the DVDs but she'd had company, and tomorrow she would start on stuff she hadn't been able to grasp from the diagrams on the pattern instructions—things that her twelve-year-old tutor could grasp, but Tess wasn't going to dwell on that.

"We can't come by tomorrow," Emma said as the three

of them walked to the door, "because we have a 4-H meeting, but we can come back the day after."

"Just practice your seams," Darcy warned. "Don't screw
up the dress."

Tess fought a smile. "Yes, ma'am." She gestured toward
the porch. "Any hints on how to make your sister feel more
at home?"

"Ignore her," Darcy said.

"Seems harsh," Tess answered.

Emma scrunched up her nose as she said, "It'll work.
Always does. And if it doesn't, try sugar."

Tess laughed as Darcy opened the door. Lizzie's head
came up at the sound and then she abruptly turned away.

"See you day after tomorrow," Emma said and then a
second later the girls were gone.

And Tess was alone.

CHAPTER TWELVE

WHEN JIM ANDERSON had owned the place, Zach would check his cattle every week or so—mainly by driving by and taking a look. But Tess O'Neil wasn't cow-savvy, so he needed to keep a closer eye on them.

He was lying to himself, of course.

It didn't take long to check the cattle, see that everything was well and the fence was fine, and it didn't long to figure out that Tess wasn't going to leave her house.

Zach solved that problem by tying Roscoe to the fence before walking up to the front door and knocking.

The dogs made a huge racket and a second later Tess opened the door with the dogs poking their sharp black noses out from either side of her.

"Is there a problem?" She'd forgotten her glasses again and again he was struck by the unusual color of her eyes.

"No. I—" *feel ridiculously self-conscious after our last parting* "—was checking the cows. Thought I'd let you know."

"The dogs already informed me."

"I imagine they did. So, anyway." He raised a hand in a less than suave salute, and started back across the porch when he stopped and turned back. "I was wondering after our last conversation…would you like to learn to ride?"

Those green eyes widened slightly. "Why would you do that?"

"Teach you to ride?"

"Yes."

"Just being neighborly." A patently disbelieving look crossed her face. "And I'm grateful that you've given Darcy a mission. She thinks she's the answer to all your sewing problems."

"She is," Tess said, folding her arms over her chest. Was she backing off? "I know nothing and she's helped me make sense of the DVDs. I bought too high of a level."

"You should have seen how she fought learning to sew."

"Really? She seems to love it now."

"Stubborn kid. If my sister-in-law hadn't been more stubborn, you wouldn't have a tutor right now."

"Your sister-in-law who lives with you." It was more of a question than a statement. A request for clarification.

"In the hired hand trailer. She's been a lot of help since… my wife died."

"I'm very sorry about your loss," Tess said. Again, simply spoken, but he did not doubt her sincerity. Tess, too, had suffered loss.

"It was not an easy time." Still wasn't, but something had shifted since meeting Tess. He didn't know if she was simply there at the right time, when his grieving had finally hit the point where he could move on, or if she'd somehow prodded that part of him he'd buried away after Karen's death back into being.

Tess idly reached up to touch her scars, a gesture he noticed she made when she was thinking. She didn't look at him for a long moment and he wished he knew what was going on in her head. A yes or a no. That's all he needed.

When she did finally meet his eyes, he saw that she was torn. "After what happened to you, I'm not exactly anxious to get on a horse," she pointed out.

"I have other horses."

"Then why do you ride *that* one?" She gestured at Roscoe, who was happily eating her flowering bush. Zach made a shooing motion and the horse stopped, bobbing his head with flowers sticking out both sides of his mouth.

"He understands cows and I can ride him for fourteen hours straight if I have to."

"Unless he leaves you on the mountain."

Zach gave her a smile. "He doesn't shy at all after hour ten. If I can stay on him for that long, I'm good." He waited then to see what Tess would say. He wanted her to say yes.

"Tempting," she finally said.

"Then…?"

"I'll think about it."

"Fair enough," he said.

TESS SHUT THE door as Zach started down the steps, refusing to let herself watch him walk away—even if those short, fringed leather chaps he wore emphasized his butt in a good way. How deeply involved could she allow herself to become with her neighbors?

You've encouraged the girls to drop by after school…

That was a way to give herself some company—even if Lizzie wasn't about to forgive her. But this…thing with Zach…this felt more like pursuing an attraction.

Mainly because that was exactly what it was—and it went two ways. He was attracted to her, scars and all.

So why her?

Because he'd lost his wife? Because she was handy?

Was she someone safe to dally with—a first dip back into the dating pool? Someone who wouldn't expect him to hang around for long?

Tess clapped both hands on top of her head, which reminded her it was time to redo her roots, cover the good half inch of dark auburn that was showing. Her drugstore order hadn't arrived and she was on her last box of dye, but hopefully the next shipment would get here before she had to touch up again. And she'd forgotten her glasses the past few times she'd been with Zach. She was getting complacent. It was one thing to get on with her life as Detective Hiller had told her, and another to totally shove aside the possibility of being recognized.

Not knowing how careful she had to be was hell—and made it so tempting to grasp at any straw of normality she could. Like a hot cowboy neighbor who seemed interested.

And heaven help her, if he had temporary in mind, as in easing back into the dating world after a painful loss, she was very, very tempted. Temporary she could do.

Sugar didn't work.

Tess had spent the morning baking cookies, something she *could* do competently, thanks to her grandmother's best friend, Helen, who'd taught Tess to bake the summer she'd turned ten. Three years before the bad times started.

As she stirred the dough, Tess realized this was the first time she'd baked Helen's recipe since her grandmother had died. There'd definitely been no baking when she'd lived with her mom and Eddie. She'd spent those years holed up in her bedroom with the door locked—except for the time Jared had broken it down. It felt good to relive some of the happier moments of her life while making the ginger cookies, but despite the warm scent of sweet spice that hung in the air when the girls arrived, Lizzie made it clear she was not impressed. Darcy and Emma both took cookies, biting into them and making appreciative noises, but Lizzie stubbornly stood with her hands behind her back.

"Take a cookie," Tess heard Darcy order in a low voice when she went into the kitchen for the milk she'd picked up at the mercantile that day along with six plastic glasses— her company glasses.

Lizzie's voice came next. "I don't— *Mmmph!*"

Tess could only imagine what had happened, but when she went back into the room, Lizzie was chewing away at the cookie and avoiding her eyes.

The sewing lesson was slightly more successful than the ploy to win over Lizzie. They made the pleats in the dress bodice and skirt, basting them into place by hand, even though the pattern said to use the machine. Darcy had been taught the "old school" methods and insisted that Tess learn the same.

"You can always fall back on basic skills," she said.

"Did someone say that to you?" Tess asked.

"About nine hundred times," Darcy muttered.

Lizzie sat in the recliner, which was better than exiling herself to the porch where the dogs lay in the sun. Progress. Tess's sketch pad lay on the overturned crate she used as an end table and Lizzie started flipping through the pages. When Tess smiled at her, she instantly stopped, but a few minutes later, when she thought Tess wasn't looking, she picked up the pad again.

Once the pleats were done and they started constructing the bodice, Darcy frowned. She read and reread the instructions, then handed them to Tess. "I don't quite understand this part about turning the corner at the small dot. It's like there's something missing."

"That's how I feel every time I read these things." And she'd read the instructions a lot, trying to visualize what she'd be doing.

"Let's try this," Darcy said, pinning the fabric and then comparing it to the diagram.

"It doesn't look right," Emma chimed in.

"Okay, then maybe..." Darcy unpinned and repinned.

"Uh-uh," her sister said. Across the room Lizzie was

deeply involved with the sketch pad, which was now on her lap.

"What do you think?" Darcy asked, comparing her pin job to the diagram so that Tess could see.

"Doesn't match." Tess took the fabric and had to agree with Darcy. There seemed to be a step missing.

"Take it to Tia," Emma said.

"Yeah," Darcy agreed. "It'd be better than picking out a bunch of seams later."

"I thought this was easy."

"It is. Except for this part." Darcy folded the instructions. "Would you care if I took this home and showed my aunt and dropped it off tomorrow on my way home from school?"

"Sure," Tess said with a small shrug. Why should she care if Zach's sister-in-law thought she was an idiot?

When she looked over at Lizzie, her hands were in her lap and the sketchbook was back on the crate. Tess took a chance.

She walked over to the girl and crouched down so that they were at eye level. "I'm sorry I told you a lie about my face and scared you."

"I wasn't scared."

"I'm sorry I told you a lie."

"Grown-ups aren't supposed to lie."

Tess exhaled, hoping she hadn't lost the moment. "*I* was scared," she said.

"Of what?" Lizzie asked, showing more interest.

"Strangers. When you guys would walk by my house, my dogs would go nuts and it scared me. Every time it happened it scared me, since I live alone, so I wanted you guys to stop walking by."

"Then why didn't you just tell us that?" Lizzie asked.

Tess gave a weary smile. "I should have. I didn't. I'm sorry."

Lizzie considered for a moment then cocked her head. "So what really did happen to your face?"

Tess was ready. She'd known she'd have to eventually come up with some kind of an answer, so she'd worked on it and, heaven help her, she was about to tell another grown-up lie using Darcy's theory about the car wreck as a springboard. "I got into an accident. A piece of metal slashed my face."

Lizzie's eyes were huge. Tess truly hoped she hadn't made a mistake telling her.

"A car accident, like Daddy said?"

Tess sidestepped the question. "I'm kind of shy about people seeing my face now, so that's why I wasn't very friendly."

"Your face isn't *that* bad," Lizzie said, repeating what Darcy had said when she'd come looking for the cat.

"Thanks," Tess said, getting to her feet. "You want to take a few cookies home? I can't eat all of these. Maybe you can put them in your lunches tomorrow."

"Great idea," Darcy said from behind Tess, but she needn't have given her sister the blatant hint as to how to respond, because the little girl was smiling now.

"I'll put them in some foil," Tess said.

ZACH RODE OVER to Tess's house on his way to check the last stretch of fence on the mountain. He didn't bother pretending to himself that he was checking the cows, although he'd give them the once-over on his way by. He was going to see the neighbor lady, following instinct, cautiously seeing where it was leading him. For the past several days he'd been thinking about something other than the ranch slowly slipping into the red or worrying about whether he'd be able to give his girls the life he wanted to. For the past several days he'd been feeling alive again.

Tess wasn't home. Her car was gone so Zach reined Roscoe around and headed out for his last long day on the mountain.

When he got back to the ranch six hours later, Beth Ann was sitting on the porch.

"Where are the girls?" he asked as he dismounted. Roscoe put his head down and started eating.

"They walked home."

"And they're not here yet?"

Beth Ann shook her head. "Nope. They were going to stop over there—" he pointed at Tess's house "—to drop off the pattern instructions I explained to Darcy last night."

"You don't look happy about it." Zach hadn't seen this coming, but maybe he should have. Beth Ann was very protective of the girls.

She shrugged casually. "What do we know about her?"

"Not a lot," Zach conceded. He swung his leg over the saddle and dismounted. "But the read I'm getting now isn't the same as the one I was getting before."

"Oh, really. Have you been spending a lot of time reading with her?" Zach's eyebrows lifted at her snarky question and Beth Ann let out a huff of breath. "Never mind. It's just that those are your daughters over there and you don't know this woman."

"I'm getting to know her."

The startled look Beth Ann gave him made him feel suddenly guilty. Was her reaction because she sensed that he was attracted to Tess? Was she upset because somehow that made him unfaithful to her sister?

Logically, probably not, but there were a lot of emotions tied up in losing a sister, and a wife. For a long time he hadn't been ready to move on. He still wasn't certain he was ready, but he couldn't deny that he found Tess intriguing.

"Here they come," Beth Ann said, lifting her chin toward the county road. Zach turned to see his three girls passing the gate posts.

"None the worse for their experience, it seems."

Beth Ann sent him a sharp look, but didn't answer. Instead she pushed herself to her feet and dusted off her pants. "I'll go see if they need help with their homework."

She started down the walk to the driveway.

"Hey," Zach said. She turned to look at him and he realized he didn't know what he wanted to say. He just didn't want her going away mad or thinking he didn't appreciate all she did. "Come by for dinner tonight."

She hesitated for a moment then said, "Okay."

Zach picked up Roscoe's reins and led the horse toward the tack shed, where he unsaddled him and turned him out into the pasture with the other horses. By the time he was done with the evening feeding and got back to the kitchen, the girls had the table set and Beth Ann was making a salad to go with the slow cooker stew. She smiled at him when he came in, a peace offering, then went back to mixing greens.

Everything was back to normal. The way he liked it. The fragile status quo they'd maintained over the past three years was back in place and he felt himself relax.

THE GIRLS STOPPED by Tess's house after school as they'd promised the day before, when they'd visited to drop off and explain the pattern instructions. The dogs rushed to the door as the kids clamored up onto the porch and knocked, their tails wagging excitedly.

"I hope you guys haven't lost your edge," Tess said as she went to the door.

Lizzie smiled as she walked in, a different kid than the last time. "Can I look at your dress drawings?"

"Sure," Tess said.

"Any cookies?" Emma asked, setting her backpack on the floor next to the door.

"Not today, but maybe next time."

"We still have a bunch at home," Darcy said.

"We're not *at* home," Emma pointed out.

Mental note—have after-school snacks on hand. Tess smiled a little as she followed Darcy to the sewing table. Her grandmother had kept snacks. It'd been nice. Funny how she was thinking about her grandmother so much more than she had in several years.

Because her time with her grandmother had been the most stable time of her life? And she wanted a stable life more than anything?

Probably.

Modeling had been anything but stable—talk about a career rife with uncertainty. Surviving in the business had given her a boost in confidence...confidence she was struggling to get back after the slasher had shot it all to hell.

Darcy waved her over to the table. "So here's what we do..."

Half an hour later when the girls were ready to leave, Tess had a nicely pleated and draped bodice finished.

"I'm going to try to do the rest of the dress on my own," Tess told Darcy as they walked to the door.

"All right. But call me if you have any problems. Or better yet, stop and we'll figure them out."

Yes, ma'am. Tess smiled. Lizzie looked up at her after putting on her oddly colored purplish-gray coat.

"Can I have one of your pictures to put on my wall?" she asked.

"Liz!" Darcy said irritably.

"It's okay," Tess said. "Why don't we look at them and you can pick one next time you come."

"Thanks." The little girl grinned and Tess could see a

gap where she'd lost a bottom tooth. But she didn't comment because she had no idea if the gap made Lizzie proud—or self-conscious. Funny how a very visible injury gave one a whole new perspective.

Tess watched the girls go, feeling unexpectedly depressed that things could not be different. That she couldn't tell Zach the truth about herself. He seemed trustworthy.

You don't know him. You can't take that kind of risk.

Personal safety aside, her trust issues were too deeply ingrained to be easily set aside—issues intimately tied to her experiences with her less than trustworthy family. Her mother, who would always take Eddie's side. Jared, her older stepbrother, who'd become more sexually aggressive as she matured. Sometimes she wondered how she'd gotten out of that house without being raped. It'd been coming though.

Tess had run away after he'd broken down her door. The only thing that had saved her that day was that Jared hadn't realized Eddie was still home, in a stupor in his bedroom.

What an irony. Saved by Eddie. He'd staggered out demanding to know what the hell had just happened and Tess had grabbed her pocketbook and ran. She'd never gone back. Instead she'd borrowed some clothes and fifty bucks from a friend and taken a bus to Seattle. There she'd lived with the older sister of the same friend for a couple weeks, then eventually ended up in a halfway house.

Not a good time. The only decent memory she had was of Mikey, who'd spent most of his time with her and her grandmother instead of at home with his own family. He hadn't been able to stand life with Eddie, either, and left home before Tess had, even though he'd been a year younger than her. She'd never heard from him again, didn't even know if he was still alive. Sometimes she considered doing an internet search, but what was the point? A lot of the memories they shared were not good ones. The good days had ended when her grandmother had died and then had picked up again—for her anyway—on that marvelous day when she'd been taken on by the Dresden Agency.

The years in between had been tamped deep down into a dark place she'd rarely visited...until Eddie had come back.

CHAPTER THIRTEEN

ZACH WAS changing the oil in the tractor when a shadow fell over him. He looked over his shoulder, still hanging on to the funnel stuck in the crankcase, to see Tess standing in the open barn door.

She stayed right where she was, the early-afternoon sun behind her throwing her face into shadows.

"Hey," he said as he turned back to pour the last quart of oil into the plastic funnel.

"Hey, yourself." The shadow moved as she came closer, crossing the short distance between the door and tractor.

"Are you here to learn to ride?"

"Yes."

Her matter-of-fact answer surprised him. "I didn't think you were going to." It had been several days since he'd made the offer.

She folded her arms over her chest, looking as if she was protecting herself. "I've been known to take my time before coming to a decision."

"But now you have." He shook the funnel, then lifted it and held the oil rag onto the bottom. Then he set the funnel aside and replaced the cap on the crankcase. He took his time wiping his hands and realized he was moving slowly, treating Tess like a spooky colt. Sudden movements were not going to send her running.

He hoped. He still had no idea why he was so drawn to her, especially after their shaky beginning. Part of it was physical—scarred or not, she was one of the most beautiful women he'd ever met—but the attraction went deeper than that. Beyond the face and the long legs and perfect ass. He loved it when she smiled at him. When she trusted him enough to joke with him, gave him glimpses of who she really was.

"Dirty work," he said as he bunched up the rag in one hand.

"I'm aware."

And then those translucent green eyes were on him. Wide. Thoughtful. And still a touch wary, as always.

"I'm glad you came over."

"Yeah?"

"Yeah. Roscoe needs the kinks worked out of him."

She gave a surprised laugh, her uninjured eye crinkling at the corner, the wariness melting away. For the moment anyway. He'd seen her relax, then retreat moments later many times. He didn't want that to happen today.

"Well, you're in luck because I brought my spurs," she said.

"Spurs don't work on Roscoe."

"No?"

Zach shook his head as he came closer, still dabbing at his hands with the rag, more for something to do than because of the remnant oil.

"He's too tough for spurs. Besides, spurs are really for guidance."

"I thought they were for jamming the horse in the ribs to make him go."

Zach laughed. "Trust me, the last thing you want is for Roscoe to *go*. And spurs are just extensions of the rider's heels. For nudging, directing, communicating. Never for pain."

"Hmm," she said thoughtfully. "Learn something new every day."

"Do you want to go and meet your mount?"

Tess gave a quick shrug, a shadow of uncertainty crossing her face now that the zero hour had arrived. A second later the bravado was back.

"Sure." She smiled up at him. "Lead the way."

TESS FOLLOWED ZACH out of the barn, savoring the warmth of the sun. Being nervous always made her feel cold. She hadn't intended to be nervous, but between Zach and the prospect of climbing up onto a beast that weighed ten times what she did, yeah, she was a bit jittery.

"I'll put you on Lizzie's horse."

"Is it taller than my dogs?" she asked.

"Barely." Zach walked to a large corral with four horses inside eating hay. There was Roscoe, the horse that had bucked off Zach, a striking black-and-white pinto, and a very short black horse with a white spot on its nose and a yellowish horse. "That's Snippy," he said, pointing at the black. "Lizzie learned to ride on her. She's very steady."

"How long ago did she learn to ride?"

Zach considered for a moment. "About two years ago. We took a lot of family rides after Karen died. Before that she rode with me. Took the reins and steered." He smiled distantly.

"Whose horse is that?" She pointed at the pinto.

"That's Emma's mare, Belle. Emma gets to go to 4-H horse camp this year, so Belle's getting a lot of attention. And the buckskin is mine, but Beth Ann rides him when we gather."

"Gather what?"

"Cattle." He pointed out into the field beyond the corral where two more horses grazed beside two small calves.

Tess wondered if he was going to tell her his horses also acted as surrogate mothers, since there wasn't a cow in sight, but instead he said, "That sorrel out there, the red-dish horse, is Darcy's."

"And the other?" She knew the answer before she'd fin-ished the question and wished she'd kept her mouth shut.

"Karen's." One corner of Zach's mouth tightened. "Bing's getting pretty old. She bought him when she was in high school and I think he was twelve then. He was her first horse."

Bing...

Mr. Bingley from *Pride and Prejudice*. It had to be. But Tess wasn't going to ask.

"So…" He put a hand on the fence and turned to her with a half smile. "I'll saddle up Snippy and let's get you a' horseback."

Tess nodded with more confidence than she felt, although she wasn't certain if it was Zach or the prospect of horse-back riding that made her nerves hum—or perhaps a com-bination of the two.

TESS HAD NEVER been near a horse. That much was evident from the way she cautiously approached Snippy. When she gingerly stroked the little mare's neck, the horse turned her head to put her nose on Tess's arm and Tess stepped back—but not as fast as she had that day Zach had taken her elbow when she was about to trip.

"She doesn't bite or anything," he assured her as he put the blanket on then settled Beth Ann's saddle in place. He had to readjust the cinches and lengthen the stirrups, guess-ing at Tess's length.

"Okay." Tess stroked Snippy's neck again then ran her fingers through the mare's long mane. When she stepped back she sniffed at her hand. "Horses have a rather distinctive smell."

Zach grinned as he tightened the cinches. "It's a good smell," he assured her. One that made him feel good anyway.

When he was done he crossed the reins over Snippy's neck and stood back. Tess stayed right where she was on the other side of the horse.

"You need to come around to this side. Horses have a near side and an off side. You're on the off side. You mount on the near side."

"There are rules?"

"There are," he assured her. And he wasn't quite sure how he was going to help her onto the horse without touching her.

She walked around the horse and stopped beside him. "What now?"

"You're going to put your left foot in the stirrup, grab the saddle horn and use it to help you swing your other leg over. And you're going to try to keep your weight centered over the horse's back when you do it."

"Is that all?"

"Pretty much."

"Care to demonstrate?"

He shrugged. "Sure." He patted Snippy's neck then slowly mounted, demonstrating everything he'd just said.

"All right," Tess said, approaching the horse. She lifted her leg, placed her foot in the stirrup and hopped in place as she tried to get her balance, then pulled her foot back out of the stirrup again and stood back. She cast a sidelong look at Zach.

He pressed his lips together momentarily, then said, "If it doesn't bother you too much, I can help you into the saddle and we can work on mounting later."

"That's fine," she said. They faced off awkwardly for a few seconds, the incident where she'd jerked away from him obviously on both their minds. She moistened her lips and then said, "I don't mind being touched, as long as I know it's coming."

The elephant was now squarely in the center of the room, but Zach let it be. If Tess wanted to tell him what had happened to her, she would.

"Okay. I'm going to make a stirrup with my hands. You're going to step in it and I'm going to boost you into the saddle."

"If you say so," Tess said cautiously.

Zach laced his fingers together and held them near the saddle's stirrup. Tess took hold of the saddle horn and put her foot into his hands. "Give a jump." She did, he boosted and Tess landed neatly in the saddle.

"Top of the world, Ma," she said with a laugh as she awkwardly gathered the reins.

"Here. Let me show you how to hold them." Zach arranged the leather in her hands, thinking it really had been a long time since he'd touched a woman. Tess's hands were soft and she smelled good, like a field of grass and sunshine.

When he glanced up at her, she was biting her lip.

"It's normal to be a little nervous," he said quietly.

"This feels strange. And wonderful."

"You're good to go."

"Go where?" There was a touch of panic in her voice, but she was still smiling. She was loving this. He could see the excitement in her eyes.

"Nudge her with your heels and we'll walk to the end of the driveway and back."

"Nothing fast."

"I'll be on foot," he assured her. "Today we'll just walk

for a bit and then if you're still game, maybe I'll saddle up Roscoe another day and we can ride across the field."

Tess nudged Snippy, who obediently moved forward. Tess lurched slightly, but kept her balance without grabbing the saddle horn and off they went down the driveway. She didn't look at him the one time Zach shot her a quick glance, but he could see she was getting a kick out of the experience.

"How's your balance?"

"I haven't fallen off yet."

"Doing better than me, then." She laughed and he was struck by how warm and husky it was.

"Would you like to go a little faster?" he asked when they got to the county road and turned around.

"I, uh…"

"No faster than I can jog in work boots."

"All right."

"Hang on." Zach made a clucking noise and started to jog. Snippy jogged beside him as she'd been taught. She had a wonderfully smooth trot, not like Roscoe's pile-driving gait, and when he glanced back at Tess she was smiling widely.

Damn but she was beautiful when she smiled.

ZACH SLOWED TO a walk as they approached the barn and Tess let go of the saddle horn she'd been clinging to for dear life, even though the horse hadn't been going that fast. "Wow," she said. "I had no idea how much fun riding was."

"Then maybe we can do it again."

She dismounted before he could tell her how, and did a fair job of it, hopping a little as she pulled her shoe out of the stirrup.

"Want a beer?" he asked as he took the reins from her.

She would have loved a beer, but she shook her head.

"It's too late." She wanted to get out of there before the kids got home.

"Big date?"

Tess snorted. "As if."

When their eyes met, she could tell that he'd read more into the statement than she'd intended—he thought she was saying she was too ugly for a big date. She should have kept her mouth shut. She wasn't looking for sympathy or empathy. She was looking for…what?

"I have to let the dogs out. They've been in the house for a long time."

He nodded, but when he spoke it wasn't about the dogs or her getting home. "What happened to your face?" he asked softly.

"I had an accident." The words fell out of her mouth and then she firmly shut her lips.

Zach waited, but when it became obvious she wasn't expanding on her answer, he reached up to lightly touch the right side of her face, the good side, tracing the back of his finger from her cheekbone to her jawline. Her eyes wanted to drift shut from the sheer sensuousness of his touch, but she forced them to stay open as she reached up to take his hand by the wrist, stopping his movement.

"I need to go home."

"I understand," he said as she slowly let go of his wrist, taking a step back. Once there was some space between them, she felt like she could breathe again.

"I don't think you do. I—" she pulled in a very deep breath, feeling like she was about to dive off a cliff "—I don't mind it when you touch me." *I like it.* "But—" she tightened one corner of her mouth "—you've probably noticed I have some issues I'm working through."

A faint smile tilted his mouth. "Yeah. I noticed."

"It's something that's going to take me some time to

work through." Damn. Could she get any more cryptic? She wouldn't blame him if he just told her to go to hell—that he wasn't into games. But he didn't.

"You want to come back and ride again sometime?"

"Yes." She spoke without giving herself time to think because she didn't want to think. She wanted to spend time with him. She didn't want him to touch her too much. Yet. Not until she had a read on the situation and what they both expected from it.

"Day after tomorrow? Two o'clock?"

"Sounds good." And then Tess turned and started down the driveway before she agreed to anything else she wasn't certain she should do.

"YOU SHOULD see the pretty dresses that Tess draws," Lizzie said when Zach tucked her in after getting home late from a Wesley supply run. Apparently she and her sisters had stayed at Tess's for such a long time that afternoon that Beth Ann had called and asked Tess to send the kids home.

"Yeah?" Zach asked, smoothing back the wisps of hair on Lizzie's forehead. His baby was still young, but she was growing up so very fast.

"She draws them and then she colors them and she's going to make one special for me. And after Darcy teaches her all the sewing stuff she needs to know, she might make the drawings into *real* dresses!"

"Really?" Zach said.

"Mmm-hmm." Lizzie nodded adamantly. "She got a dress dummy today in the mail to put her fabric on."

"We named it Sylvia," Emma said from the doorway. "Darcy and I helped her put it together. That's why we were there for so long tonight."

"Darcy already explained." Zach stood after kissing Lizzie on the forehead.

"And there was also the matter of the cookies," Emma said as she stepped out into the hall. "Lizzie was eating them as fast as Tess could pull them out of the oven."

"Was not," Lizzie called from deep in her blankets.

Zach and Emma walked down the hall toward her room. Emma stopped at her door, her forehead wrinkling. "Tia got really bent out of shape about us being late."

"She was worried. You should have called her," Zach said.

"We did," Emma said.

"Maybe she didn't understand." Although Zach had no idea how she couldn't have understood.

"Maybe," Emma said slowly, but she didn't sound convinced.

Zach debated then headed back downstairs without knocking on Darcy's door. As she got older, she valued her privacy, so he did his best to respect that. But when he started down the stairs, she opened the door a crack to call out, "Good night, Dad."

"Good night, kiddo. Sleep well."

He paused on the landing, looking out the small window there. Tess's lights were off except for one.

How things had changed, for both of them, in just a matter of weeks.

TESS LOOKED FORWARD to her next riding lesson more than she wanted to admit. As she walked down Zach's driveway, she told herself that, her attraction to Zach aside, it was also a matter of being hungry for adult company, that she spent too much time alone. But ten minutes later, after she'd mounted Snippy and Zach had casually put his hand on her knee to demonstrate exactly what he wanted her to do with her feet and legs in order to communicate with the horse, Tess admitted to herself that she was hungry for more than just adult company.

She nodded as he explained how to gently press the horse's side with her left or right knee while she used the opposite rein to turn, but she barely heard what he said.

"Got it?" he asked.

"Got it," she lied, trying to remember the last time she'd reacted like this to something as simple as a touch on her knee. Just a touch. Not a squeeze or a stroke. A touch.

Which made her wonder, where was all this heading? Were they on similar courses? Or did they have totally different objectives? Did it matter as long as they had the same goal?

For a person who hated questions, Tess had a ton right now.

Zach's wife died three years ago, and from the way the girls chattered during their visits, it appeared there wasn't a woman in the picture except for their aunt. Was he done grieving and ready to move on? If so, Tess could see where it would be intimidating to jump back into the dating game after a long layoff.

Which made her wonder if she was a nonthreatening way to do just that. The scarred woman next door hungry for any attention? Tess gave a soft snort at the thought. No, she hadn't exactly been giving off the I-need-attention vibe.

So, in the end, the big question was what was Zach interested in and would it mesh with what she wanted? If he was looking for a person with whom he could get deeply involved, then she was not what he was looking for.

Zach mounted in one smooth move and Tess swallowed dryly. He was so damned sexy. No getting around that.

Picking up his reins, Zach gestured with his head at the open gate leading to a vast green field. "Ready?"

"Ready," she said, even though she wasn't. Sometimes you had to make a move even if you weren't fully ready… in many areas of life.

CHAPTER FOURTEEN

"DAD, Dad, Dad!"

Zach dropped his razor in the sink, where it landed with a splash, and yanked open his bathroom door, ready to deal with an emergency, just as Emma appeared in the doorway of his bedroom. She thrust her hands out in front of her, an expression of sheer joy lighting her face.

"It's a kitten," she explained, not trusting him to properly identify the tiny black-and-white creature that barely filled her palm, its eyes little more than barely open slits.

"I see that."

"It's *Misty's* kitten. She just brought this one to the house and disappeared. Tia said she's going to get the others. I need to get this one back to the mitten box, where Misty left it." She grinned happily at him. "And I thought she was getting fat because I was feeding her too much."

Zach felt a ridiculous surge of relief. Okay, one small disaster avoided. He'd lived in fear of the girls finding what was left of Misty along the edge of the road or in a field.

By the time he got down to the kitchen, Misty had dropped off another kitten and Beth Ann was helping the girls make a box.

"I think we should follow her," Lizzie said, cuddling the first kitten close to her chest.

"Let her do it her way," Emma said sternly. "She's following her instinct and we don't want to mess it up." She looked up at Zach as he came into the kitchen. "Do we, Dad?"

"Probably not," Zach agreed.

"We get to keep the kittens, don't we?" Lizzie asked, shielding the tiny animal she held as if someone was going to snatch it from her.

"We could use help with the mice," Zach said.

"But maybe we'll take advantage of the spay/neuter clinic we should have taken advantage of earlier," Beth Ann said, catching Zach's eye over the girls' heads.

"If we'd done that," Darcy said under her breath as she arranged the blanket, "then we wouldn't be having all this fun now."

"Fun or not, we need to be responsible," Beth Ann said with a snap in her voice. "A couple of cats are fine, but if we have three or four ready to multiply, we're going to have cats coming out our ears."

"Here comes another," Lizzie announced happily as Misty trotted in the door, looking right and left as she traveled, holding a yellow kitten by the scruff of its neck. "Oh, I can't wait to tell Tess." She smiled up at her dad. "Can I tell her now?"

"How?"

"I can call her!"

"Yeah," Emma said. "Maybe she'd like to come over and see them. Maybe she'd like to have one!"

"With those dogs?" Darcy asked.

"She says they are super well trained," Emma said, "but we'd better check before we give her a kitten."

"I get to call her," Lizzie said, clutching the kitten as she headed for the phone.

"No." Beth Ann spoke before Lizzie had gone two steps.

The girl turned toward Beth Ann with a perplexed frown. "Why?"

Beth Ann drew in a deep breath and looked at Zach.

"It's almost dinnertime," he said, pulling the excuse out of the air.

Beth Ann turned her attention back to the mother cat, who deposited the kitten in the box with the other and then settled in with them and began cleaning the closest kitty's ears.

"You'd better put the one you're holding back," Beth Ann said to Lizzie.

"All right," Lizzie said sullenly.

"That must be all," Emma said, sounding decidedly disappointed.

"Hey, three's a good number," Zach said. "One for each of you."

"Then Emma will have two cats," Lizzie pointed out. "I think we should give one to Tess."

"We'll keep them all," Beth Ann said.

Zach watched as his sister-in-law, who was not a cat fan, began taking plates out of the cupboard, her movements short and jerky.

Darcy met his eyes with a slight frown and then got to her feet and started helping Beth Ann set the table. Dinner was a fairly stilted affair. Emma and Lizzie were focused on the kittens in the box behind the stove and Darcy was focused on Beth Ann. He wasn't the only one who noticed that his sister-in-law was mad about something.

As soon as dinner was done, the girls started the dishes and Beth Ann said good-night. Zach followed her out the door.

"What's going on?" he asked flatly.

She simply shook her head.

"Beth Ann…"

"I think the girls are getting a bit carried away with their new friend."

"Tess."

"Tess." She looked at her trailer, then back at him. "Do you honestly think she's here for the long haul?"

"Does it matter?"

"What's going to happen when she leaves?" She folded her arms over her chest. "The girls lose again. How fair is it to allow Lizzie to fall in love with someone who has no plans of sticking around?"

"What do you suggest?"

"I suggest less time at her house for one thing. They don't need to stop by every single day." She let out a sigh. "It's setting them up for a fall later, Zach. And I know you worry about that as much as I do."

"We can't control everything in their lives, Beth Ann."

"But there are some things we can control, and we can keep them from getting involved to the point that it'll be devastating when…Tess…leaves."

Zach rubbed his fingers over his eyes.

"Think about it, Zach. They get attached, she takes off. I can't blame her, because she obviously doesn't belong here, but the girls tend to hold on tight." One corner of her mouth tightened. "For obvious reasons."

"People are going to come and go from their lives, Beth Ann."

"Yes. Of course they are. But right now, they're still re-covering."

Them? Or her?

"It's been three years."

"I know how long it's been," she snapped and then she pressed a hand to her forehead. "I'm sorry, Zach."

He reached out to touch her shoulder. "It's all right."

"I know this woman is novel to the girls. She draws and bakes cookies and there's this air of, I don't know, mystery about her. But when Lizzie starts wanting to call her on the phone, I think enough is enough. But they're your daughters, Zach. You have to do what you think best."

Zach could so remember his mother using similar tactics—laying everything out logically and then basically daring him to do the right thing. It was still a surprisingly effective tactic.

So the big question was whether Beth Ann had a legitimate concern, or whether she was unhappy seeing the girls bond to someone else.

He could understand her concern…but that didn't make it right.

Tess's new lawn mower was nice. Very nice. As usual, she found the box waiting for her on the porch and after tearing into it and reading the directions, discovered that all she had to do was put the handle on with a couple of bolts—and get oil. The fuel she'd anticipated, but oil…not so much.

The mercantile had oil. The mercantile had everything except for actually fresh "fresh produce."

A small school bus idled next to the school a few blocks down the street from where Tess parked in front of the mercantile. School had to be out for the day, but there were no cars in front of the store, no one picking up a few things before collecting the kids after school. And the store was blessedly empty, or so she thought until Tess rounded the corner at the end of the first aisle and ran smack into the woman she'd seen driving into Zach's place more than once. This had to be his sister-in-law, Beth Ann.

For a moment the woman simply stared at her, then her expression hardened slightly.

"I'm sorry," Tess said. She adjusted the hair over her scarred cheek before attempting to squeeze past her in the narrow aisle.

"My fault," Beth Ann said, standing square in Tess's path. "Are you settling into your place okay?"

"I've been here a couple of months," Tess said with a slight frown, "so yes, I'm settled."

"Are you staying long?"

What the...? "I signed a lease on the place," Tess said shortly. Something was going on here and she didn't like the feel of it one bit.

Beth Ann smiled apologetically. "I'm not trying to be rude. It's just that rural life is sometimes different than people expect."

"How do you know I've never lived rural before?" Tess asked with a clip to her voice. But before Beth Ann could come up with an answer to the question, Tess said, "Never mind. If you'll excuse me?" and edged past her. She didn't want a confrontation with Zach's sister-in-law and she felt one brewing.

"Zach and my nieces have been through a lot," the woman blurted from behind her. Tess turned slowly to face her, a disbelieving frown on her face. She was going to go into this here? Now? Color rose in Beth Ann's face, but she didn't back down or apologize. Instead she said, "They don't need more loss in their lives."

"I can't believe you're telling me this." The one thing that Tess had in her life that made her feel a spark of joy and this woman was trying to ruin it.

"My nieces are still fragile. They cling tightly to people they get attached to and they're getting attached to you."

"So what do you want?" Tess asked.

Beth Ann pointed a finger at Tess. "I want *you* to be very careful not to hurt my girls any more than they've already been hurt."

Tess opened her mouth to respond, then thought better

of it and turned and walked away without a word. She was not getting into this discussion here. Now.

Never.

She walked to the rear corner of the store where the oil was stored, found the type she needed, despite the fact that she was so upset she could barely read the label, then brought it up front and plopped it down on the counter. Ann made no comment as she rang up the single purchase and Beth Ann had either left the store or was down an aisle.

Tess stalked out of the store, got into her car and dropped the bag on the seat beside her. Had that really happened? Had she just been blatantly and unexpectedly warned off?

Yes.

It was almost as if the woman was jealous. Of her. A scarred woman with a local reputation for bitchiness.

How much did Beth Ann know about the time Tess had been spending with Zach? Or was this only about the girls?

And more important, was Beth Ann in love with her brother-in-law? Was that why she'd warned Tess off? She was living on the ranch. Still. And her sister had been married to him. Perhaps she had the same taste. The theory made sense.

Tess lowered her forehead to the steering wheel. It was not her intention to put herself in the middle of a situation she didn't understand—especially not under these circumstances—but she hated someone else trying to control her. She had little enough control of her life as it was. And more than that, she was surprised at how much she hated the idea of this woman being in love with Zach—or of Zach loving her back—even if she was certain she didn't want to go any further than friendship with Zach.

Okay, maybe friendship with benefits, if she was honest about the fantasies that edged into her mind, but that was it. What more could she have without confessing her whole ugly life—past and present—to him? When she might have to go into hiding at a moment's notice if Eddie ever discovered her whereabouts?

Not a hell of a lot. Nor did she want more than that.

Tess raised her head, shook her hair back.

Zach is not in love with his sister-in-law. Whatever Beth Ann felt, it was not reciprocated.

She was fairly certain of that. Zach wasn't the kind of guy to chase after her when he was involved with someone else. She'd run into enough of those kinds of guys to know them when she saw them. Zach wasn't one.

What now?

She was so damned tired of backing off, running, hiding, at the first sign of trouble—especially since she hadn't done anything wrong.

Tess shoved the key into the ignition and started the car. Even though she wanted very much to drive straight to Zach's place and sort things out, she went home. She'd sleep on the matter, take action—whatever that may be—tomorrow.

TESS WOKE UP the next morning knowing what she had to do. She enjoyed her time with Zach, enjoyed not living in total solitude, but realistically, how long could they go on like this? Sooner or later they'd have to make a move one way or another and Tess did not want to hurt anyone in his family—which could well happen.

How fair was it to let the girls get wrapped up in helping her and then find out she had to leave?

How fair was it to flirt with their father with every intention of walking away? It wasn't like he was a single guy with no encumbrances. What he did affected his family—just as Beth Ann had intimated.

Beth Ann may have pissed her off, but she'd spoken the truth about Tess's situation with Zach and his kids.

By midafternoon Tess had screwed up the courage to do what she had to do. She drove to Zach's house instead of walking, wishing she'd followed her gut and done this yesterday when she'd been angry. It would have been so much easier then.

After parking next to Zach's truck, Tess walked to the house and knocked on the front door. She waited for several seconds then tried again. He wasn't in the house. But he was here. Roscoe was in the corral, the four-wheeler was parked by the barn and she'd parked next to his truck. All forms of conveyance were accounted for.

She started across the driveway when she heard the sound of metal hitting metal followed by a string of muffled curses.

The barn. As usual. A veritable man cave, that barn.

She walked through the open door into the cool interior of the old wooden building. It took a moment for her eyes to adjust and by the time they did, Zach had set aside the torch he was using on the frame of a trailer and pulled off the protective goggles.

"Hey," he said as he set the goggles on the bed of the trailer. "I didn't expect you today." But he did look happy to see her, which stirred something deep inside, but she did her best to ignore it.

"I came to talk about riding."

A shadow crossed his face at her cold tone. "What about it?"

She walked over to the trailer and put a hand on the steel side rails and spoke the blunt truth. "This isn't going to work, Zach."

"What isn't?" he asked, but he knew exactly what she

was talking about. She was damned certain of it, but if he wanted her to explain, then she would.

"The riding lessons. You. Me." His eyebrows lifted and Tess gestured impatiently before blurting, "There's more going on between us than riding lessons and maybe there shouldn't be."

"Why not?" he asked after a few long seconds of silence.

"*Why not?* Fewer complications."

"Complications like my daughters?" Now there was a cool undertone to his voice.

"No. I enjoy your kids," Tess responded automatically, truthfully. She did like his kids. "But if you and I—" she spread her palms "—then things might get, well, complicated. For them. Your kids, I mean." Now she was babbling. It'd been a while since she'd broken off a relationship and she couldn't remember it being this difficult. The crazy thing here was that she and Zach didn't even *have* a relationship.

"I see your point," he said.

"My life right now is…"

"Complicated?" he asked. He didn't smile, but somehow managed to project a feeling of reassurance.

Ignore it.

"You could say that," Tess said.

Zach took a couple of slow steps toward her, moving as if expecting her to bolt—a wise course of action and one she didn't take. "I'd never do anything to hurt my daughters. Or anyone else."

Tess cleared her throat. "Meaning me?" She needed to take a step back…really she did.

"For one. Me, for another. But," he said as he continued to close the space between them, until her breasts were lightly touching his chest, "I don't see any reason we can't proceed…as long as we understand each other's limitations." She'd wondered what it would feel like to press herself against him and now…now she wanted to do just that so badly she almost shook. This breakup was not going according to plan.

"How will we do that?" she asked.

His hand came up to cup her injured cheek, his touch warm and reassuring and yet somehow deliciously sensual. "Communication."

That word came close to jerking Tess back to reality. "I don't—"

"I'm not asking for full disclosure," he said. "Just honesty."

"I can honestly tell you I don't do well with questions."

"Then I can honestly tell you that I'll keep them to a minimum. And if you don't like the questions I do ask, you don't have to answer."

"You could do that?" she asked on a note of disbelief, trying not to let the way his thumb lightly caressed her scarred face sway her into believing something she shouldn't.

"Sometimes I'm surprised by what I can do," he said.

"Limitations," Tess said.

"We both have them. We will not ignore them."

That was reassuring. The words Tess needed to hear and to believe. She brought her hand up to his cheek, mirroring the way he was touching her. "Promise?" she asked softly. Her hand slid around the back of his neck and when she felt the corded muscles there, she realized that for all his calmly reassuring words and movements, he was as tense as she was. And she really, really needed to kiss him.

Zach was of the same mind. His free hand settled on her lower back, gently pressing her into him, as his lips came down to hers. Tess met him halfway, touching, tasting. Savoring.

Zach gathered her against him as the kiss deepened and

it was only when the workbench was pressing into her back that Tess realized they'd been moving backward.

Tess's knees were shaky when Zach finally lifted his head. One thing was certain—this was not a mercy kiss, a you're-okay-despite-the-scars kiss—and any minuscule doubts she'd had on that front dissipated. Zach wanted her. She could feel him pressing against her thigh, hard as hell, making her want nothing more than to haul him home, take him to bed. It'd been such a long, long time for her. Probably for him, too.

"I won't ask for anything you can't give," he said softly.

"All right." Her voice was so husky she barely recognized it.

"The girls will be coming home soon, so maybe we can talk about this later?" He smiled a little. "At the next riding lesson?"

Tess smiled back then pulled his head down to kiss him one more time. Just because she wanted to. "Later," she said against his mouth.

The words had barely left her lips when she heard a car drive in. Beth Ann, of course. She smiled at Zach, wryly, then stepped away from him.

"Tess," Darcy called a few seconds later as the girls came racing into the barn. "What are you doing *here?*" The girls didn't know about the riding lessons, and they almost certainly didn't know that she and their father had been spending so much time together. But they seemed so happy to see her it made her heart twist a little.

"Just stopped by for a minute to talk," she said.

"Can you stay for a while and see my dolls?" Lizzie asked.

"Sorry." This time she did chance a look at Beth Ann, whose face was unreadable. The woman was good. "Maybe another day. I have to get home now."

"Where are you at in your sewing project?" Darcy asked.

"About to set in the sleeve."

"Good luck with that," she said on a sputter.

"Thanks," Tess said. She glanced up at Zach, smiled quickly. "See you all later."

Her breathing was still not quite normal when she opened her car door and got inside.

CHAPTER FIFTEEN

This isn't your first rodeo. You've been kissed by hotter guys than Zach Nolan.

No, you haven't.

Tess pressed her fingers to her still warm cheeks as she got out of her car and started for her house, more oblivious to her surroundings than she'd been since moving to this place. And now that she was away from Zach, she was thinking straighter. Kind of.

Damn but that guy could kiss. And she wanted to do so much more. She wanted to feel a man's body against hers, in hers, feel whole again…but she didn't want to hurt anyone in the process.

Was that possible? Could they operate within the parameters Zach had suggested? Observing each other's limitations, answering only the questions they—technically she—felt comfortable answering?

She had secrets, he had kids. Zach was a protective dad and Tess knew instinctively that his needs would not override his daughters' happiness…but that didn't mean he didn't want some action on the Q.T. He was a guy, after all.

Was she willing to give some action on the Q.T.?

A tingle of anticipation went through her at the thought. Question answered.

The dogs went nuts when she opened the door, turning circles in their joy to see her alive and well. "Settle down," she said, fighting a tired smile. They both sat, grinning doggie grins at her.

"I wish you guys could give advice," Tess muttered as she went to the kitchen to get the dog treats out of the cupboard. Or that she could call a friend. She couldn't—not without answering a lot of questions, like what had happened to her and where she'd been.

The sad thing was that she didn't have a friend she trusted with the answers to those questions. Tess had never let herself form truly tight relationships because she hated losing them later—which inevitably happened. Everyone she'd loved or cared about had disappeared from her life. Her friends from the halfway house, her grandmother, Mikey, her youngest stepbrother, whom she'd adored, her mother…

Tess squeezed her eyes shut. She *had* loved her mother—before drugs and Eddie had taken over her life—and for years had hoped to get her back. It hadn't happened. Another loss.

Zach's kids had also lost their mother. Maybe that was why she felt such a bond with them. Tess knew the pain of not having a mom around to help with the traumas involved in growing up.

So was it stupid to pursue something with Zach, even if it couldn't go anywhere? Were they setting themselves up for a whole lot of hurting later? Or indulging in some mutual healing?

Questions without answers. She hated them.

ZACH SIGNED HIS name on the check, stuck it in the envelope and sealed it. For the second month in a row he hadn't been able to make the full payment to the hospital, but he sent most of it. He and Jeff had decided to ship cows at the end of the month to give Zach operating capital. Cow prices were down and he hated to sell, hated that Jeff was also taking a loss, but there wasn't much else he could do.

Zach dropped the pen on his desk next to the nearly empty checkbook. Two and a half more years and he'd be out from under the medical bills…and it wouldn't be long after that he'd start paying for Darcy's college expenses. Then Emma. Then Lizzie.

The checkbook was going to see a lot of action in the next fifteen years. He just hoped that after this month he'd be able to start making full payments to the hospital again.

He stood, stretched and then reached for his hat, which was hanging off the antler hat rack his dad had made, and then headed out the door to change the irrigation lines.

His dad had done okay on the ranch before selling it to Zach and Jeff and moving east to the Denver area, where he'd been raised, but he'd never embraced the life the way Zach did. Zach's mother had said more than once that the only reason his father ranched was that when he married her, the ranch came along as part of the deal. Well, Zach did love the ranch and his girls loved the ranch. He truly wanted to pass it along to them. They'd never get rich off it, but it provided a decent income and a unique lifestyle—if one didn't get hit with over a hundred grand in medical bills.

When he and Karen had bought the ranch, they'd gotten the only medical insurance they could afford, primarily for the girls. It had turned out to be woefully inadequate, as was the policy he had now. All he could do was soldier on.

The setting sun was just touching the top of Lone Summit as he changed the wheel lines in the north pasture, allowing a new part of the field to get water. After he was done, Zach sat on the tailgate of his truck and watched the sun disappear. Benny worked his way under Zach's arm and he idly stroked the dog's silky fur, trying to pretend the only thing on his mind was irrigation and finances.

It wasn't.

It'd been a little over twenty-four hours since he'd kissed Tess. And though it'd just been a kiss, which shouldn't have been a big deal between two adults, it was. They'd turned some kind of corner and now they had a new, wide-open playing field to explore...with new obstacles, no doubt.

Tess had wanted to kiss him. Had responded as intensely as he had, and she hadn't backed off as quickly, or as far as usual.

But he'd had to promise not to push things, not to expect answers to the questions he might have and he had many.

Who or what was she afraid of? How did it relate to her injury, if at all? Was she on the run? Had she committed a crime?

If Tess had come here to hide out, she'd picked a place that would be hard for a stranger to navigate without people noticing. She obviously had money, or she couldn't have afforded to lease the Anderson place, which he knew sold for cash after being on the market for almost five years. Anderson hadn't gotten his asking price, but he'd snapped up whatever it was she'd offered.

So what he knew about Tess boiled down to she'd been injured, possibly been assaulted, possibly hiding out and she had some resources. And he felt comfortable talking to her, really liked kissing her, wanted to make love to her— and not just for sex. There was a connection between them that neither had worked at developing, but had sprung up anyway.

That was worth exploring, at least as far as he was concerned. So did he make a move? Wait for Tess to make a move?

Under normal circumstances he would do the honors, but Tess's circumstances were not normal.

The sun had barely disappeared behind the mountain

when Zach noticed a vehicle slowing at his driveway. Sure enough it pulled in. A large silver SUV that he'd never seen before.

He slid off the tailgate and walked around to open the truck's door. Benny shot into the passenger seat.

Strange to have visitors this time of day. Zach had an uneasy sensation that only grew as he drove close enough to recognize the man standing next to the SUV talking to Beth Ann.

Bradley James. Husband of hospital administrator Marcela James. Zach's mouth pressed into a flat line as he stopped the truck in its usual parking place and crossed the distance between it and James's expensive vehicle.

"Zach," Bradley said, extending a hand and smiling that too-toothy smile of his. Zach only knew him casually from the occasional bull sale or rodeo. The guy oozed money and he fancied himself a gentleman rancher. Few people took him seriously as a rancher, but money tended to give one a lot of sway and Bradley was quite aware of that fact.

"I was hoping we might have a few minutes to discuss some business," he said with a dismissive smile aimed at Beth Ann, who frowned deeply at the announcement.

"Sure," Zach said.

"Well," Bradley said, "I came to see if you were interested in selling that parcel of land."

"No."

"Hear me out," Bradley said patiently. "I'd pay you more than it's probably worth."

"Out of the goodness of your heart?" Zach asked politely.

"Because you've had a rough road, son."

Don't call me son. Zach tilted his hat back. "Why now? The long drive out to talk to me in person when a phone call would have been much easier?" Bradley shrugged. "It couldn't be because your wife is releasing confidential information to you?"

"What kind of information?"

"Financial," Zach said. As in that he hadn't paid his monthly installment in full.

"No," the man blustered as if such an idea was utterly crazy. "Of course not. You know that I've been interested in that land for some time now."

He had offered Zach a goodly sum for the forty acres last year, too. "Sorry you made the drive for nothing, Mr. James."

James's expression was no longer congenial. "You need to think about this, Zach. With a family to support, the extra money could come in handy."

Indeed it could.

"This is not a time to be selfish," Bradley said when Zach made no response. Zach's eyes snapped up to the older man's face. "You could provide a lot of security for your daughters."

And drive by the castlelike second home the Jameses would no doubt build on the acreage and be reminded that he'd sold off part of what was his, and had been in his family since the valley was homesteaded in the 1860s.

"The land will always sell," he said, although that may not be totally true considering how long it had taken Anderson to lease his place to Tess. "For now that answer has to be no."

Bradley shook his silver head in a way that indicated Zach was being ridiculously foolish and opened his vehicle door. "If you should change your mind, I'd appreciate a call."

"You bet," Zach said, keeping his face as expressionless as possible, trying not to show the depth of his anger. "And if you'd tell your wife to keep my financial information quiet, I'd appreciate *that*."

Bradley climbed into the SUV and started the engine. Zach stood stone still, watching the man drive back the way he came.

"What'd he want, Dad?" The sound of Darcy's voice startled him. He turned to see his three girls standing together on the porch.

He wanted your future. "He was just here to talk some business."

"You're not selling Roscoe to him?" Emma asked in alarm and Zach couldn't help smiling. He'd threatened to sell the horse often enough.

"No, kiddo, I'm not selling Roscoe. I'm not selling anything unless I absolutely have to."

"That's too bad," Lizzie said in a small voice.

"Why, honey?"

"Because I want a pair of sparkly shoes and a new bike that's bigger and Darcy says we don't have money."

Knife to the heart. Zach briefly met Darcy's eyes, saw the stricken look mixed with an unspoken apology and tried to smile. "We may not have a lot of money, Liz, but we have horses to ride and lots of land that belongs to us instead of someone else."

"I guess," Lizzie said, but she didn't seem impressed to have a legacy.

"Dad—" Darcy started after Lizzie and Emma went back inside, but he touched his finger to his lips.

"You didn't say anything that wasn't true." The relief on her face before she smiled and followed her sisters made him wonder just how stressful their financial situation was to her. He'd thought he'd been hiding things pretty well. Lots of folks in the community were struggling to make ends meet. His family just happened to be struggling a little bit more.

He'd have to be more careful not to let his stresses affect his kids.

ZACH HAD FULLY expected to say no to Bradley James and have the matter over and done with. Except that it wasn't. The situation ate at him for the rest of the evening and he lay awake that night, thinking about how much the money from selling the forty-acre parcel would help him ease out from under the medical bills.

And how he was basically robbing from his daughters if he did sell. He didn't have much to leave them, but he had the ranch. Even if they decided to sell and split the money after he was gone, the more land there was, the more they would have.

He got out of bed and quietly walked upstairs to check the girls. Benny slept on Emma's bed, having resisted the impulse to roll in something nasty after his last bath. The dog raised his head then dropped his chin to rest on Emma's legs. Zach moved on. Lizzie's sneakers were lying on the floor next to her bed, well worn and not at all sparkly. And she was right. Her bike was too small for her.

Darcy's door was closed and Zach left it that way. As he walked down the stairs, moving slowly to keep them from creaking, he paused at the window on the landing and looked toward Tess's house. It wasn't lit up like it'd been after she'd first moved here, but there were lights.

Three in the morning. Was she awake? Or sleeping with the lights on? The only reason he could think of for her to do that was fear, pure and simple.

The thought made Zach's gut twist.

Or maybe, like him, she was wide-awake because she had a whole lot to think about. Maybe part of what she was thinking about was him.

AS A RULE, Zach was not an impulsive man. If anything he was overly cautious, but after one hell of a long sleepless night, he didn't think twice about following impulse and saddling both Roscoe and Snippy. He wanted to think about something other than money and Bradley James.

Benny slunk off to pout in his doghouse after Zach put him in the fenced yard. It couldn't be helped. Zach was on a mission and he didn't need a dogfight sidetracking him.

He rode Roscoe across the county road and down Tess's driveway, leading Snippy behind him. Tess's dogs raced around her house as he approached, but Roscoe did little more than snort when the dogs' heads appeared above the fence and they commenced barking and growling.

Today, however, the mock canine attack lacked conviction and after a few seconds the barking stopped and the dogs dropped out of sight on the other side of the fence—just as Tess came around the corner of the house, carrying a rake. She stopped when she saw him, appearing…uncertain. Ready to disappear back inside her house at any second.

"Are you busy this morning?" he asked before she could say anything.

Tess pushed her hair back from her forehead, frowning as she shaded her eyes from the sun. "Why?"

"I thought we could go for a ride."

Her expression clouded as if this was too much, too soon. "Zach…"

"Come and ride with me, Tess."

She dropped her hand and stared at her feet. For a moment he thought she was coming up with a way to say no—and if she did, he'd turn around and ride home without pressing the matter—but instead she raised her eyes back up to meet his. "Can I ride in these?" she asked, pointing at her athletic shoes.

"No reason you can't." The saddle had *tapaderos* covering the front of the stirrups, so her foot couldn't slip through, get caught—the danger of riding with shoes without heels. "Just don't tell Emma or Darcy."

"Why not?"

"They're studying for an equestrian safety test they have to take at horse camp and have safety rules coming out their ears."

"I wouldn't want to be unsafe," Tess said. There was a world of meaning in her words. Zach wondered if she was aware of whether she'd voiced the major issue in her life unconsciously.

"Grab a sweatshirt," he said. "And a hat if you have one."

"All right. Be back in a sec." She called the dogs and started for the back of the house, moving quickly, as if she was afraid if she slowed down she'd change her mind.

TESS TOOK THE blue cloche out of the closet, then put it back and instead grabbed the complimentary bright red ball cap that had come with her new lawn mower and slapped it onto her head.

Zach had brought the horses to her, wanted her to ride with him…she was more touched than she wanted to admit. And nervous as hell.

She'd spent the night thinking about him and the kiss and how very much she wished her life was different. When she'd rolled out of bed this morning, she'd been no closer to a decision as to how to handle the situation than she'd been the night before. One thing she did know, though, was that pretending she and Zach had no unfinished business between them, staying in her house and avoiding him, wasn't going to resolve anything.

Tess sucked in a fortifying breath and headed out the door. She tried to smile as she opened the gate and stepped out onto the driveway.

"Nice hat," Zach said with an easy smile. He'd dismounted and was coiling Snippy's lead rope, and, as always, Tess's eye was drawn to the long lean lines of his body.

"You think so?" she asked blandly. "Does it give me attitude?"

"You're doing okay on the attitude front without the hat," he said, a smile in his eyes. He tied the coils of rope to the saddle with the leather thongs attached near the front and then handed Tess the reins. This was her third time mounting and her best effort yet. Snippy stood steady as a rock as Tess swung up into the saddle. Zach nodded his approval and then mounted Roscoe with a kind of fluid grace that made her want to ask him to do it again—just so she could watch.

"I thought we could ride the trail along the base of the mountain, have some lunch…ride back."

Tess lifted the reins and Snippy stepped forward. "So, this is kind of like a date?"

"Kind of like two people having lunch by a stream."

"Afraid I'll back off if you call it a date?"

"Yes." Zach smiled at her and again she thought of how much her photographer, Jonas, would have loved to have photographed Zach…and how much Zach probably would have hated it.

"I'm not afraid of a date," Tess said. She was afraid of she and Zach wanting, needing, different things from each other. But they were going to communicate. And he wasn't going to ask for anything she wasn't able to give. That was the pact.

"Good to hear," Zach said. He turned Roscoe onto the county road and Snippy obediently followed his buddy. Tess did little more than hold on, which was fine.

She had things other than riding on her mind right now.

CHAPTER SIXTEEN

Tess and Zach rode across Murray's field and onto a narrow overgrown dirt road on the other side that wound through the sage toward the mountain.

"Are you doing all right?" he asked.

"Fine." And she was, riding along on the placid horse with the sun on her back, lulled by the creak of the leather saddle, trying hard not to think about anything but how much she enjoyed being on horseback.

Zach turned Roscoe off the road and onto a trail which led to a stretch of grass next to a wide, shallow stream. He dismounted and waited for Tess to do the same, then led the horses into the shade of a grove of white-barked trees, where he tied them before pulling an insulated carrier out of Roscoe's saddlebags.

He carried the lunch to the grass and Tess followed, taking a seat as he silently unpacked the food—sandwiches, chips in plastic bags and beer.

"I have water, too," he said, looking up at her. "I didn't know if you liked beer since you said no the last time I offered."

"I like beer," she said with a slight smile.

Zach opened a bottle and handed it to her and she took a drink before picking up a sandwich. When was the last time she'd eaten anything a guy had made for her?

Never. Until the assault had changed her life, she'd had to watch her weight so closely that eating had never been a big part of going out. Drinking, yes, but even then, she'd had to watch the calories, sticking to lower-cal drinks and club soda.

They ate in silence and it was, for the most part, relaxing, but the mood between them reminded Tess of a calm lake. Lovely and still, but at any moment something could happen to ripple the water. She wasn't yet ready for ripples.

After they'd eaten, Zach stowed the remnants back into the saddlebags and then stretched out in the grass. Tess sat near him, nerves humming as she wondered what was going to happen next.

Did they talk? Sleep in the sun? Ride back home?

Or...

Zach reached out and took her wrist in a loose hold. Tess's eyes shot to his at the unexpected contact, and he gave her a lazy smile. "Relax so I can relax, okay?"

"You aren't?" she asked, frowning down at him. "Funny, but you look relaxed all stretched out in the sun like that."

"As I'm sure you know, appearances can be deceiving." His thumb moved over her wrist, slowly, caressingly.

"Why aren't you relaxed?" she asked.

He gave her a wry look. "This is the closest I've come to a date in over a decade."

"Zach—"

"And I'm trying to figure out how to walk the thin line between asking questions you don't want to answer and just accepting the here and now." Tess pulled in a deep breath. She understood his position and was about to say so, when he added, "I like spending time with you," as his thumb continued to caress her wrist.

"That goes two ways," Tess conceded. A small insect climbed over the toe of her shoe and she brushed it away. "I wish things could be different."

"How so?"

She met his eyes candidly. "I wish I could be more up-front with you."

"Have you committed a crime?"

She drew back, genuinely shocked. "No." She pushed back her hair as she turned to stare off into the distance. "Wow," she murmured. "Did you really think I had?" But why wouldn't he think that, the way she'd been acting?

He shook his head. "I think you're very afraid of something that you won't talk about."

"It wasn't a crime. At least not one where I was the perpetrator."

"How about the victim?"

She turned back to him. "For not asking questions, you're asking a lot of questions." But there was no sting to her words, because he hadn't said anything that wasn't obvious to someone who'd given the situation some thought.

"Come on," Zach said, getting to his feet, his fingers sliding from her wrist to her hand. "Let's check out the water."

Conversation done, dicey issues put on hold. Tess was good with that.

"With your boots on?" she asked, allowing him to haul her to her feet.

"I guess not," he said on a heavy sigh before he let go of her and reached down to pry off first one boot and then the other. His socks followed. Tess wondered if he was going to stop at the socks, thinking she could come up with worse things to do than skinny-dipping with this guy—except that the creek water appeared to be about four inches deep. There wouldn't be a lot of dipping going on. Zach rolled up the legs of his jeans, exposing his muscular calves and answering her question.

No skinny-dipping. Too bad, because she could deal with the strictly physical. It was what she needed, what she wanted. It was the emotional that gave her pause.

Tess loosened her laces and pulled the shoes off her bare feet, leaving them next to Zach's cowboy boots.

Zach led the way into the shockingly cold water, which rushed over Tess's feet and splashed against her calves as she followed him across the stream to the smallish granite boulders near the center of the streambed. He held out a hand and once again Tess took it and she scrambled up out of the frigid water onto the rock.

"Did you know it was that cold?" she asked, dancing a little on the sun-heated rock, trying to bring some blood flow to her calves.

"I suspected," he said with a crooked smile, pointing at the snow-topped peaks behind them.

"I'm a city girl and didn't realize."

For a moment they stood balanced on the low granite boulder, the light breeze blowing over her damp feet, chilling her. She shivered and Zach closed his arms around her from behind, steadying her, warming her.

"Maybe this was my plan," he said.

It was a good plan. Tess closed her eyes, allowed herself to lean into him for a moment. He smelled so damned good. More than that, he felt so damned good.

He leaned close to her ear, his breath caressing the side of her face, and then he pressed a kiss to her temple. Tess shivered again. This time cold had nothing to do with her reaction, but Zach ran his hands up over her arms, trying to warm her. Oh, he was warming her all right.

She turned in his arms, looped her hands around his neck and pulled his mouth down to hers, kissing him.

He leaned back, brushing the hair away from the injured side of her face, his touch butterfly soft. "You're beautiful," he said.

"Thank you for not saying 'still beautiful.'" He shook his head, as if the thought had never occurred to him—

though she knew it'd had to have—then leaned down for another kiss.

The sun disappeared behind a small cloud as a gust of wind came up, whipping Tess's shirt around her, but she barely noticed as Zach's mouth closed over hers.

"Maybe we should go back," he said against her mouth as another, stronger gust nearly knocked them over.

"Maybe I don't want to," she said. Heat sparked in his eyes as the next gust swirled Tess's hair up and around her face. "Okay," she said, brushing her hair out of her eyes and conceding to Mother Nature, who was trying hard to knock Tess off the rock.

Zach stepped into the water with a small splash. Tess took the hand he offered, gripping it tightly as she jumped down beside him. With the exception of William, whose kindness she could never repay, how long had it been since she'd depended on anyone for anything?

The water didn't seem as cold this time. In fact, it felt good on her heated skin. They waded back to the shore, hands still linked together.

"I've never waded in the creek before," she said as they crossed the grass to where their shoes lay in a small pile.

"What kind of childhood did you have?" It was a rhetorical question, but Tess surprised herself by answering it.

"The awful kind." She said the words casually, avoiding his eyes as she picked up a shoe.

Zach didn't ask for elaboration, but she'd suspected he wouldn't after the previous conversation.

"You seem to be giving *your* girls an excellent childhood," she said as she pulled on a shoe. Hard to believe they were getting dressed instead of the other way around, but the wind was getting worse, not better.

"I hope." He sat down and started dragging his socks

onto his damp feet. "There's a lot of stuff I wish I could do for them—things I may never be able to do."

"You're giving them a stable upbringing."

"Unlike yours," Zach guessed, jamming his foot into a boot.

She smiled slightly, wishing she could pour out her soul to him. "I had some good years."

Zach left it at that. When she finished tying her shoes and stood, he reached for her, smoothing her hair back with both hands, framing her face as he kissed her. Several times, the heat growing with each one. His hands left her face, skimmed down her sides, his thumbs moving over the curve of her breasts, and then settling on the curve of her butt, pressing her into his erection, making her insides go liquid.

After he raised his head, Tess leaned her cheek against his shoulder, catching her breath as his hands moved soothingly over her back. She sighed deeply and then said, "I guess we should get back before we blow away."

The wind began to die, but clouds continued to build as they rode back home and by the time they got to Tess's place a light rain had started to fall. Tess dismounted at her gate, her feet stinging a little as she made contact with the ground, and then she handed her reins up to Zach.

"Next time," he said with a half smile, rain sparkling on his dark eyelashes, "we'll bring sunscreen."

Tess touched her hands to her cheeks. In spite of the rain, they felt warm—or at least the unscarred one did. Crazy. She never forgot sunscreen.

"I'll be cutting hay the next few days, and that eats up most of my time, but when I'm through…"

"Give me a call," Tess said, anticipating his question.

He smiled, a heartbreakingly sexy smile, before he reined Roscoe around and headed off down the driveway, Snippy in tow.

Tess watched him go for a moment before slowly walking to her door as the rain drizzled down on her new red hat. Her world had shifted. Again.

THE UNFAMILIAR SOUND of Tess's cell phone ringing jerked her out of a sound sleep two days after the picnic. Heart racing, she jogged down the stairs. It had to be Zach—she'd given him the number after they'd returned from their last ride and no one ever called her cell.

Sunlight was just beginning to streak across the kitchen floor when she came down the stairs and grabbed the phone off the top of the fridge. She answered with a quick hello.

"Terese Olan?"

Tess's heart stopped for a moment. "Detective Hiller?" she asked, even though she instantly recognized his brusque voice. The detective had never called her cell phone— mainly because she'd always called him.

It had to be something about Eddie. What had he done? Was he going back to prison?

"Yes. I'm calling to tell you that your stepfather applied to have his parole transferred to Nevada."

"What?" Tess's fingers went slack and the phone nearly tumbled out of her hand before she tightened her grip. "Why? When?" She inhaled sharply. "Can he *do* that?"

"It takes time and approval from a board."

"How much time?"

"A couple of months."

A couple of months—if he did things in an aboveboard manner, which was not Eddie's modus operandi.

"Why would he want to do that?" Tess asked. "Unless…" She couldn't say it out loud. Didn't even want to think it.

"He has an offer of employment from a mining company. As you can imagine, the pay is better than the car wash. His parole officer said it was an excellent opportunity."

"Well, bully for Eddie."

"There's no guarantee the board will approve his transfer."

"But there's a chance."

"Yes."

Tess realized she was now sitting at her kitchen table. She didn't remember moving away from the fridge, sinking down into the chair. Propping one elbow onto the laminate wood tabletop, she pressed her forehead into her hand.

"Do you think he knows I'm in Nevada?" she asked.

"*I* have no reason to think that. Do you?"

"No." Her voice was barely audible.

"I don't think you have cause for concern—"

"Yet," Tess muttered.

"I'll keep you apprised of the situation," the detective said. He cleared his throat. "Unofficially you understand?"

She did. Because officially Eddie had not been implicated in her attack. The detective, who had so pissed her off the last time they'd spoken, honestly was trying to watch out for her. "Thank you," she said.

"I'll be in touch."

Tess pushed the end button and carefully set the phone on the table—mainly because she wanted to refrain from throwing it across the room and watching it smash against the wall.

She'd had a lovely vacation from the edgy, certain-that-Eddie-would-show-up-at-any-moment state she'd been in during her first month in Barlow Ridge and now here he was, back again. Front and center in her thoughts.

Did she have to start running? Was she safe staying here?

Was he even looking for her?

There was no reason for Eddie to move to Nevada, because Tess didn't believe the employment story for one minute—Eddie hated to work—so the only conclusion the very-paranoid part of her could accept was that he thought he could find her here.

And if he did find her, what if he chose to hurt those she was close to?

Tess shoved her hands into her pockets and started pacing the kitchen, trying to talk her paranoid side down.

Right now Eddie was in California. There was no reason to believe he'd actually *found* her, only that he might possibly be looking in the correct state. A very, very big state. Detective Hiller would call her when there was information she needed to know. He'd keep her on top of the situation, as he'd just proven.

For right now, she'd stay put. She would also take whatever steps were necessary to ease herself away from the Nolan family, because although she might take a risk with her own safety, guessing that she hadn't been found, she wasn't risking theirs. Just in case.

It'd been stupid to allow herself to get involved in the first place. Stupid to think that she could start living a more normal life.

Tess pulled in a shaky breath as she paced through her house, hands pressed so deeply into her sweatshirt pockets that she stretched the seams. Big deal. She owned a sewing machine and although she may still be learning the ropes, she could probably fix a pocket or two.

Too bad she couldn't fix her life so easily.

Yanking her left hand out of her pocket, she scrubbed it over her injured cheek, tears starting to well up as she once again inventoried everything that asshole Eddie had stolen from her. Her mother, her face, her career, her sense of safety.

And he'd now made it impossible for her to continue having contact with people she was beginning to care for.

Before she could talk herself out of it, Tess dialed Zach's

home number. He didn't answer, even though it was early, so she called the cell number he'd given her after catching the escaped calf. Best to end this now, when he'd think it was because she'd decided their relationship was too much, too soon.

He answered almost immediately, his voice hard to hear over mechanical racket in the background.

"Hi, Zach…" *We need to talk. Can you come by tonight?*

No. She was doing it now.

"I've been doing a lot of thinking, and this thing between us isn't going to work." For a few seconds she heard only the sound of the machine, so she continued on, hoping he was still there. "It's better if we stop now. Before… before—" she pressed the heel of her hand to her forehead, cursing the way stress stole her words, her train of thought "—it gets out of hand. Trust me, Zach. This will be best for all of us." Tess pressed her fingers to the bridge of her nose, thinking that this hurt more than it should have, or would have, if she'd followed her own rules and never gotten involved to any degree.

"Tess—"

"I'm serious. I'm done."

And then, coward that she was, she hung up the phone. A few minutes later she was dressed and loading the dogs into the car. If Zach was going to show up to discuss things, which he well might, then she was going to be somewhere else.

TESS SPENT TWO days avoiding her place. The first day she spent aimlessly driving, trying to talk herself down.

Eddie may not be looking for her. She may be overreacting.

But if that was so, then why in the hell would he want to

come back to Nevada? He'd made no secret of hating the two years they'd lived in Reno.

Not knowing was killing her, making her think in circles again, making it impossible to sleep.

The second day she had a legitimate excuse to leave the house early—she had to take Mac back to Dr. Hyatt for one final checkup and while she was in Wesley, she'd also stock up on everything Ann's mercantile didn't have. Once again she resorted to dark glasses, hoods and hats, hid herself behind her pseudo-disguises because she didn't feel safe not doing that.

Déjà vu. She hated it.

On both days she arrive back home well after dark, trying not to look at Zach's house as she turned into her own driveway. Getting semi-involved with the neighbor had been a major, major mistake.

Tess had just begun unloading groceries from the trunk of her car when she heard the sound of the four-wheeler as she came back. Sure enough a headlight cut through the darkness as it approached her place.

Zach.

Tess ducked back inside the house even though the trunk of her car was still open. A few minutes later Zach mounted the porch steps and she realized she already recognized the cadence of his walk. Another bad sign. She took a deep breath and pulled open the door, keeping the expression on her face carefully neutral. Just a landowner speaking to her very pissed off lessee.

Zach didn't bother with a greeting. "Tess, your life is none of my business—"

"But…?"

"Who are you hiding from?"

"If you're here to check the cows—" *in the dark* "—great. If not, then you need to go."

"Don't," he said softly.

"What?"

"Play games."

Tess gripped the edge of the door. "I'm not. I just realized that I wasn't being fair to you or me or anyone."

"Bullshit."

"Believe what you wish."

"So you back off, hole up in your house. Hide yourself away."

"It's a habit of mine."

Zach leaned his shoulder against the newel post, his eyes narrowed as he studied her. "*Why* is that a habit of yours?" he asked in an annoyingly reasonable voice.

Another question she wasn't touching. Better to go with a distraction. "I like you, Zach, and we obviously have some chemistry, but I don't want to—" she gripped the door tighter as she sought the right words and finally came up with the epitome of lameness "—explore it further."

"You were doing pretty good exploring a few days ago."

"I agree," she said softly. And she'd very much enjoyed that exploration. Had looked forward to more until reality had reared its ugly head.

"Why are you trying to push me away?"

"I told you why," she snapped, taking a step backward, ready to close the door in his face again. This time, however, he stuck his boot out so she couldn't get the door all the way shut.

"Move your foot."

"Open the door." For a moment they faced off, then Zach pulled his foot back and because he did, Tess refrained from slamming the door shut. But she wanted to. Zach was a decent guy and she'd come very close to using him to help deal with her own loneliness. It wasn't right.

"I'm not going to force my way in," he said coldly, "but I

have the right to know if whatever it is you're running from poses a danger to my daughters."

"The girls shouldn't come by anymore."

It killed her to say those words. She would miss their visits more than she would have ever dreamed possible a few weeks ago.

Zach's expression shuttered. He stepped back, raising his hands in a gesture of surrender. Then he turned and walked to the four-wheeler. A few seconds later the headlights once again cut the darkness.

Tess was shaking by the time she'd shut the door. She'd lived alone, responsible only for herself for many years, so why did she have the feeling that she'd just cut her lifeline?

Deal with it.

Zach was not coming back and the girls wouldn't either, and that meant she was well and truly alone. But this time it felt different.

Tess finished with the groceries, then picked up a pattern envelope and pulled the tissue out. She still needed to focus on learning to set in a sleeve and there was no time like the lonely present. But she couldn't focus, so she dropped the tissue in a heap on the rickety sewing table and set the pattern directions beside it.

She was making headway in her sewing, even without Darcy's help, but wasted a lot of time trying to figure out what the pattern wanted her to do. Once she figured that out, she could usually find a video or online tutorial to help her out. Unfortunately, a ten-minute video took about an hour to download on the ridiculously slow internet connection. Darcy had been right—it was better to have an actual person helping her. Keeping her company. Charming her and making her laugh.

Well, you don't get to have that.

She shouldn't have allowed herself to get involved with

the family because she'd gotten a taste of something she did not want to give up. She'd been so gung ho on convincing herself she was safe and life was normal, that she hadn't considered what would happen to those around her if she was wrong—that she may have been putting the girls in danger if Eddie ever did find her.

The thought of the girls being collateral damage ate at her, as did the thought of Zach despising her for being a flaky coward. True, that solved matters, but she couldn't shake the thought that she owed him the truth. Not so that he wouldn't despise her, but so that he would see how very important it was to keep his family as far away from her as he could.

DARCY WAS WORKING at Zach's desk with the afghan Karen had made her draped over her shoulders.

"Is something wrong, Dad?"

There was no easy way to do this. "You won't be going to Tess's place anymore."

Darcy's mouth dropped open then her expression became one of outrage. "Why? Because Lizzie wanted to phone Tess about the kitten? I know Tia talked to you about it."

The kid honestly did hear everything. Zach shook his head. "No."

"Then what?" Darcy demanded.

"I don't have all the facts, but Tess wants us to leave her alone."

"Since when?" Darcy demanded.

"Since today. There are…things…going on in her life that she wants to handle alone."

"What kind of things?"

"Things that are none of our business."

"It's whatever made her so afraid when she first got here, isn't it?" His thoughts exactly.

"I don't know, Darcy."

"We can't just abandon her, Dad."

"We don't have a lot of choice. She asked me to leave her alone. I'm going to abide by her wishes. You're going to do the same. No more creek path. No sewing lessons."

"But, Dad…" His daughter's voice quavered a little before it trailed off. Darcy rarely if ever cried. And if she did, it was almost always in private.

"We'll give her some time, Darcy. I'm not saying it's forever, but for right now, we're going to respect her wishes. And I need you to back me on this with Emma and Lizzie."

Darcy swallowed, gave a quick sniff then wrapped the afghan a little tighter around her. "What do you think is happening, Dad?"

"I don't know," he said.

But sure as hell wished that he did. He was angry at Tess's attitude, but still hated the thought of her facing whatever it was alone. Was it an angry ex-husband or ex-boyfriend? The person who'd assaulted her?

Whatever it was, he didn't have it in him to walk away.

CHAPTER SEVENTEEN

"Daddy, have you seen Scamper?" Lizzie asked as she came into the kitchen where Zach was getting ready to spend the day on yet another stretch of fence now that the meadow hay had been knocked down.

Scamper was a kitten no doubt. They were still too young to scamper, but they were crawling out of their bed and wandering around, much to Misty's consternation. "Which one is that?"

"The yellow one," Lizzie said with an air of indignation.

"I saw the black-and-white one under the sofa a few minutes ago."

"That's Timmy. I'd better go find him." Lizzie ran off into the living room. At least she was talking to him. For two days after he'd told his girls they couldn't go back to Tess's, Lizzie had pouted.

"I told you they'd get over it," Beth Ann said from the kitchen table. The girls had told her they couldn't go back to Tess's house for sewing lessons and cookies, and while she'd commiserated, Zach could see that she'd been relieved. Beth Ann didn't want Tess in their lives.

Zach picked up his gloves from the table and shoved them into his back pocket. "Roscoe and I will be on the mountain." Beth Ann raised her eyebrows. "Just in case he comes home without me—you know where to start looking."

Which, the way things had gone that week, was a very real possibility.

"Sell that horse," she said just as Emma came into the kitchen.

"For what? Two dollars?" Zach asked.

"Two dollars more than you have now and you won't get stranded on the mountain."

"And I'll be in great shape hiking after the cattle." The four-wheeler simply couldn't handle some of the places he needed to go, the things he needed to do.

"Don't sell Roscoe," Emma said, stopping dead, her expression alarmed. "He's part of the family."

Beth Ann met Zach's eyes, her message clear. These girls clung to family, even the equine members, and it was better to ease Tess out of it now than later. He started for the door.

"See you guys tonight," he said.

Zach rode into Tess's driveway for a quick cow count, since he'd had to mend a section of fence along the road where one had jumped yesterday, but he did not go to the house. He stopped Roscoe by the gate and counted the cows and calves. Everyone was where they should be. Before he turned the horse and started back to the county road he glanced up to the window where he'd seen Tess watching him more than once before she'd gotten to know him.

She wasn't there.

He told himself that was a good sign…but he didn't believe it. There was unfinished business between them and it would probably remain unfinished, which he didn't like one damned bit.

ROSCOE WAS SLATHERED in sweat by the time he and Zach came off the mountain. Zach could almost hear the horse sigh as he set foot on the level trail leading through Murray's field to the county road. They were halfway through the field when his cell phone rang.

Zach answered it automatically, assuming it had to be his family.

"State your emergency," he said, expecting one of the girls to launch into a description of some pressing matter.

"I need to talk to you."

Tess. Zach's grip on the phone automatically tightened. "When?"

"Now? It won't take long. I can meet you at the gate."

Now didn't work for him, because if he was going to talk to Tess, it wasn't going to be standing on the county road—although that was perfect neutral territory directly between their two ranches.

"I'm coming off the mountain. Let me take Roscoe home and feed him. Then I'll stop by your house." His suggestion was met with silence. "Does that work?"

"Yes," Tess finally replied. "I'll see you in a bit."

Once home, Zach unsaddled Roscoe and sluiced off the gelding's back using the hose. A quick curry, then he released him to happily roll in the dirt and join his buddies out in the field.

Zach stowed the tack, then went in the house and took a quick shower. Tess may not want to talk for too long, but she probably wanted to be able to breathe while she did it. Six hours on the mountain in the hot late-spring sun did things to both guys and horses that made them unfit for polite company.

He slapped a ball cap on his damp hair and went outside to fire up the four-wheeler. For all he knew, Tess was going to give him the thirty days' notice required for her to break their contract...but somehow he didn't think so.

Tess opened the door after he parked the four-wheeler, and stepped back so he could come inside. No glasses today. Her dark hair was pulled back in some kind of a headband, for once fully exposing both sides of her face. And he noted with a fleeting touch of amusement that they were dressed almost identically—jeans and white shirts. The difference was that she looked hot in her jeans and white shirt.

She closed the door behind him and walked a few steps into the almost empty living room. The dogs, who'd been flanking her, followed for a few steps and then went to the far side of the room to stretch out on the hardwood floor. But they kept their amber eyes firmly fixed on Tess—perhaps because she was practically radiating tension.

"I owe you an apology," she said. "For not telling you the facts you needed to know. For not thinking about the safety of your daughters before I allowed them to stop by so frequently. So…I'm going to tell you everything. So you can be prepared…in case something happens."

"What might happen, Tess? Who are you hiding from?"

"My stepfather." Her words were little more than a whisper, but she cleared her throat and said it again, more loudly. "My stepfather. Eddie Napier. The drug-dealing ex-con."

Sounded like a person one would want to be afraid of.

"Did he do…that…to you?" Zach indicated her injuries with a nod.

"I think he had it done." Tess pressed her lips together briefly. "I'm sure of it. When I first moved here, I was a nervous wreck, thinking he was going to find me. Somehow. Drug people talk. Word travels. But—" the breath she pulled in quavered slightly "—after talking to the detective on my case, several times, I managed to convince myself he couldn't."

"Where's your mother?"

"She died after I left home. Eddie went to prison for dealing about six months before, but she kept using, because she died of drug-related causes."

Zach took a couple steps toward her but her barricades were up so he didn't make a move to touch her.

"I'm afraid that if Eddie does find me and discovers I'm...close...to you and your family, he'll do something bad. He's a sadistic man." Obviously, if he destroyed her face.

"Why'd he slash you?"

"He thinks I have money he left with my mother," Tess said. "I don't and I told him so. I thought he'd believed me, even though he told me he wasn't done with me."

"How would slashing you get him the money?"

"The guy who did it told me Eddie would keep taking pieces off from me until he got what he wanted."

Zach's gut twisted. Shit. He leaned back so he could look down into her face. A face that was still beautiful. Marred, but striking. He wanted to haul her up against him, but instinctively knew that Tess would never stand for that. Not right now.

"Does anyone know?"

"You," she said simply. "And the attorney who handles my business stuff. A guy I fired once."

"You fired him?"

"He didn't hold a grudge," Tess replied, dragging a hand over the tense muscles at the back of her neck. "I found an attorney who was more familiar with my particular business situation, and William actually told me I'd made the right decision. We kept in touch over the years and he was the only person I could think of who could possibly help me hide."

"Is there any way that your stepfather could possibly track you here?" Zach asked, still trying to imagine what she'd gone through, being assaulted and having her face ripped like that. He was not a violent man by nature, but he wanted very much to clean house with the guy who'd done this to her.

"I can't think of any...unless someone recognized me and word got back to him...or to the media."

"I'm missing something here," he said with a slight frown. "The media?"

"I was a model, Zach. I worked quite steadily right up until…" She touched her cheek and Zach felt another surge of hot anger. "I have magazine ad campaigns that are still running. May run for a long time yet." She turned the uninjured side of her face so that the light from the living room hit her cheekbones just so. "Imagine red hair and lots of it."

He couldn't say that he recognized *her,* but he recognized the classic buy-this-makeup/perfume/whatever-and-you-can-look-like-me pose.

"Which is why your stepfather slashed your face."

She dropped the pose. "Which is why I'm afraid of him. He isn't known for his mercy. He likes to mess with people. Torment them before he hurts them." She touched his hand. "I thought he'd burned my barn down. That had I been home it might have been my house. He did that once—burned down a guy's house that owed him."

It all made sense in a sad, sad way.

Zach brushed the hair away from her face, his fingers brushing lightly over the scars.

"And this is why you broke things off with me?"

She pressed her lips together briefly. "I got a call from the detective in charge of my case telling me Eddie had applied to have his parole transferred to Nevada. Apparently he has a job offer here, but…I don't believe it. I think he wants to look for me."

"Why?"

"I don't know," she said on a whisper. "But I can't take the chance that he'll find me and hurt people close to me. That's the kind of thing he does." She inhaled deeply, exhaled again. "So now you know everything. Why I behaved so poorly when I first arrived, why the girls can't come over. Why I can't…you know…with you."

Zach shook his head. "I don't understand that last part, Tess."

She cast him a frowning sidelong look, but didn't say a word, so Zach plunged on. "Now that I know the score, I don't see why we can't be together."

"Did you not hear everything I said?" she asked incredulously.

"I did."

"Maybe you didn't understand. Eddie applied to transfer his parole to Nevada."

Zach rubbed a hand over the back of his neck. "But he's not necessarily looking for you."

"Are you willing to take that chance?"

He dropped his hand back to his side. "I'm willing to be there if you need me."

"You don't get it," Tess said intensely. "Eddie will hurt you. I couldn't handle that."

"And I don't want to see you hurt because you're trying to handle things alone."

Tess pressed her fingertips to her temples. "You need to go."

"You need to wake up and accept help. Law enforcement—"

Her eyes flashed, truly alarmed. "No."

"Tess."

"No one can know I'm here."

Zach wondered how the hell he was going to deal with this. He couldn't, really. Not if she wasn't going to let him.

He let out a frustrated breath, started for the door. It wasn't over in the long run, but it was for the moment. He was thinking war, not battle.

"Zach!"

He stopped with his hand on the doorknob, brought up

short by the desperation in her voice. Slowly he let go of the knob and turned back toward her.

Tess stood in the kitchen doorway, color staining her cheeks. "You need to understand…it's…really important to me that you understand—" she sucked in a long breath "—I couldn't handle it if you got hurt."

"Same here," he said. "If you're kicking me out of your life because you don't want anything to do with me personally, I'm gone. But your stepfather…you're not getting rid of me on that front, even if we don't see each other. I won't let him hurt you."

For one long silent moment they faced off across the room.

"If he finds me," she said quietly, giving Zach a glimmer of hope that she wasn't using her asshole stepfather as an excuse for backing away from him.

"If he finds you," he echoed. "He may not be looking for you, Tess."

"Agreed," she said in a low voice. "I really want to believe that." She cleared her throat before continuing, "I… have been told I may be suffering from post-traumatic stress."

He took a few slow steps toward her, cocking his head slightly to one side. That made perfect sense. He stopped several feet away, hooked his thumbs in his pockets, allowing her space.

"I know Eddie, though," she said, glancing down. "And I am not reacting entirely from stress. I've had days to think about this. I know how he would respond if he did find me." She pressed her lips together then looked up at him. "But what if he isn't looking for me? What am I losing if he isn't looking for me?"

Her expression was so intense that it was all Zach could do not to cross the distance between them and haul her into his arms. Hold her against him, make her feel safe. But he didn't move.

"He's already taken so much, Eddie has." Tess drew in a long breath before saying, almost more to herself than to him, "I can't let him keep taking stuff from me."

"Agreed," he said quietly.

"I want to be with you, Zach."

"I'm glad to hear that." An understatement, that. He ached to be with her.

"But if I tell you I can't do this anymore, you have to back off."

He raised his hands. "The only thing I can't promise is to back off if that asshole tries to hurt you again. Other than that, our deal stands as it was. We respect our limitations. You say stop, we stop. And vice versa."

Tess jammed her hands into her back pockets and walked closer, focusing on the floor as she moved. She stopped less than a foot away, close enough to touch—but he didn't. This had to come from her.

"I agree," she said, her beautiful green eyes coming up to meet his, her expression thoughtful, yet shrewd.

Zach felt a surge of relief, but he had to make one more thing perfectly clear. There was a point he would not negotiate on. "But you need to understand that I mean it when I say I will not let that bastard hurt you."

She reached out to lay a hand on his cheek. "I truly hope Eddie never finds me."

It FELT LIKE slow motion as Tess took Zach's face between her hands, the stubble on his cheeks rough against her palms, and tilted her lips up so that he could cover her mouth with his. He brought his head down slowly, his mouth hovering for a moment, as if he was making a decision, before he touched her lips, sealing the bond.

She wouldn't allow him to get hurt, to get sucked into *that* part of her life. Somehow she'd make sure that didn't happen…but right now she needed him. When he lifted his head, she brought it back down, telling him with her tongue, with the heat of her mouth, how very much she needed him. His hands settled on her hips, pulling her against him, telling her he was getting the message.

Tess pressed her lips to the underside of his jaw, felt his intake of breath as she let them travel down to the V of his shirt. She pulled away slightly to give herself room to unbutton his shirt, except that there were no buttons. He had snaps. So she popped the top one open. Then another. His hands were resting on her hips and he made no move to stop her.

Emboldened, Tess glanced up to meet his eyes, saw the heat there, felt an answering surge deep inside her, and then her fingers stilled. If she sent him away now…

He covered her hands with his. "He's not going to find you," Zach said.

Tess bowed her head, but Zach raised her chin. "You're right," she said. And he probably was.

Zach released her chin and lowered his head to nuzzle the sensitive spot near her ear, sending a shiver through her. Slowly he worked his way along the edge of her jaw to the corner of her mouth then up across her cheekbone while his other hand cupped her breasts through her clothing, moving slowly from one to the other, tracing the contours through the cloth of her shirt. Tess's eyes drifted shut, then suddenly came open again as he scooped her up in his arms.

What the…?

"Where?" he asked. With next to no furniture in the house there was only one where unless they chose the floor, which right now, in her heightened state, Tess would be fine with. She'd also be fine with walking.

"The bedroom's upstairs," she said. "You can't—"

"If I can wrestle a steer to the ground, I can carry you up a few stairs."

And he did, though he was a bit winded at the top, where he lost his footing and Tess slipped out of his arms, laughing.

"Now that," he said in a low voice, backing her up against the wall, "is more of what I want to see."

"Laughing?"

He was now the one in control, capturing her mouth, one hand on either side of her head, his body pressed against hers, flattening her breasts against his chest, the wall hard against her back. "Yes."

But that wasn't what he meant and she knew it. He wanted her to not be so damned afraid and distant all the time.

"I'll try," she said, smiling up at him as he eased back, his eyes down as he once again caressed her breasts. "Too many clothes," she said, taking hold of the hem of her T-shirt and pulling it up over her head, tossing it aside. And now she was exposed, having brief second thoughts.

What if...?

But Zach reached behind her, undoing her bra and letting it drop on the floor, and then his hands were on her breasts, his tantalizingly rough skin against her soft flesh, snapping her nipples to full attention. And then he put his mouth where his hands had been.

Oh, yeah. His mouth.

Tess sucked in a breath through her teeth, tilting her head back against the wall as he took his mouth lower, and lower, exploring her breasts, teasing a trail down her abdomen and back up to her breasts. She was going to explode right there. And he still had too many clothes on. Her hands fisted in his hair, urging him to stand, and he abandoned his exploration of her breasts to once again take her mouth.

She reached between them, took hold of his shirt and pulled, popping open the remaining snaps, and Zach fell back, giving her more access. When she saw the lean lines of his torso, the dark hair covering hard, very hard, muscle, she felt like melting. She touched him, ran her hands over his muscular abs, thinking of how Jonas, her photographer, would have also melted. Talk about a body meant for the lens. She smiled to herself, then Zach caught his breath as her fingers glided over his skin and she felt a surge of sensual power…until she remembered that she might well be the first woman to touch him since he'd lost his wife.

Her hands stilled, but he covered them with one of his, pushing them lower, to the edge of his jeans. Tess did not need a second invitation. She unsnapped, unzipped, set him free just as his mouth came down on hers in a kiss that seemed to meld their souls, making Tess thankful she had the wall behind her to hold her up. And then the wall was gone and once again Zach was carrying her, this time into her bedroom, where he sat her on the bed.

They peeled out of their remaining clothing, tossing it piece by piece on the floor near the bed, making Tess think Zach was going to take her fast and hard, reflecting their need. But instead, once they were naked and she was finally going to feel this man's body against hers, as she'd so often fantasized, he gently pushed her back onto the pillows.

Zach's hands shook slightly as he caressed Tess's body, slowly, tenderly, making her wonder if it was nerves or need. Both broke her heart a little. He came up to kiss her as his hands continued to explore, his clever fingers somehow finding all the right places as Tess returned the favor, skimming her hands over long, lean muscle, her fingers circling his erection, stroking, feeling it throb in her palm.

Tess had intended to get to know every inch of his body, as he had come to know hers, but she never got the chance as the heat flared into flames of urgency.

Tess sucked in a sharp breath as he parted her thighs, her hands clutching his shoulders as he slowly eased into her, filling her as she arched her body up to meet him. So hard, so hot. So much.

He held for a moment, meeting her eyes, making certain she was with him, and then he started to move. Tess stayed with him, matched his movements, their bodies becoming damp with sweat and need. Too late she thought about a condom.

"Zach...protection?" she asked, eyes wide, hating the thought of stopping, even if there were other avenues to pleasure.

"No worries," he said in a low voice.

No worries? It took her a second to realize his meaning. Three kids...no worries. *Ah.*

And then need took over rational thought and Zach became the center of her world, filling her, moving her, making her feel whole and good again.

Tess hadn't expected an orgasm—rarely came the first time she made love to a man—and she fully expected to wait until the second time she and Zach made love, so when the waves hit her, making her back arch and her mouth O at the intensity, it stunned her.

Seconds later, Zach plunged into her one last time, his body shuddering slightly as he came. He held for a few silent seconds, then brought himself down to sprawl on top of her, shifting his weight to the side as his head came to rest against the hollow of her sweat-slicked shoulder. Tess splayed her fingers through his damp hair, trying to catch her shaky breath as their hearts pounded together. Dear heavens.

"I should have told you I can't get you pregnant before we started," Zach said against her skin.

Tess smiled a little, continuing to thread her fingers through his hair. "No worries," she said.

"I need to get home before my kids," Zach said.

"You have a couple hours."

"Mmm," he said, easing his body so that it was half on her, half off.

The next thing Tess knew, he was asleep. And she was good with that.

CHAPTER EIGHTEEN

"Is SOMETHING wrong, Dad?" Emma's question snapped Zach out of deep thought and he flipped the pancake he was cooking.

"Just tired," he said. Tired and worried and wishing he knew whether Tess's fears were realistic or an aftermath of the assault. Wishing he could head over to her place, make sure she was safe, make love to her again.

"But all the cows have calved."

He smiled a little. "I wasn't checking cows, I was just up late." Worrying. Wondering. Emma held out her plate and he dumped two pancakes onto it. Lizzie came into the kitchen as Emma went to the table, her shoes still untied, got a plate out of the cupboard and took her place next to the stove where Zach was cooking.

"Two?" he asked.

"Yes, please. Shaped like hearts, okay?"

"You got it," Zach said, smearing the batter into the requested shape as he poured it into the hot skillet.

"Dad, I didn't mean it about buying the sparkle shoes, okay?" she said in a small voice. He could practically hear one of her sisters coaching her. "Or the bike."

"Hey," he said, smiling down at his youngest. "It's okay to want stuff, kiddo, as long as you understand that you can't always get what you want." *Even if your dad really wants to give it to you.*

"Yeah," Lizzie said wistfully, tapping her plate against her leg. "I heard about that."

Zach flipped the heart cakes and a few moments later put them on Lizzie's plate. She went to join Emma at the table.

"Where's Darcy?"

"Oh," Emma said, stopping her fork in midair, "she went down to have breakfast with Tia. They're talking about the quilt. We're supposed to meet her down there."

"Great." Zach turned off the burner and set the spatula and batter bowl in the sink.

"Aren't you going to eat?" Lizzie asked.

"After you guys go to school," he said, turning on the faucet.

"But you put water in the batter bowl," Emma pointed out.

"I'm in the mood for eggs," he said. Actually he was going to make a sandwich to take with him when he went out to check the fence. Karen had always insisted on a hot breakfast and he wasn't going to tell the girls how often he skipped that meal.

Once the girls had left for school, Zach sat at the kitchen table wondering what his next move should be.

Last night, when Zach had stopped by Tess's on the way home from his volunteer firemen's meeting and ended up in her bed again, she'd given him more details after they'd made love, letting the story slip out in bits and pieces.

The stepfather was a cold-blooded bastard. According to the L.A. detective handling Tess's case, however, the guy held down a job and attended his parole meetings. Kept his nose clean.

Was it possible that he'd changed his mind about going after Tess? That he'd realized after the slashing how easily he could end up back in the penitentiary? Because he hadn't done it himself, which meant that there was a guy out there who knew the truth. A possible loose end…who may be as afraid of Eddie as Tess was.

Jeff's truck pulled into the driveway just as Zach was leading Roscoe out of the corral. He tied the horse to a post and walked over to meet his cousin.

"This is the guy I want you to check out." He handed Jeff a slip of paper containing Eddie Napier's name.

"Something to do with Tess O'Neil?" Jeff said after he read the name.

"Why?" Zach asked, startled because he and Tess had only been together a few times and as near as he knew, there'd been no witnesses. He sincerely hoped there'd been no witnesses.

Jeff smirked at his expression. "You didn't think you could fly under the radar, did you? Especially after last night when the taillights of your truck were seen turning right, into her place, instead of left into your own."

"What I do is no one's business."

Jeff shrugged. "Of course it isn't—in Fantasyland. Here in Barlow Ridge everything is game." He slipped the paper into his pocket. "The name?"

"I want to know who he is and what he's done."

"And I want to know what I'm getting into."

Zach had debated about this for more time than he cared to think about. Keep his promise to Tess or find out what he was up against?

Jeff frowned. "This isn't like her ex-husband or something?"

"I just want to know about him." Jeff was not wearing his cooperative face. "We'll talk after you look him up, okay?"

His cousin exhaled loudly. "I take it this is on the Q.T.?"

"Yes. If you can't do that, then—"

"I'll do it. But only because I don't want you getting into anything you shouldn't."

"Me, neither. How long?"

"I'll get back to you tomorrow. I'm spending most of my day in the county," he said, meaning he would not be back at the sheriff's office until late. "I'll let you know as soon as I have something." He walked back to his truck muttering about pain-in-the-ass cousins and Zach went back to saddling his horse.

He didn't know what would come of this, but the more information he had, the better he'd feel. His hope was that Tess was overreacting. Hell, the thought of being attacked, slashed...he couldn't begin to imagine the terror she must have felt. She'd definitely been suffering from post-traumatic stress when she arrived in Barlow Ridge and probably still was.

Now the trick, once he knew what was going on, was to convince her she didn't have to face these traumas alone.

"HEY, Dad?"

Zach looked up to find Darcy standing in the door of his office, dressed for school and carrying her quilting tote bag. "I know you don't want us to go to Tess's house, but I was wondering if she could come over here."

Zach was glad he wasn't drinking his coffee, because he might have choked on it.

He didn't want the girls to know that he was seeing Tess, at least not until he was fairly certain they had a chance of building something together. There would be no women popping in and out of his girls' lives, and he did not want them to think he was replacing their mom.

He also didn't want to spend his life alone.

"Why?" he asked in a fairly normal voice.

"Because we miss her." Zach believed her simple statement, but watching her face, his dad radar went up...there was something else going on.

Shit. What had she heard through the gossip mill?

"Well—"

"I don't think she *wants* to be alone." Darcy jumped in, interrupting his half-formed reply. "I mean, okay, she has something going on and asked us to stay away, but I don't think she meant it."

Zach blew out a breath. "Next time I see her I'll talk to her about it." Which would give him a little time to sort through this.

"Do you think that will be anytime soon?" Darcy asked a bit too innocently.

"I don't know." Zach met his daughter's eyes in a conversation-ending way. She simply smiled at him.

"See you after school," she said, leaving Zach with a lot to think about—as if he didn't have enough already.

If only this was as simple as introducing a woman into his daughters' lives. But no. He had to fall for a woman with some serious baggage. The solution, of course, was to either get rid of the baggage, or make sure it had no way of doing harm.

ZACH CAME OVER to her place around noon, as they'd planned yesterday, riding Roscoe. He tied the horse behind the lilac bush and knocked on the door. The dogs, who had gone to the door, did not bark.

"Hey," he said to the dogs when he came inside. "No greeting. What's up with you guys?"

"Maybe we're all relaxing," Tess suggested as Zach pulled her up against him for a kiss.

"Not to put you on edge again, but our secret might not be a secret."

"You mean…" She pointed first to herself, then at him.

"Yes."

"How?" she asked.

"Apparently someone saw my truck turn the wrong direction after the firemen's meeting night before last." He still wondered who'd spread the word. Jack Killian? He gossiped like an old lady and had been right behind Zach when he'd left the firehouse.

"Maybe you came by to drop off the lease check," Tess suggested.

"At midnight."

"It could happen."

"I guess." He took her by the hand and went over to the recliner, sitting down and pulling her onto his lap. Tess curled into him, debating the consequences. For herself, not many. She was no more visible as his lover than simply being the standoffish, rude lady in the old Anderson place. But Zach had more at stake.

"I imagine gossip travels fast here."

"Let me put it this way…Beth Ann knew about you not accepting Melba's casserole before school let out that day."

Tess put a hand on his chest and pushed herself up until she could see his face. "Do you think the girls will hear?"

She did not like the look on his face. "I think they already have. At least I think Darcy has."

Tess laid her head back against his chest as his arms closed around her. To be here in her house, midday, cuddled up against this guy who she was beginning to suspect she was falling in love with felt so perfect…or would have if she wasn't worried about devastating his daughters.

"I don't know what to say, Zach."

He inhaled deeply, his chest rising beneath her cheek, and then falling again. "I think Darcy likes the idea, but I don't know how to proceed with this."

Tess lifted her head at that. "We're not going to proceed beyond what we're doing now, Zach. Not for a long time.

This is good, or it would be if only you and me are involved and not the rest of the community."

"So this is all you'll ever want?" he asked in a low voice, those blue eyes drilling into her.

"I have to take this day-to-day, Zach. I can't do it any other way until I have some answers about Eddie." She ran the flat of her hand over her injured cheek.

"I understand," he said in a low voice, pulling her back against him. "I wish I didn't, but I do."

But something had shifted. Tess could feel his tenseness. She closed her eyes, wishing things could be different. They'd made a deal for the here and now and that was what she had to stick to until she knew for certain she could handle it. She would not be the source of further disruption to this family.

"I need to get to work," he finally said before pressing a kiss against her hair.

"Just stopped by for a cuddle?" she asked.

"You never know who's watching," he said.

The words sent a shiver through her, although she knew that wasn't his intent.

"Is this worth it?" she asked quietly. "For you?"

For a minute she didn't think he was going to answer, then he cupped her face between his hands and kissed her in a way that made her knees go weak.

"What do you think?" he asked when his hands dropped back to his sides.

Tess cleared her throat. "I think you'd better go back to work right now or you won't be leaving for a while."

BETH ANN DID not stop by to help the girls with their homework that night and Lizzie warned Zach to watch out for Tia because she was grumpy.

"Any idea why?" he asked Darcy after Lizzie went into the kitchen.

"Nope, but Liz is right. Tia has been kind of mean lately."

Normally Zach left Beth Ann to her business and vice versa, but something had felt off between them over the past couple of days, so after dinner Zach left the girls loading the dishwasher and walked to his sister-in-law's trailer. She opened the door almost as soon as he knocked…an uncapped marker in one hand. He could see a poster she'd been working on lying on the table—no doubt another lame assignment.

"What's wrong?" she asked.

"I came here to ask the same question."

Beth Ann's mouth tightened as she glanced over his head in the direction of the Anderson place and Zach knew.

"Tess."

"It's none of my business, Zach. I mean if you want to… date…it's been three years. You should."

She didn't mean a single word of it. "If you're worried about the girls," he said, "I'm not going to do anything to upset them."

"How can you not upset them, Zach? I mean, this woman is not hanging around this valley for any longer than she has to."

"You don't know that," he said quietly.

"I know she doesn't belong here!"

"She got a rough start here."

"A rough start? Come on, Zach! She kicked Melba Morrison off her property."

"Maybe she had reason."

"To send a grandma packing. With her casserole."

"Is this about Karen?" he asked.

Beth Ann dropped her chin for a moment. When she raised it again, he could see tears glistening, but they didn't fall. She shook back her hair and said, "I don't expect you to be celibate, Zach."

"Fair enough. But you want to okay who I date?"

"I want my nieces' lives to be stable."

"So do I. It's my top priority." And she knew that. Zach had a sudden unsettling thought. "What is this really about, Beth Ann?"

"This is about me not wanting to lose out on my nieces' childhood. I need to be here, for Karen's sake. And for mine."

"Why wouldn't you be here?" Zach asked.

"Because if you do get serious about someone, then she is not going to want her former sister-in-law living a stone's throw away from her marital bed." Beth Ann snapped her mouth shut then half turned away, letting out a shaky breath, telling Zach how much she already regretted blurting out her feelings.

"Beth Ann…" He reached out to touch her shoulder. The muscles were tense beneath his fingers. "That day is probably a long way away."

"Maybe it is, and maybe it isn't," she said.

"You will always have a place here."

"I know," she said quietly. "But will I feel welcome?"

JEFF TOOK HIS sweet time getting back to Zach, although he assured him it was because it'd taken him a while to hear back from his sources, which surprised Zach, who'd assumed he'd simply run the guy through the National Crime Investigation database.

"This Napier guy is bad news," Jeff said over the phone. "*Major* drug dealer. Arrested in both Nevada and California. Did time in both places on various charges. The last stretch was for dealing, extortion, assault with a deadly weapon— two counts. One of the weapons was a car."

"Great," Zach said, his stomach knotting.

"The good news is that he's flirting with the three-strikes law. If they put him away again, he may never get out."

"Good to know." Although if the asshole did what he wanted to do—hurt Tess—then that didn't do either of them a lot of good.

"He's a model parolee," Jeff said with a touch of irony.

"How'd you get all this? NCIC?"

"I called a cop buddy in Los Angeles. That's what took me so long getting back to you." There was a brief silence and then he said, "This lady of yours…do you know her background?"

Zach hoped he did. "Maybe."

That was all the encouragement Jeff needed to fill Zach in on who Tess was and what had happened to her. His story matched Tess's exactly, the only additional information being her name. Her real name—Terese Olan.

"How easy was it to get that information?" Zach asked, very afraid that Tess might be easier to find than she had hoped.

"Napier got called in for questioning concerning an assault on his former stepdaughter. A model whose face was slashed. It wasn't hard to put it all together." Jeff let out a low snort. "No wonder she was so jumpy when she moved to Barlow Ridge."

"Nobody can know about this, Jeff."

"Give me a break," his cousin replied harshly. "I have no reason to tell anyone anything. It's her secret. And yours."

"Dad!" Emma came flying into the room clutching a flyer with a 4-H emblem in one corner and Zach held up a hand to quiet her. She skidded to a stop, still smiling widely.

"I have to go. Thanks, Jeff. I owe you."

"No problem. But, Zach?"

"Yeah?"

"This guy's a real scrote, but there's nothing, not one thing, connecting this guy to Tess's assault. The official case report concluded that it was a random attack."

"Thanks again," Zach said. "Talk to you later." He'd barely hung up the phone when Emma slapped the paper onto his desk in front of him.

"I have my horse camp list!" she announced.

"Let's take a look," Zach said.

After helping Emma go over the checklist of what she had to find/purchase/procure for a successful week at horse camp, which was almost two months away, Zach sat back in his office chair and pulled the whiskey out of the file drawer. After making sure there were no children lurking in the hallway, he took a swig straight from the bottle. It burned all the way down to his stomach. And then he took another. Half an hour later, while the girls were watching TV, he told Darcy he was going to check cattle and to call Beth Ann for any emergencies. She gave him a distracted nod, being deeply involved in the animated adventures of some kind of undersea kingdom. Emma and Lizzie didn't even look up.

Satisfied that his girls were occupied for the next hour at least, he went outside, climbed onto the four-wheeler and went to check cattle. At Tess's house.

TESS AND THE dogs recognized the sound of Zach's four-wheeler, but while the dogs lazily ambled toward the door, Tess crossed the room quickly. He'd never stopped by at this time before. It'd always been when the girls were at school, except for two nights ago, when he'd knocked on her door close to midnight—and put them squarely on the gossip radar.

When she answered the door, she could see by the intense

look on Zach's face that something was wrong. But before she could ask, he took her face in his hands and kissed her.

Tess kissed him back, deeply, and soon there was a trail of clothing, leading from the living room, up the stairs to her bedroom. But when they got to the bedroom, Zach did not lay her down as usual. Instead he boosted her up by her bottom and she automatically wrapped her legs around him, surprised that he could lift her so easily. But this was a man she'd once seen tackle a man-size calf and bring it down. He set her butt on top of the single bureau and then slowly, oh, so slowly, impaled her on his erection, his eyes locked on hers.

Tess's breath caught as he buried himself fully within her, and then he started moving, thrusting hard and deep in a slow rhythm as Tess wrapped her legs around him even tighter. Tess clung to him as her head fell back and she gasped for breath.

It was only a matter of minutes until Tess all but exploded. Zach gave a few more thrusts before burying himself to the hilt as he emptied himself inside her. For a moment they held then Tess's forehead came down to rest on Zach sweat-slicked shoulder.

"Well," she said as he slowly stepped back a few minutes later. "I kind of like how you say hello."

He smiled then started gathering his clothes, pulling them on as he went. Tess did the same, following him down the stairs.

"I didn't come here just for a quickie," he said after he'd zipped his jeans.

"You know," Tess said, shrugging her black T-shirt over her head, "I kind of suspected that." The smile she wore faded. "Why are you here?"

"I want to make a few things clear, so you know where I'm coming from."

"Okay…" Her stomach tightened.

"I sincerely hope your past does not come back to haunt you, but if it does, I'll be there for you."

"I know." So far he hadn't said anything he hadn't said before.

"I care about you, Tess. The more time I spend with you, the more I care."

That one was new. Tess felt herself start to withdraw, but before she could get the shutters up, he was there, in front of her, tipping her chin up.

"I will not push you. I will not ask for anything you cannot give. But it's only right that you know how I feel. If you need to back off because of it, that's something I'll have to deal with." Tess simply stared at him, eyes wide, not certain what to say. "But even if you do back off, I want you to promise that you'll call me if you ever need any kind of help. With anything."

"Clogged drain?"

It was a poor joke, one meant to give her a little breathing room. It didn't work. There was a glint in Zach's eyes as he said, "I'm an excellent plumber. And you know what I mean."

Tess felt her skin warm. Again. "I do know what you mean." It was as close to a promise as she could get at this point and Zach seemed satisfied. Or, if not satisfied, smart enough not to push.

"I have to get back to the ranch," he said, dropping a kiss onto her lips.

"I know." And it suprised her how much she wanted him to stay.

After Zach had gone, she sat in her chair, dangling her sewing shears from one hand, watching as the shiny stainless steel caught the light of the late-afternoon sun.

He cared for her…

Well, she'd be lying to herself if she pretended she didn't care for him, too.

Could it be possible that this could work out? That signing with the agency wasn't the only break she was ever going to get in her life?

That maybe Eddie would continue putting in his time in the car wash and she could happily settle in this valley, close to the man who was getting deeper under her skin every day?

Was that too much to hope for?

Maybe not.

THE SENSE OF promise was still there the next morning when Tess got out of bed, wondering what it would be like to wake up next to Zach, and continued through the morning almost until noon—when the phone rang and a few seconds after answering it, Detective Hiller brought Tess crashing back to earth.

"William Abbott was attacked in his home last night."

A numbing sensation traveled up her spine. *No. Not William.* "Is he all right?"

"The attack was interrupted by a neighbor before he was hurt too badly. He spent the night in the hospital as a precaution and was released this morning."

"I see." The calm words sounded inane to her. *Yes, I see. William Abbott was beaten because of me.*

"He contacted our office to let us know what happened and he wanted me to pass along the message that he hadn't told the guy anything."

"The man who attacked him asked about me?"

"Yes."

She had to stay calm. Think clearly. Get all the information she could. Later she could break down.

"What's being done to protect William?" she asked.

"William is protecting himself. He's arranging to visit a friend who lives out of the country." She heard a rare touch of humor in Detective Hiller's voice when he said, "He also told us to contact him when the assailant was caught, because he intends to sue."

Tess smiled grimly. Of course he did.

"Did he give a description?"

"It matches that of Jared Napier."

Tess's heart stopped beating for a split second. "No. He's in prison." But even as the words came out of her mouth, she knew what the detective was going to say.

"He was released two weeks ago. They had no reason to inform our office."

"I guess they have one now," Tess said, pressing her hand against her eyes. *Think. What are you going to do?*

"When I got the report, I checked all of Eddie's known associates, since he's—"

"Working at the car wash and never misses a day," Tess said bitterly. But the detective wasn't going to say he'd been wrong when he'd told her to get on with her life, that Eddie wasn't a threat. Technically he wasn't—to her. At the time. But William probably had a different take on the matter.

"That's when I found out his son had been released from prison, pulled up his profile and the description fit."

"Then can't you just pick him up?" Tess asked, a note of desperation working into her voice.

"We had the authorities in San Jose do just that. He has a pretty solid alibi."

"Wonder how much he paid for it."

"There's nothing we can do until we get more substantial evidence, and that isn't likely. I want you to call if you have any concerns. Any concerns at all."

That was a change. Tess agreed, then after she'd hung up

the phone, she slammed her palm against the wall. It wasn't fair. Not freaking fair!

She'd had what? Two weeks of feeling like she had a life.

And what about the girls and Zach? What if Eddie or Jared came gunning for her and they were around? She could only think of one possible solution—to give Eddie and Jared what they so desperately wanted—before they hurt someone else she cared about.

TESS GOT INTO the car after dropping her dogs off at Dr. Hyatt's vet clinic to be boarded, and hoped she would be back to get them.

She had to end this craziness once and for all and the only way she could think of to do it was to give Eddie what he wanted. She couldn't give him the money he thought she'd stolen from him, but she had money in the bank. A good deal of money even after leasing the ranch. Once she found out how much her mother had stolen from Eddie, she'd replace it. If she played things right, they wouldn't even know it wasn't the same money. What better way to spend what was left of her nest egg than to buy her freedom?

The only problem was Zach. She'd wanted to tell him what was going on. To confess. But in the end she'd decided that the less he knew, the better. He was too damned protective. There was no way he'd agree to her plan, because he didn't understand her family's mind-set the way she did.

Hey, Zach. I need to run to Reno where my stepbrother Mikey is going to help me broker a deal with the rest of my felonious stepfamily.

Oh, yes. That would have gone over well.

This was her life, she reminded herself as she backed the car out of the parking space. Her business. She'd come close to putting his family in harm's way and she needed to do something about it. If this worked out, she'd come back

to Barlow Ridge, tell Zach the truth. If it didn't work out…
well, Zach wouldn't have to worry about her running out
on him because she'd be long gone.

Tess checked the time as she pulled onto the highway.
Twelve-thirty. She'd pull into Reno at about five-thirty, ditch
her car in a parking garage, take a cab to the casino where
she'd meet Mikey at seven o'clock. Once there, she'd take a
good look at the place. Get to know her escape routes. Hope
to hell this deal worked so she could get on with her life.

It hadn't taken long to track down her stepbrother, since
he went by his real name, had a sedate career as an IT guy,
a wife and two kids. He'd been stunned when she'd called
out of the blue, but after hearing her story, had reluctantly
agreed to meet her in Reno, which was only an hour and a
half drive from where he lived in Sacramento. Tess wanted
to meet in Reno because it wasn't in California where both
Eddie and Jared were paroled, she was moderately familiar with the town and she wanted a place that had lots and
lots of cameras. Nothing better than a casino for that. She
wasn't certain yet that he would agree to play middleman,
but he was her best shot. There was no way she would dare
contact Jared directly. Too dangerous.

If Mikey couldn't broker this deal, then she had a feeling
she would have to disappear again. She was taking a big
chance, but Tess could no longer stand the idea of spending
her life looking over her shoulder—or endangering anyone
who eventually came to care for her.

THE HOUSE WAS empty, Tess's car was gone. And Zach's bad
feeling was working its way into a really bad feeling.

He flipped open his cell phone and dialed Jeff.

"What?" his cousin answered.

"Tess is gone. She's not in her house. Hasn't been there all
night." He'd told himself when he'd stopped on the landing

after tucking in Lizzie and noticed that Tess's lights were off that it was because she finally felt safer. What an idiot.

"Maybe she went somewhere."

"I've called her cell. No answer."

"Zach—"

"She's never not been in her house at night and she agreed to tell me if she was in any kind of trouble." Which was why he hadn't tried to contact her the night before. She needed her space and he wasn't going to shadow her every move. But being gone all night without telling him didn't seem right. Especially when they were supposed to ride today.

He heard his cousin exhale loudly. "What do you want me to do?" he asked. "Put out a BOLO?"

"I want you to ping her phone."

"Shit, Zach, do you have any idea what that involves? Especially when we don't know for sure that something is wrong?"

"Do you think I care?"

"Just…give me a minute. Let me check into some stuff. I'll call you back."

The phone went dead and it was all Zach could do not to throw it against the side of the house.

He was glad he didn't because less than an hour later Jeff phoned back. "I called in a favor. I know where she is and you are not to ask how."

He couldn't care less how. "Where is she?"

"A casino in Reno. And, yeah, she's been seen there alive and well."

Zach felt a swell of relief. She was fine. In Reno, but that was her business. As long as she was safe.

"There's more," Jeff said quietly. "Her stepbrother just got out of prison and I guess he's already been questioned on a possible assault charge."

CHAPTER NINETEEN

TESS FROZE at the knock on her hotel room door and waited, hoping to hear a member of the housekeeping staff announce their presence.

There was nothing but silence on the other side of the door.

Had Jared found her? Was that why Mikey had delayed the meeting until that evening?

If so, how? She'd paid for the room in cash, declined incidentals so she didn't have to leave a credit card.

Heart hammering, she slowly approached the door and peered through the peephole, fully expecting to call security.

And then, when she saw the very angry man on the other side of the door, she didn't know what she was going to do.

Zach. And he wasn't alone. For a wild moment Tess thought the other man might be Jared, but the guy moved and she could see that it was Zach's cousin. The deputy.

Tess leaned her forehead on the door. What freaking now? She'd left to try to protect this guy and here he was. And how the hell had he found her?

The knocking started again, more insistent this time.

"Let me in, Tess."

Let him in. She'd done that. In many different ways and none of them had turned out well for him.

"Don't make Jeff have to call his cop buddies," Zach said in a voice barely audible through the thick door, but

Tess made out what he was saying. Jeff probably did have law enforcement buddies here and the last thing she needed was law enforcement.

Slowly she unbolted the door and opened it. Zach briefly met her eyes, his expression the picture of cold anger, before he stalked into the room. Jeff followed, taking the door from her and closing it after a quick check of the hall.

"Why are you here?" Tess asked. She knew that if she was going to remain in control, she had to be the one asking the questions.

"Why did you run?"

"I didn't run. I have some personal business here. I was coming back."

"I know about your stepbrother, Tess." Her eyes widened.

Tess went to the sofa and sat, pressing her hand against her forehead. Then she looked up at Zach, who was silently staring at her small bag, still zipped shut because she'd had no intention of staying here tonight. Once she talked to Mikey she was grabbing a cab and doing her best to lose anyone who might be interested in where she was going.

"Why didn't you tell me about this, Tess?"

"Because you didn't need to get sucked into the cesspool of my former life," she said harshly before she pushed her hair back with both hands, angling her face so he got a good look at the scars. "I didn't want you involved with people who would do this. *And*—" she met his eyes accusingly "—I was coming back."

"After you took care of this problem on your own."

"It's my problem." She shook her head and stepped toward the window, wishing she hadn't seen the icy anger on Zach's face when he'd walked into the room. She so much preferred remembering him smiling after they'd made love that last time.

"Law enforcement made it pretty clear that there wasn't

a lot they could do until someone actually assaulted me," Tess said before glancing at Jeff. "No offense intended." She ran her fingertips over the scars on her left cheek. "I, uh, decided I didn't want to go through that again."

"There are other options."

"Yeah?" Tess said. "Tell me one."

"No," Zach said. "You tell me one. Tell me what you're going to do."

"I'm giving them what they want. Then maybe they'll leave me alone."

"What do they want?"

"Money," Tess said with a small shrug. "Of course. All anyone in my family wanted, except for me and Mikey, was money or drugs."

"Mikey?"

"My younger stepbrother. I'm going to meet him, arrange to give Jared, my older stepbrother, and Eddie the money they think I stole from them. I'm giving them my money," Tess said, so there'd be no confusion on that point.

Zach's expression was a study in disbelief. "Paying them off?"

"I want them out of my life."

"How much?" Jeff asked.

"I don't know. That's what I'm going to find out from Mikey. The biggest deal Eddie made that I knew of was in the 50K range."

"You're going to give a criminal fifty thousand dollars," Zach said.

"This is why I didn't discuss it with you," Tess snapped. "You come from a decent place where stuff like this doesn't happen. I didn't think you'd understand."

"Of course I don't understand, because it's a stupid idea to buy off criminals. What keeps them from coming after you for more?"

"Because I don't have any more and I'll make sure they know that."

"Can you trust this guy?" Jeff asked, drawing her attention away from Zach. "Your younger stepbrother?"

"He's different. He left home before I did, for almost the same reasons I did."

"Almost?"

"I don't think Jared wanted to rape him, but you never know."

"Did he—Jared, or whatever the hell his name is—rape you?" Zach asked in a deadly voice.

Tess shook her head. "I left after a close call."

"That was why you ended up in the group home?"

"After I ran away." She glanced over at the dark window. There was so much she hadn't told him, but that had been the deal. He'd agreed to it…just as she'd agreed not to face danger without him.

"I came here because of what happened to William. I didn't want them getting anywhere close to the girls." *Or you. It would kill me if something happened to you.* "I knew you wouldn't back down if I told you the truth, wouldn't like my plan. So I didn't tell you."

"When are you meeting your stepbrother?" Jeff asked.

Tess glanced at the digital clock next to the bed. "In twenty minutes. Downstairs." She met Zach's eyes. "It's the only way I can hope to get out of this." Then she looked away as she ran a hand over her upper arm.

"I want to be there," he said.

Her eyes shot back to his. "You *can't* be there."

"*We're* going to be there," Jeff said.

"No. This is my one shot and I can't screw it up."

"We'll be nearby," Jeff said. "Unobtrusively nearby," he repeated with a significant look at Zach, who nodded back, looking none too happy.

Tess simply shook her head, overwhelmed by how this situation was already barreling out of control. As if she'd ever had any control.

"Mikey isn't a criminal, but if he suspects anything, he'll walk. We're not a very trusting family."

"These guys aren't your family," Zach said in a low voice.

"But they were and I'm still dealing with the fallout."

"Where are you meeting him?" Jeff asked.

"The Xanadu Bar downstairs. Lots of cameras there."

"That's good," Jeff said. "And then what?"

"I'm checking out of this room before I go, then I'll grab a cab after I talk to Mikey." She took pains not to look at Zach when she said, "Disappear so they can't find me."

Neither Jeff nor Zach said a word and Tess refused to look at them. Instead she focused on her fingers which seemed unable to stay still.

A silence hung over the room and Tess continued to study her hands, wishing Zach had simply let her be. Let her work this out.

She couldn't keep from raising her eyes and of course she found him studying her the way she'd been studying her hands. Intently.

"We should go down to the bar now," Jeff said to Zach.

"You go," Zach said. "I'll join you."

"All right," Jeff said. He looked like he wanted to say a whole lot more, perhaps something along the lines of "Don't hurt each other while I'm not here to referee," but instead he grabbed his hat and headed out the door.

"Are you really meeting this guy in the Xanadu Bar?" Zach asked when the door closed.

"I wouldn't lie about that."

"You might if you thought it would protect me," he said.

Tess's mouth fell open. "Yeah. I figured it out."

"Why did you come?" she asked as he let himself out the door.

"Because I'm in love with you," he said, sending a wave of shock shooting through Tess. She could deal with it when he said he cared about her. But love…love meant…she didn't know what it meant.

"You can't love me."

"Yes, I can." And then the door clicked shut.

TESS BARELY RECOGNIZED Mikey. The last time she'd seen him he'd been fourteen, a skinny towheaded kid who'd never gotten enough to eat because food wasn't a high priority in their house. That probably explained why he now weighed well over two hundred pounds.

But his hair was still blond and his face was the same, once she got used to it being broader, and the teeth were actually better.

"Terry," he said, getting off the stool as if to give her a hug, but she automatically stepped back then turned her face so he could see the scars in the dim light of the bar. He gave a low whistle.

"You really think Eddie did that?"

"I think he hired the guy as a warning to me…a warning I feel I have to take seriously."

Mikey sat back down and Tess gingerly took the seat across the table, holding her oversize bag on her lap as a barrier.

"You want something to drink?"

"I just want this to be over," she said. No drinking, no reminiscing. "Have you talked to, you know?" Damn. She couldn't even bring herself to say his name.

"Yes," he said patiently. "And…you know…said if he gets what's his, then yes, he's done with you."

Tess nodded, wondering if that was really true. If they

had the money, there really was no reason to do anything but forget about her. It wasn't like she could finger them for anything. After all, as far as they knew, she was passing along drug money, which made her as liable as they were for criminal prosecution.

"Look," she said, leaning closer even though the bar was noisy and it was unlikely anyone could overhear. "I don't know how much is my mother's and how much is Eddie's. If there's anything that's not Eddie's I want it."

"Meaning?"

"How much do I owe Eddie?"

"Five hundred thousand."

For a moment, Tess simply stared at Mikey as a wave of what felt like hysteria washed over her. Then she pressed her lips together before she started laughing insanely, managed a small nod and wondered if she was going to have a heart attack. If so, then her problems were over.

No wonder Eddie had been adamant about getting the money. Who in their right mind would have left half a million dollars with *her* mother?

Eddie wasn't in his right mind, but he wasn't stupid, either. He must have put the fear into her mother, but never dreamed she'd up and die on him.

"My mother didn't give me that much," she said, her voice low, firm. She only had one hundred thousand if she cashed in everything. She'd hoped that Eddie might have only given her mother 70 or 80K, so she'd have a little left. Five hundred thousand? There was no way she could come up with that kind of money in the time frame Eddie would want it.

What choice did she have?

"How much did she give you?"

"A hundred thou."

Mikey shook his head. "That may be true, because, no

offense, but your mom was kind of a skank, but Eddie won't care. He'll want all of his money."

"Maybe I could broker some kind of a deal." Or spend her life looking over her shoulder.

Mikey gave her an are-you-kidding look. "Like make payments?" he asked skeptically.

"I can't give him what I don't have."

"Then it's going to be a matter of convincing him you honestly don't have it." He gave his blond head a shake. "And you know how that's going to go."

Tess closed her eyes for a moment and Mikey reached out to gently touch her cheek. She instinctively jerked her head sideways then heard the slide of a chair close by. A quick shift of her eyes and she saw Jeff pushing Zach back down into his seat. She had to get this meeting over with, then figure out a way to ditch her guardian angels. Zach didn't belong in this mess. He didn't understand how these guys operated. His world was so far removed from theirs.

He thinks he loves you. What's he going to think when he finds out you owe criminals half a million bucks?

"Will you talk to him?"

"Not unless you have the money, Tess. I can't get involved. I have a wife and two kids. You're lucky I'm doing this."

She gathered her bag, prepared for flight. Perhaps a flight that was going to last until her family screwed up and ended up back behind bars. It was going to be fun explaining that to Zach. Who thought he loved her.

Maybe now that he knew the cold hard facts, he'd change his mind on that, because come hell or high water, she was not going back to her ranch and leading Eddie right to someone he could terrorize in order to get at her.

"Thanks, Mikey. I hope you have a good life."

Tess got out of her chair and quickly threaded her way

through the crowd, wondering if Jeff and Zach were even aware that she was on the move. What now? Did she just get that cab as she'd planned? Did she send Zach a note or letter or something?

He deserved that. He deserved to know that he was the closest she'd ever come to loving someone and she would have given almost anything to have been able to see if they could work things out.

Tess blinked a little as she walked out of the dim bar and across the lobby, eyes on the ugly carpet, heading for the cab stand as fast as she could go without drawing attention.

Five hundred thousand...

How was she ever going to come up with that amount of money to buy her freedom?

She was almost to the door when she ran smack into a solid chest. The guy had to have stepped directly in front of her, because he hadn't been there a split second ago. He gripped her arm firmly, to steady her, Tess thought until she glanced up and stared into the face of her worst nightmare.

"Jared."

"Got it in one," he said in that nasty voice she remembered so well. She could feel her arm bruising as he yanked her up against his side so tightly that the knife he held under his sweatshirt jabbed her.

Mikey had sold her out. She'd known she was taking a risk contacting him, knew she'd have to lie low afterward, but never had she dreamed that Jared would risk coming after her in public. This was not part of the scenario.

"There are cameras everywhere."

"Hat, hoodie and glasses," he said with a complacent smile, indicating how he'd hid his face pretty damned successfully. "I see you're wearing glasses now, too."

Tess jerked her arm, but he only held tighter, steering her toward the door. "Make a scene and you'll regret it. A knife between the ribs is a nasty thing and I only have to run a few feet to get out of here. You on the other hand… let's hope you don't bleed out."

Tess had every intention of making a scene, risking the knife rather than let him haul her off and play with her before he killed her, but the words were barely out of his mouth when Jared's head suddenly snapped backward. It took her a second to realize that Zach was there; that he'd taken hold of her stepbrother's hood and yanked. Jared did not let go of her, but Tess stomped on his instep as hard as she could, jammed her elbow into his solar plexus, and when he grunted, twisted free.

Less than a second later, Zach's fist crashed into Jared's jaw, knocking him sideways. Jared retained his balance, barely, but Zach was on him again, jamming his foot into the back of Jared's knee and sending him down, then locking his arms around his neck the same way she'd once seen him headlock a large calf. And like the calf, Jared toppled, struggling on the floor, bellowing, until Zach nailed him in the kidney.

Security came rushing in, pulling Zach off Jared. Jeff flashed his badge, said a few words to the uniformed man, and then Tess watched numbly as her stepbrother was handcuffed.

Zach looked up at her, breathing heavily, a smear of blood across his face.

But he was very much alive, and as she stared at the knife lying a couple feet away from him, she realized he could have been very, very dead.

"What in the hell do you think you're doing?" Tess demanded.

"Saving your hide?"

"You could have been *killed*. He had a knife!"

"Well, I'm not killed," Zach said, his chest still heaving from the exertion. Tess was not mollified by his answer.

"What would have happened to the girls if things hadn't ended in your favor? Did you think about that?" she asked, pointing a finger at his chest. It was too much. Tess turned and started pushing her way through the people that had gathered around. A security guard took her arm. "Ma'am, you can't go. The police are coming and you have to make a statement."

"Fine," she said, looking down at the ugly casino carpet. Pale blue and violet circles on a black background. A carpet meant to keep patrons' eyes up, on the machines.

Zach could have been killed. Because of her.

Because of his own stubbornness.

She chanced a glance in his direction, saw that he was getting to his feet and seemed none the worse for wear. Jeff handed him his hat.

She was so damned mad at him.

CHAPTER TWENTY

IT DIDN'T take long for the police to show up and haul Jared away. Mikey, Tess, Jeff and Zach all made statements in various casino offices and then, apparently in an effort to make certain they weren't sued for being on the site of an attempted kidnapping, or perhaps out of the good of their corporate hearts, the casino offered Tess, Zach and Jeff rooms, gratis.

The three of them walked to the elevators without speaking, Zach carrying the light bag that contained Tess's few belongings. When the elevator hit the fifth floor, the floor his and Jeff's room was on, only Jeff got out. He walked down the hall alone without looking back.

"Don't you have a room?" Tess asked pointedly when the elevator doors closed.

"I'm not leaving you alone after what just happened."

"Zach...this is what I do," she muttered without looking at him. "I handle things alone."

"Do you want to keep doing that?" he asked quietly as the door opened on the eighth floor.

She didn't have an answer so he took the key card from her and opened the door. Tess stepped into the room and then stopped dead as reaction started to set in. A different kind of reaction than she'd expected. Not anger. Not fear—not the kind of fear she was used to anyway. It was more like...disorientation. Being set adrift in unfamiliar seas.

She'd been running on autopilot and adrenaline up until she walked into the room.

And now she didn't know what to do.

Eddie was still out there somewhere, but Jared was a recent parolee in possession of a weapon on the wrong side of the California state line. According to Jeff, he'd be going back in prison for the rest of his sentence and then some for attempted kidnapping and assault with a deadly weapon. Everything was on camera and the hoodie hadn't saved him once Zach knocked him onto his back.

She suddenly turned to Zach. "Why did you do that?"

"Tackle him? I think that's pretty obvious."

"You could have been killed."

"Me? What do you think that guy was going to do to you?"

Jared had probably planned to do a lot to her, whether he got the money or not. She hadn't fully trusted Mikey, but she'd never expected Jared, fresh out of prison, to do something so brazen as to try to nab her in a crowded casino. He never had been big on brains.

"I didn't want to drag you into this," she said.

"I believe you've made that point," Zach said, setting her bag on the desk. "I dragged myself into it and I don't regret it." He took her hand and led her into the room without bothering with the lights. The curtains were open and Reno fanned out beneath them, a brilliant sparkling mosaic of white, yellow and red. It was beautiful and she was tired.

Tired of just about everything, but most of all tired of having such a screwed-up life.

"It's done," Zach said close to her ear, his breath warm against her skin.

"I'd love to believe that," she murmured.

His lips touched the base of her neck and she shivered then took a step away, putting distance between them. "It's not over," she said. "And why are you here after I lied to you?"

"I told you why."

"Zach—"

"Shh," he said before he covered her mouth with his in a kiss that stole her words. When he raised his head, he pushed his hands into her hair, brushing it back away from her face, smiling ever so slightly as his thumb moved over the scar as it always seemed to do. Then he kissed her again, more deeply. Tess closed her eyes, let her arms wrap around his solid body, spreading her fingers out over the muscles of his back. "I did what I did out of sheer instinct. You were in danger and I acted."

"You took him down good," she murmured.

"Physics," he replied as his mouth traveled over the scars to plant a kiss at the corner of her injured eye. Then he took a step back, his hands still on her upper arms. "Come on. We're going to bed…and we're going to sleep."

Tess could see he was serious. So she stood there and let him undo the buttons of her shirt and slide it down over her shoulders. She pretended not to notice his erection when he undid her bra and tossed it onto the sofa with her shirt. With an intent expression that made her want to smile, he lowered the zipper of her pants and slid them down her legs. Tess stepped out of them and he tossed them onto the sofa, too, leaving her in her bikini underwear.

"I have to use the bathroom," she said.

When Tess came back out a few minutes later, he was in bed, his clothes in a stack next to hers on the sofa. She slid beneath the covers and he pulled her against him, cradling her.

"Just go to sleep," he said.

Tess took a breath, inhaling his scent deep into her lungs, and feeling ridiculously comforted by him just holding her.

Maybe she didn't have to live handling everything alone…maybe knowing that she was quite capable of handling everything alone was enough.

ZACH COULDN'T SLEEP. He held Tess as if he was going to lose her if he let go, which he well might. He'd lost one woman that he loved deeply and he wasn't ready to lose another before he found out what they might be able to make together.

Tess would have denied it with her last breath, but she'd been in shock the night before. Who wouldn't have been with the ape that had once tried to rape her forcing her out of the building with a knife to her ribs?

His grip tightened on Tess's shoulder at the thought, causing her to stir in her sleep. He relaxed his hand, stroking her arm as he pressed his lips against her hair.

It was going to take her a while to get over this, and to believe she no longer had to fear her stepfather. Eddie was going to get the message, via his P.O., that there was no money and if anything happened to Tess, his life was going to be a living hell…

When Zach woke up Tess was gone. He lay still listening, wondering how the hell she'd slipped away. How far she'd gone and if she was going to come back. Because if she'd left again, things were out of his hands. She knew how he felt. The next step was up to her.

That didn't make it any easier to accept, though. He tossed the covers back and got out of bed. The bathroom was empty, her clothes and her purse were gone. *She* was gone.

The sound of the door opening startled the hell out of him and he grabbed a pillow off the sofa, holding it in front of his crotch.

Tess came in the door, took one look at him and put her hand to her mouth, fighting back a choked laugh. But a second later her smile disappeared.

"You thought I'd left again." He didn't answer, didn't even toss the pillow aside. He just stood there. Tess held up a paper bag. "I needed some essentials and I didn't want to wake you."

"Why?"

"Because every time I woke up last night *you* were awake. I thought you might need some sleep."

Now he did toss the pillow aside and went to sit on the bed. Tess sat beside him.

"I feel better," she said without looking at him, holding the bag on her lap. "I went downstairs without an escort. I avoided the lobby where Jared nabbed me, but I did go downstairs."

"You did good," Zach said, realizing this was territory she had to cover alone, no matter how much he wanted to help her.

"Last night I…" She let out a breath, her shoulders slumping. Then she looked sideways at him. "Not just last night. For a long time I've been letting knee-jerk reactions rule my life."

"I did the same thing after Karen died. I wasn't myself for months."

Tess nodded. "I can't promise I won't keep doing that. Eddie is still out there."

"And I'm still right here."

"I screwed up because now he thinks I have the money."

"I think the California authorities will have a long talk with him."

Tess looked into Zach's very blue eyes. "I love you and the girls," she said simply. "I can't put you in danger."

"We'll come up with something," he said, closing his arms around her. "We'll sell land, pay criminals, whatever it takes. We'll come up with a way for us to be together and safe."

Tess laughed a little. "Right."

"I mean it. We'll take things slow and when the time is right, we'll tell the kids and they'll be happy for us."

"Beth Ann?"

"We'll work on her."

"I don't know, Zach." She dropped her chin and focused on the paper bag. "Kind of sounds too good to be true."

He tilted her chin toward him. "Sometimes things are like that."

"Too good to be true?"

"Let's just stop at too good. That's how I think things can be between us."

Tess smiled. "In spite of everything you think they can be good?"

"Look at it this way…you don't have to explain a convoluted past to me. I'm familiar. And we've been through a tight spot together."

"Yes."

"And I love you."

"You've been saying that."

"Probably because I'm also meaning it."

Tess took his hand and held it tightly in hers. "I guess since I wanted to kill you for almost getting killed…that might mean I love you, too."

"Yeah," he said, leaning over to kiss her. "It might. And everything else we'll deal with as it comes along."

EPILOGUE

JARED WAS a self-serving scumbag—as his father found out not long after his eldest son had been arrested. Jared cut a deal and gave up the name of the man who'd slashed Tess's face in return for a reduced sentence. The slasher had given up Eddie and Eddie had just swung his third strike.

"He got life," Tess said after hanging up the phone six months after her stepfather's arrest. Zach took her hand, bringing her to sit on his thigh behind the desk.

"Now maybe we can have a life," Zach said, nuzzling her neck.

She leaned back against him, looking at the photos on the office wall. Emma and Darcy at horse camp. Lizzie with her new bike. Beth Ann and Tess at the Father's Day picnic. Although awkward at first, the relationship was getting better, and sometimes Beth Ann came to eat with the family on the same days that Tess stayed for dinner after sewing lessons.

The girls seemed to enjoy the fact that their dad had a girlfriend, especially because it was Tess. Lizzie asked if she had to put her mama's photo away and Tess had told her it would make her very unhappy if she did that.

Zach splayed his hand out over her abdomen. "Ever think about having kids?" he asked.

"Only if they're over the age of six," she said. And she meant it. Zach's kids made her happy. They were enough for her.

"Ever think about being a wife?"

Her heart skipped a beat. "Only if the guy is a dark-haired, blue-eyed cowboy," she replied casually.

"Then darling," he said as he pulled her lips down to his, "you are in luck."

* * * * *

COMING NEXT MONTH FROM
HARLEQUIN® SUPERROMANCE™

Available January 2, 2013

#1824 THE OTHER SIDE OF US
by Sarah Mayberry

After a few less-than-impressive meetings, Mackenzie Williams and Oliver Garrett have concluded that good fences make good neighbors. The less they see of each other, the better. Too bad their wayward dogs have other ideas, however, and won't stay apart. The canine antics bring Mackenzie and Oliver into contact so much that those poor first impressions turn into a spark of attraction...and that could lead to some *very* friendly relations!

#1825 A HOMETOWN BOY
by Janice Kay Johnson

Acadia Henderson once had a secret crush on David Owen. Then they went their separate ways. Now they're both back in their hometown trying to make sense of a tragic turn of events. Given what's happened, they shouldn't have anything to say to each other. Yet despite the odds, something powerful—something mutual—is pulling them together. Maybe it's the situation. Or maybe they're finally getting their chance at happiness.

#1826 SOMETHING TO BELIEVE IN
Family in Paradise • by Kimberly Van Meter

Lilah has always been the quiet, meek Bell sister, the one to follow what everyone expects from her. Then she meets Justin Cales. The playboy turns her head and she allows herself to indulge in a very uncharacteristic and passionate affair. But when that leads to an unexpected pregnancy, Lilah discovers she has an inner strength she has never recognized!

#1827 THAT WEEKEND...
by Jennifer McKenzie

A weekend covering a film festival is what TV host Ava Christensen has been waiting for—her dream assignment. But not if it means being alone with her boss! Jake Durham recently denied her a big promotion, so Ava wants as little to do with him as possible. That's virtually impossible at the festival. Somehow, though, with all that time together, everything starts to look different. Must be the influence of the stars...

#1828 BACK TO THE GOOD FORTUNE DINER
by Vicki Essex

Tiffany Cheung has tasted big-city success—and she's hungry for more. So when she ends up at home, working in her parents' restaurant, all she wants is to leave again. Nothing will change her mind. Not even the distraction of Chris Jamieson, her old crush. Yes, the adult version of him is even more tempting—especially because he seems equally attracted. But her dreams are taking her somewhere else, and Chris's life is deeply rooted here. There's no future...unless they can compromise.

#1829 THE TRUTH ABOUT COMFORT COVE
It Happened in Comfort Cove • by Tara Taylor Quinn

The twenty-five-year-old abduction that cold-case detectives Lucy Hayes and Ramsey Miller are working together is taking its toll—especially with their attempt to ignore the intense attraction between them. The effort has been worth it, because they're close to solving this one. And once they do, then maybe they can explore their feelings. But as they get closer to the truth, they aren't prepared for what they discover!

Coming January 2013

THE OTHER SIDE OF US
A brand-new novel
from Harlequin® Superromance® author
Sarah Mayberry

*After a not-so-friendly introduction to Mackenzie Williams,
Oliver Garrett is looking to make a better second
impression...and he may have found it, thanks to
their dogs! Read on for an exciting excerpt
from THE OTHER SIDE OF US by Sarah Mayberry.*

OLIVER searched the yard for his dog, Greta. Finally he spotted her doing a very enthusiastic doggy meet and greet with Mackenzie's dachshund.

How did he get over here? Obviously there must be a hole in the fence between their properties.

Suddenly Oliver saw his best chance at a second meeting with his neighbor. Mackenzie would be grateful if he returned her wayward pet, wouldn't she?

He scooped up the dachshund, who wriggled desperately, but Oliver kept a tight grip the entire walk to Mackenzie's.

"Why do you have Mr. Smith?" she asked, frowning as she answered his knock.

"Your dog was in my yard. Seems our fence has a few holes."

"Thanks for bringing him back." Her tone was warm, even a little encouraging, he thought.

As he was about to respond, the phone rang inside her house.

"I need to get that." She was already closing the door.

HSREXP1212

"Fine. But we should talk about the fence or the dogs will keep visiting."

"I'm sorry, but I really need to take this call." There was a distracted urgency beneath her words.

He opened his mouth to respond, then stared in disbelief as the door swung shut in his face for the second time that day.

"You cannot be serious."

Okay, so he got the message. She was too busy for a friendship. Fine. He and Greta could live here happily *without* knowing their neighbors.

Oliver may have given up on a relationship with Mackenzie, but it seems Greta and Mr. Smith may have other plans! Find out in THE OTHER SIDE OF US by Sarah Mayberry, available January 2013 from Harlequin® Superromance®.